IVRRAC

"A murderer?" Asked the dark haired one, "You think we can handle a serial killer?"

"I'm sure you can handle a serial killer, Andrew," was her reply.

"We cannot afford any mistakes, Christine,"

"You're right, Andrew, we cannot. But I've had a look at the psych assessment the judge ordered. If he's insane, then anyone who believes in any cause, from religion to saving the whales are insane. It's just that, unlike them, his beliefs are screwed. That's what IVRRAC is designed to fix, isn't it?"

"Screwed is putting it mildly." Andrew looked directly at Christine's eyes, "Murder is a lot different from thieving. You can't give back life. There's a big chance this guy is going to come out worse than he came in, but I warn you." Andrew got up to leave, just as he got to the door he turned around. "One mistake, one tiny error in that psych report, the treatment won't hold and that will spell disaster; suicide or massacre, or most likely both! I'll stay with him and watch events carefully, but I won't be held responsible."

Published by
Trentsworth Press
A division of Spyral Enterprises Limited
Geraldine
New Zealand
www.trentsworth.com

Printed by Lightning Source Inc.

ISBN 978-0-473-15409-7

Forward

Welcome to the world of IVRRAC. All characters and organisations in this story are of course fictitious and do not represent anyone living or dead. Even Trentsworth is fictitious, based on the train set of my younger years. The history and rough layout of Trentsworth were created in the early eighties. Trentsworth is roughly based on Queenstown in New Zealand. Basically all the good things about Trentsworth are Queenstown, all the bad things are not. So if you wish to visit Trentsworth, you won't go far wrong taking a trip to Queenstown instead.

IVRRAC itself began in 1994 at a café bar while waiting for my bus in Auckland, New Zealand. The café is now no longer but I thank the barman for the many free filter coffees each night that gave birth to this story. The start and the main twist remain the same but it was not until 1998 that I found the missing ingredient (romance) to make it the great story it is now.

Thanks to my wife, Diana, who has supported my writing since I met her. She has been my rock and valuable critic for all my stories. And her work friend, Helen, who is responsible for any grammatical errors that follow. Actually her editing has been invaluable and any such errors are more likely my own changes post-edit.

Diana has also been very patient with my mad ideas and even accepted to own and manage a Backpacker Hostel with me. There we met many wonderful people as our guests from around the world. A couple of these guests were willing to read a hand bound version of this story and the comments were all good. I especially thank Michael, whose expertise was in the printed word, for his comment that IVRRAC needed to be published which gave me the required push to finally get it to this stage.

With his confidence in my work I resubmitted my work and finally managed to get IVRRAC into print for everyone to read and hopefully gain some insight into their own lives as well as being entertained. So sit back with a cup of coffee and start reading all about Simon and his interactions with IVRRAC.

The Final Insult

The rich protected each other. Because they caught him that first time, he was a marked man. No rich employer looked at him kindly once they found out he was a warrior for the poor. But they deserved it. All of them knew who he was. They feared him secretly. They wanted to put him away. Get him out of the picture. He had to be careful, the law was on their side. They owned the law. Didn't they?

He tried to smile at the attendant at the fast food counter as she stated, "Have a nice day." His heart wasn't in it. He had just been refused another job, and it still was another fortnight until the unemployment benefit kicked in. After rent he had twenty dollars to last him. He couldn't really afford to eat out, but he had to do something to keep himself sane. He took the paper bag and walked outside. He eventually found an empty bench opposite a café seating area. He looked around him. The cafés and restaurants were filling up quickly with office workers and tourists stopping for lunch, most of them ordering the latest in espresso coffee.

He watched as a lady sat down at a table facing him. She looked at him and then down at his bag, smiling at him as she waited for her order. How dare she smirk like that at me. No rich person would actually smile at a warrior for the poor. He paused for a while, wondering whether to stay or find another bench away from this awful lady, when the waitress arrived with her food. He decided he had every right to be there and opened up his crinkled bag.

There she was smirking, looking down at his five dollar budget-meal, while she ate up thirty dollars or more with her salad filled fancy breads. Her coffee expressed through the finest coffee beans; her four dollar dash of cream on the side, which she'd probably discard, because she is on a two hundred dollar a month diet plan. He could almost see her thoughts, 'Why do they allow such scum to eat in this pristine area?' He knew if she had her way, he'd be made to eat in the dark alleys with the rats. To her, he was lower than even a plague-ridden rat. He tore at his burger in anger, as she finely cut off another small sliver of walnut tort. He slammed the polystyrene cup down on the bench as she carefully replaced the fine china cup back into the saucer.

Her very actions mimicked his own. Well, two could play at that game. He would mimic her, right until they were alone. 'Careful,' he reminded himself, 'don't let anger rule the day, remember the first time. The law is their law. Don't do anything stupid. Don't get caught.' They had pushed him to avenge the poor six times before, and five times he had managed to avoid their law. This lady had to be the seventh. She asked for it with every pore of her body. "I am rich!" She seemed to cry "You, poor scum, are nothing!" He heard her scream in his head. Like the others, she needed to be taught a lesson. How dare the rich refuse him employment; how dare they remove him from their office just for voicing his rights. She will pay for all the injustices he had to suffer that morning.

The rich deserved everything he gave them and more. Occasionally he wondered how many other warriors of the poor were out there. How long would it be before civilisation could again hold its head up high and announce everyone is equal? Then he noticed that she had just stood up. He stood up, too. There; she leaves half the food untouched; typical. He seethed as he thrust the cardboard remains into the rubbish. She had already started in the direction of the overbridge. He followed.

He had to stop and sit down on another bench as she had stopped ahead of him, studying some pictures which hung for purchase on the way. The sun was shining in his eyes as he watched and waited. She seemed interested in a particular painting. She went into the shop entrance. The gallery assistant came out and placed an orange sticker on the frame. The rich lady exited behind the assistant and continued toward the car park overbridge.

He moved, but paused for a second at the painting. The sticker proclaimed it was sold. Under the orange sticker, one thousand two hundred dollars was brandished as the cost. 'Right!' He thought 'That's it! There are starving thousands out there and she wastes twelve hundred dollars on a poster. She is going to pay for that.'

He was quite close as she finished paying the parking fees at the machine at the overbridge. She then started walking along past the parked cars. It was either now or never; once in her car, he would not be able to do anything. As she stopped by a highly polished luxury car with new license plates, he could not stop himself. Such a blatant display of "I'm rich, so there, poor scum!" He pulled his knife from his belt.

She stopped still as she felt a slight pressure on her back. By the time she realised what was happening, she was unable to yell out, her lungs punctured. Once more he stabbed her with the knife, again hearing the silk tearing from her designer dress. He knew better than to scream the revenge. He drove the knife into her again and again.

She was dead by the fifth stroke. Blood was all over her car and the concrete floor where it flowed freely over the edge to the level below. He kept on stabbing. "For the poster, for the smirk, for the two hundred dollar diet," he cursed under his breath. He was careful not to draw attention to himself.

He was so filled with pent up anger that he didn't hear the solid footsteps behind him, until it was too late.

Who?

"Simon Harold Tallsbury, aged 23." Christine announced.

She was sitting behind an executive's desk; polished oak. Behind her hung a large picture, an artist's opinion of the New York skyline. It was the only view the office had, the four walls void of any windows. Two bright fluorescent light fixtures in the hung ceiling provided more than enough light. The blue fluorescence made her red hair sparkle. Her light brown eyes stared intently over her sparsely covered desk at the two men sitting opposite. The one to her left was dark haired and very well built, the other thin and almost bald, with oval glasses. Both their mouths dropped in surprised as she finished the name.

"A murderer?" Asked the dark haired one, "You think we can handle a serial killer?"

"I'm sure you can handle a serial killer, Andrew," was her reply.

"We cannot afford any mistakes, Christine," the bald one added, "We're running close to the line, the price we got on Geoffrey Archibald just covered our expenses. We're doing well with our thieves, why change?"

"It's time to up the anti, David. You're right we cannot afford mistakes. Wouldn't it be nice not to run so close to insolvency?" She countered, "He's been sentenced to six life sentences. It's the longest sentence in the country's history."

"Okay, so the Justice Department will save heaps giving him to us, but he's insane!" interrupted Andrew. "The only reason he didn't get insanity was that he represented himself and admitted to the seven murders. He even seemed proud of what he did. He was only up for the last murder. We cannot treat insanity."

"You're right, Andrew, we cannot. But I've had a look at the psych assessment the judge ordered. If he's insane, then anyone who believes in any cause, from religion to saving the whales are insane. It's just that, unlike them, his beliefs are screwed. That's what IVRRAC is designed to fix, isn't it?"

"Screwed is putting it mildly." Andrew looked directly at Christine's eyes, "Murder is a lot different from thieving. You can't give back life. There's a big chance this guy is going to come out worse than he came in. The programming will need to be so exact; so tight. One mistake and it will be suicide or massacre, or most likely both!"

"I trust you can do this, Andrew. The Justice Department has offered us twice as much as we would require to take him off their hands. And that's half the cost they reckon he will be to them. Especially with all these new liberal prison rules." She passed a page full of figures to the bald man. "David, your views?"

"I think we should try this, definitely," David smiled. Christine could almost make out the drool on his lower lip.

"I never doubted you would be in agreement once you saw the numbers. The decision is now with you, Andrew."

Andrew looked at Christine, his eyes a bit distant, after a few minutes of this he suddenly announced, "I'll do it! I can be that exact and you know it. That's why I'm here, but I warn you." Andrew got up to leave, just as he got to the door he turned around. "One mistake, one tiny error in that psych report, the treatment won't hold and that will spell disaster. I'll stay with him and watch events carefully, but I won't be held responsible."

Not More Doctors

Simon sat in his cell. He wasn't interested in mingling with the criminals that they had put him with. A guard came along and gestured him to follow. Another visitor? Probably another psychiatrist. Why did they think he was insane? Killing the rich was the only way to teach them who's boss. Well, at least it kept the criminals away from him. He had tried solitary, but the warden had wised in on his game and threatened to take his single cell privilege away next misdemeanor. He followed the guard quietly.

He was surprised to see a beautiful red-haired lady waiting for him in the interview room. With her was a well-built man and the psychiatrist he had met a couple of days ago.

"Hello, Simon," the lady welcomed him. "I am Christine Smythe and this is my colleague, Andrew. The doctor you've already met."

"Hello," Simon replied. He ignored Christine's outstretched

hand, thinking, 'Can't they just leave me alone?' Simon watched Christine sit down on one of the dull office chairs. She pointed to the one opposite her. He looked defiantly at her. "So what's this honour all about?"

"Sit down, Simon, and we'll talk." Christine smiled, ignoring the furious looks from him.

Simon reluctantly sat on the seat. "Cut to the chase. I am a busy man!"

"You are going to be in here for a very long time. Unfortunately for you it's election year and there are a lot of influential voters out there scared of you." The doctor stood up. He looked at her in horror. Christine waved him down. "So you got the raw end of the deal. You should be proud, you have the longest running sentence a person has ever received in the country's history."

"Yes, it's the rich men's justice, otherwise I would've been praised. But instead I am put in this hell hole with all the scum. I don't call that justice." He was beginning to regret his initial distrust, 'Finally a person who seems to understand.'

"I see your point. Here's you helping the poor men's cause, and what do they do? Place you in here with all the criminals."

"Exactly! It is nice to have someone who is aware of my

struggle, unlike this doctor here. How much do you earn a year, doctor? He's in the rich club, they stay together, you know. I can see you're on a modest wage, Christine. He," Simon continued thumbing the doctor, "Should be in here not me. So what are you going to do about it?"

"Well we, Andrew and I, have struck a deal with the Justice Department. They agree that you shouldn't be here with the criminals and are willing to let you try a new rehabilitation technique. Once you have been through our processing we will place you in a small town. There no one will know of your murders. If you last six months without attempting to kill anyone, you can go free. As easy as that."

"Who do you think I am, an idiot?" Simon looked at her. He was dubious. The richie government wouldn't make such a deal. "Nothing's that easy, what's the catch?"

"Okay," Christine smiled, "You caught us. As this is cutting edge rehabilitation, there's a slight chance of death during the final stages of our procedure. You'll need to sign a waver stating that you have agreed to assume any and all risks involved. You will not sue, nor any relatives sue, the government or IVRRAC, that's us, if any injury or death results. It's a large document. The country's laws are made to avoid such a contract, so there's a lot of loop hole text. You can read it all if you wish, and we'll come back in a week. Or you can sign it now, and you'll be out of here tomorrow."

"Give me the pen." Simon smiled, "Even death is better than spending my life with these criminals. I'd rather be a martyr for the poor, than a pawn for the rich."

Christine watched as Simon scrawled his name on the inch thick document. After taking back the document, Christine got up and knocked on the door to the interview room. The door opened and two guards came in, grabbed Simon and gently persuaded him to follow them back out.

Christine looked at Andrew. "Well?"

"He's a strange fellow, but your analysis seems to be correct. The scenario I've set up should be perfect."

"Which you'll spend all night adjusting and fine-tuning, if I know you, Andrew."

"No matter how perfect Simon is for this, the program still needs to be exact. Slightly too little and it won't last, slightly too much and it's death."

"That's why we hired you, Andrew."

"Ha ha, very funny."

The End and the Beginning

Simon couldn't get to sleep that night. Had he done the right thing in signing over his life to those people? What sort of mad experiment was he in for? Slowly the hours drifted past. He must have fallen asleep because he awoke to the sound of his cell being opened.

Two guards were there, their faces showed they were obeying orders, but weren't happy about it. "Right you!" ordered the one nearest Simon. "I don't know how you managed it, but you're being transferred to another prison. Collect your personal belongings and come with us."

Simon gathered up his small pile of clothes and toiletries and bundled them into a laundry bag labeled "Prison Property". He hadn't had time to collect many belongings. He was soon out of the cell block and on the way to the transfer station. A white nondescript transportation vehicle was awaiting him. The same guard that had spoken signed what was obviously a release form, then left him in the hands of the two new guards.

These guards were not from the prison. After a closer inspection of their coat of arms Simon realised these were private security guards. They forcibly suggested that Simon should get into the back of the van. They closed a grill gate and locked it. Then they closed and locked the rear doors. A single light on the roof of the van lit the confined space Simon now found himself in. He sat down on the narrow metal bench that was attached to one side of the van's side and threw his belongings on the cold metal floor.

The van started to move off. It wasn't long before he realised, as the engine was whining at top speed, that they had got on the motorway. The van slowed down and sped up several times. Simon rightly guessed morning traffic. He mused on the fact that theoretically, the most advanced rehabilitation firm was transporting him in what must have been the oldest paddy wagon in the country. Its engine was still whining; barely coping with the high speed.

It was a good hour, Simon reckoned, before the van gently slowed to a stop. He didn't hear the front doors open, so was surprised when the back doors swung back, blinding him with sunshine. The grill gate was opened by two new guards wearing the same uniform. They were standing on the back of another van, which had reversed as close as possible to the rear of his van. There was a slight gap between them, revealing a gravel road underneath.

"Get into this van," one of the guards commanded. "Don't! Step onto the road - jump the gap. Leave your belongings in the other van." He followed the instructions. He was amazed at the next instruction. "Now take off all your clothes. Do it now!"

He had expected a strip search, but not in the middle of nowhere. He did as he was told. The guard handed him a bright orange one piece suit in exchange. As he was undressing, he couldn't help notice the two guards were carrying a large bundle into the other van. As soon as he had all Simon's clothes, one of the guards took a long intake of breath, and dived into the shadows of the old van.

Simon looked at his new surroundings. This van was obviously the current year's model. It even had air conditioning controls behind the padded bench seats. There were still no windows. Two bright fluorescent strips took care of any murky shadows.

The other guard came back with an empty black bag. He looked slightly pale. "Okay, it's done, lets close the doors and get the hell out of here."

The guards reset the grill gate and the rear doors of the old van. They locked them in place and resealed the door with a security tag. The guard, still looking ill, thumped the van's back.

Simon felt a slight shudder as the van he was in slowly moved forward. With the back doors still open he saw the old van reversing slowly. He couldn't help notice how it kept exactly to the tracks it made in the road. Simon's suspicions reached a new level. This was not all above board. The old van slowed to a stop then started forward again slowly gaining speed but still following the original tracks.

The guards closed the back doors as the old van drove out of sight. Simon's van moved forward again, slowly. He guessed this driver also was keeping to the single set of tyre tracks in the gravel. The van drove onto a sealed road and started speeding up. The guards looked at each other and breathed a sigh of relief.

Simon sat impatiently on the middle bench seat as the new van drove on for another couple of hours. He was beginning to feel hungry; breakfast seemed a long time ago. On top of this his backside was going numb, even with the new leather seating, from sitting so long. Finally he felt the van take a sharp turn, then come to a complete stop. He heard some mumblings from the cab. Afterwards the van slowly continued on, but it wasn't long before the van stopped again.

Opening the back door, the guard motioned Simon to leave. He did so, again the bright sunlight blinding him. The van was parked outside a pyramid shaped building. It was made totally out of tinted glass. The sun reflected off it making it seem like a jewel among the perfectly manicured gardens around it. The guards ushered him down a sloping path to a set of sliding glass doors. As he walked past the doors he noticed that the glass was very thick; obviously bullet proof.

Once through, the floor sloped down further as he was led into the bowels of the building. They passed six more thick glass doors on the way down, each flanked by two cameras. By the time he was brought up to a counter, he had guessed they had gone down about two levels. Behind the counter, protected by more bullet proof glass, was a lady reading a page of names. "Mr Simon Tallsbury?" She asked, her dark brown hair, severely pulled into a knot behind, glistening in the blue fluorescent lights above.

"Yes, expecting someone else?" Simon sneered a bit. The journey had made him crotchety and her thick rimmed sixties styled glasses reminded him of his 4th year teacher. Besides, he was dying for a piss. "What was all that stuff back on the trip, why change vans?"

"All will be explained in the fullness of time, Mr Tallsbury. Please follow the guards to your room". She looked away from Simon toward the guards as she pressed a button and the solenoid locks opened. "Mr Tallsbury is in Room S320."

Taking Simon through the doorway, the guards walked along a well lit corridor passing numerous doors. They reached a door, about halfway down the corridor, with an engraved sign stating it was room S320. Stopping there, the guards opened the door and gently pushed Simon into the room.

Once inside, Simon looked around. He was surprised to note the room more resembled a hotel suite than a cell. There was a queen sized bed in a bedroom area to the right of a kitchenette and lounge. To his relief a bathroom and toilet were off to the left of the bedroom. As, Simon expected from being so far underground, the room had no windows. Air conditioning circulated a fresh cool breeze around the room.

The lounge itself was fitted out with leather seats, television and even gym equipment. "Now this is what I call a Jail!" He stated under his breath, smiling. He was now beginning to think he had chosen the correct path. After all he deserved to be treated as a guest, not a criminal for getting rid of the rich dictators.

He had only a short time to familiarise himself with the new surroundings before there was a knock on the door. "Yeah?" He queried. The door opened and a couple of guards came in, one of them he recognised from the van.

"The Governor requires your presence," the guard motioned

him out the door. "Come with us". Outside, four other guards waited and all six escorted him down the corridor.

It was a very short walk to the end of the corridor. At the end was a door with a brass plaque announcing this was the Governor's office. A gruff voice replied "Come in" to the knock of the escort guard. Simon was shown into the office. Four of the guards waited outside as the original two walked at his side into the room.

Behind a large mahogany desk opposite the door was a distinguished looking gentleman, "Sit down, Mr Tallsbury." The governor pointed to a chair in front of his desk. The guards escorted Simon to the chair and pushed him into it from behind. Simon felt their presence behind him, there was no way he could murder this rich know-it-all without instant consequences. He decided to sit and listen to what this idiot had to say.

"Thank you for agreeing to come to our experimental rehabilitation centre. Here we will make you realise that your murders have had wider consequences than you think. Many families have been affected by your actions. If we don't put a stop to it now, many more people will suffer."

"Only the rich suffered, no one important," Simon interrupted. One of the guards hit his right arm with a batten.

"Listen, don't speak until you're asked," the guard ordered.

"This is the core of our rehabilitation technique," the governor continued, "to make you realise how much suffering you have caused. We do this primarily by inducing an hypnotic suggestion into you, that will make you suffer yourself at the mere thought of killing people. In other words, the suffering you are about to cause will be revisited upon you tenfold. You will eventually get out of the habit of killing people you don't like. It's like the old trick of putting mustard on the finger nails to stop nail biting.

"I realise that you at the present time cannot see how this would be possible, but we do have an extremely powerful method of getting the message through. Our hypnosis can generate a lot of pain, pain like you will have never experienced, in such intensity as you would never think possible. Every time you even think of harming another human being, let alone put your thoughts into action.

"During your stay here, do not let the luxury fool you, this is still a high security prison. We have a very large penalty fee if a prisoner escapes, so we will not let you escape. The only way out of here is by being a supportive patient in our techniques. You will stay in your room until requested by the physicians for treatment. You have exercise equipment in your room. You are to use this at least an hour a day to keep up your strength. There will be absolutely no contact with the outside world."

"You cannot do that!" Simon went to rush the governor, but found two restrictive hands on his shoulders holding him back in his seat.

"We can, and we are! Your signature in agreeing to this process also waved all your legal rights. If you feel this is unjust, you are free to take it up with a lawyer once you have finished your rehabilitation.

'You just wait, you rich bastard!' Simon thought to himself. 'You'll be the first one dead when I have my chance. Don't need to waste money on a rich man's lawyer when a knife to do the job much more effectively.'

"Any attempt to escape, contact outside individuals, refusal of treatment, or blatant disregard of our rules, will result in loss of privileges. You will find quickly the difference between our penthouse cells and our dungeon cells. Any questions, contact me by dialling 345 on your room phone. For any other assistance, dial 0 for the operator." The governor looked up at the guards. "Escort Mr Tallsbury back to his cell."

The guards pulled Simon out of his chair and pushed him back into the hallway where the other four joined them again. Not long afterwards they reached his room and motioned him inside. Once inside he heard the solenoid locking mechanism settling into place once again. He bashed against the door to check its strength. It seemed to give quite a bit. 'Should be easy to knock down,' he thought to himself, 'Wait for a while, then, when they least expect me to escape.' He smiled and went to the living area of the cell and turned on the television, oblivious to a faint hissing sound coming from the vents in the walls.

In the hallway the governor joined the six guards. "Hi Jake," the governor greeted one of the guards as the other five went through the door labelled 319 opposite Simon's cell door.

"Hi Paul, well that's me, until the next crim comes along. Good money for a morning's work."

"Some people have it lucky", he said as the the sound of gas being released became audible. "I have to hang around until he wakes up. They're paranoid I'll have a car accident or something. Have to keep everything consistent, so it's five star accommodation for the next few weeks."

"So you have time for a coffee, then?" Jake laughed.

"Might just be able to squeeze it in." Paul held the door open for Jake as the both walked through the doorway to reveal that the corridor was just a stage set, the rows of doorways obviously false set in a wall made of wood and thick cardboard. There was a visible bulge at the end where the Governor's office was. "Perhaps next time you can be the Governor, and I get the easy job. That speech was particularly long, and I missed a few lines."

A caféteria was set up in the large open space beyond the corridor, and the seven helped themselves to coffee and cake. They sat down and watched two men in white gowns and gas masks enter the set with a gurney. Five minutes later they re-emerged with a limp body covered in a sheet and headed towards the elevator.

One of the other guards put down his mug and stood up smiling. "Place your bets."

"Two months," Paul said.

"Four months," Jake yelled, then turned to Paul, hitting his forehead with the tip of his finger. "He's insane. Four months if they're lucky. I actually believe he will find a way around their programming."

Computers and Hypnosis

The room was well lit and metal cabinets lined the walls, each one with their multitude of flashing lights. There was a faint hum with the occasional clicking as the many hard drive heads searched for the appropriate data. It seemed to be a computer geek's heaven. Positioned in the middle of all these machines was Simon sleeping soundly from the gas. Bending over him was Andrew, dressed in a white lab coat. With him was another man, light build with red hair, also in a lab coat. Christine watched from the shadows.

Both men, quietly and with absolute concentration, started placing electrodes on Simon's head. For each one they looked up to a red light and attached it to Simon's freshly shaved scalp, moving it slightly until the light tuned green. Finally after almost an hour, the panel was filled with green lights and the two men noticeably relaxed.

"Okay, Kevin, go and do your programming," Andrew commanded. "I will check his responsiveness."

Andrew watched a monitor that seemed to be displaying an EEG type graph. Andrew stayed absolutely quiet, concentrating on every peak and trough, when suddenly he exclaimed, "Yes! He is in IVRRAC!"

"Have we succeeded? Will he take?" Christine asked.

"You know better than that," Andrew replied. "We need to wait the full analysis period before we can even start counting our chickens. But as far as Simon is concerned, he is fully controlled by the IVRRAC process, which is a big step. Now we, well at least you can just sit back and watch."

Simon woke up to find himself now in bed. He looked around his cell, 'How long had he been asleep?' He remembered smelling something strange and feeling sleepy. Then it came to him what had happened. He was furious. The governor said nothing about being gassed. Picking up the phone, he paused to dial the number. He couldn't remember what the governor's extension was so he dialled 0.

"Operator, how can I be of assistance?"

"Get me the governor," he yelled down the hand piece. "Now!"

"Certainly sir, please hold," the polite voice replied and the sound of pan flutes filled the ear piece. Won't work on me, this rubbish won't soothe my anger, Simon thought.

"Governor here".

"What the hell right did you have to gas me?" Simon yelled down the mouthpiece.

"Ah, Mr Tallsbury. You have woken up", the governor quietly replied. "We have applied the hypnosis. Actually the best way to explain is face to face. I will send a guard to escort you to my office. Then we can talk about the next step in your rehabilitation."

"Fine!" Simon slammed the phone down. He'll show them, the righteous pricks. He started feeling a bit queasy as he dressed himself. After-effects of the gas, he presumed. Other than that he didn't feel any different, but he wasn't going to tell them their treatment hadn't worked, he still wanted to avenge the poor. They had to believe it had worked though, so he could leave this place and get his life back on track, a free man.

There was a knock on his door, and he went to open it. Outside was a single guard waiting to take him to the governor's office. 'Only one guard?' He pondered, they sure were certain that their hypnosis worked. He would show them, he suddenly struggled and managed to pull free of the guard and ran down the hall. He stopped at a door and tried to kick it down. The door held fast.

It did not take long for the guard to catch up. He rushed into Simon, pushing him hard against the corridor wall. The force of hitting the solid concrete almost knocked Simon out. The guard half dragged him into the governor's office, and left him slumped in the visitor's chair.

"Good to see you have fully recovered, Simon," the governor began, smirking at him. "Feeling slightly trapped are we? You are not making a good example that you are able to start life anew." The governor paused. Suddenly he was staring straight at Simon, penetrating his very soul. "You hate me, don't you. You despise my social standing. You hate that I earn six figures a year to sit here and watch people like you suffer, that I can leave at any time and go off to parties and spend hundreds on a meal without even thinking. Don't you!"

"Slightly," Simon replied. 'Smug rich bastard, sitting across the desk. He probably thinks he is safe from me. Not knowing that his death is only seconds away. Get rid of the lone guard first.' Simon's thoughts stopped. He suddenly felt a massive jolt in his stomach. It seemed as though his guts had imploded. The pain was unbearable. He could just make out the governor's voice through the anguish.

"Ah, your thoughts betray you. Now think of nice things,

fields of daisies, waterfalls, etc. Any time you think of harming someone, your subconscious will make you feel slightly nauseous. If you keep on thinking along those lines it will build up, until finally you feel that your guts have been ripped out of your body. It is a good idea to stop at the first signs of nausea, trust me."

'Trust a richie, never!' The pains got worse. Simon started to think of sheep grazing in a field. The pain subsided. "Why the hell did you gas me? How long was I out for?", he asked, trying to keep calm, but still a wave of nausea went through him as he spoke.

"You have been here for three days. It is much easier to apply the treatment when the subject is unconscious. Plus, the process has a higher percentage of lasting. Ninety five as compared to five when the subject is just in a hypnotic state."

"So can I go now, then?" Simon hopefully requested. "The treatment's finished. I am rehabilitated. So can I go home and live my life as normal?" Simon smiled. 'Idiots, no way will this hypnosis last even with being gassed. Suckers, they'll all pay for their smugness.' He stopped as the nausea began to build and thought of other thoughts. He could control it, and no one would be the wiser.

"You will never be able to live your life as normal, your

face was plastered over the news nation wide, which you should already realise. What you don't know is that over the past three days there has been a media circus around your death and why you were removed from prison. The scandal that the press are busy creating in their need for a newsworthy story, has made certain that your death is known by everyone in the country."

"You killed my identity?" Simon yelled and then twisted in pain. He then remembered the strange episode swapping vans. It was all becoming clear. 'What right had they to do this to him?'

"Yes, so now when you enter the world as Scott Harold Tallburg, people may think they have seen your face before, but dismiss the thought as easily as it arrived. And you have what many criminals never get, a clean slate for a second chance."

"Do I start with nothing at all, become a bum on the street?" Simon asked, trying to keep calm to keep the nausea at bay.

"No, we will provide you with an adequate start, the rest is up to you. But first we need to watch your steps for the next six months so as to ascertain the hypnosis has in fact taken hold successfully."

"You are taking a big risk there. I know the city's back streets, it will be hard to know where I am, I could mess things up for you and you wouldn't know about it until the next day. I'm surprised you hadn't thought of that." Simon smiled. 'They won't know what's hit them. These smug IVRRAC people. One short stab.' He stopped and tried to hide the immense pain he was feeling. 'Cannot let them see my thoughts,' he thought to himself, as he pictured more sheep in his mind.

"We had, which is why for those six months you are not going back to the city, but living in the tourist haven of Trentsworth. A town of small area, encircled by some of the highest mountain peaks in the country, and the railway is the only way in or out."

"Trentsworth?" Simon laughed, "You're paying for me to live in the most expensive holiday location in the country? You need your heads read." 'Trentsworth,' Simon mused to himself, 'Home of the rich and famous. If you have a house in Trentsworth you have made it. They are actually placing me there, the idiots. Imagine the damage I could do. All those richies, just waiting to be slaughtered.'

"Yes," the governor smiled. "Our budget has been stretched to the limit on this, but we need to make sure we can keep tabs on you. But we are absolutely confident that the process is infallible, otherwise putting you in a town full of millionaires would be like putting a tiger in a nursery school."

"So what is the catch? There must be something!" Simon asked. 'I could not be this lucky. There will be a price to pay and I want to know what it is now.'

"You cannot contact anyone from your past, ever. You cannot tell a soul who you really are. Trentsworth is unaware of the true nature of your stay. If you do, be it on your head. We are not a government department, we do not answer to the people. We will keep you in Trentsworth and the Trentsworth people will put the blame on you. All your previous paranoia about being ostracised from society will actually become true. You will be living in a hell I wouldn't wish on my worst enemy."

"I'll kill them first," Simon yelled, then doubled over in pain.

"And!" The governor continued, "You will not be able to fight back. We have seen to that. The best idea is to do what we say, Mr Tallburg. Stay quiet about your actual past and learn your new past we have given you. All the legal papers and cards are on your bed in your room. Also a book detailing the highlights of your, or should I say, Scott's, past life up to your arrival in Trentsworth. Read it and I stress again, learn it completely."

"I can't live another person's life". Suddenly it lost its appeal. If he couldn't avenge the poor, what was the use of being there. He'd rather be locked up in a cell than spend six months with richies all around him, and not being able to do anything. "I am not an actor".

"You need not be, our social experts have created a personae which pretty much is a mirror of yourself, except the absence of hating the rich. Your name is so similar to your old one that your current signature could be either. Believe me this is not going to be hard to pull off. You will have a financial start to life many of us just dream of. All moneys will be yours after this initial parole period, though the house and contents stay our property."

"And what if I say no?"

"You will go, anyway. You signed the contract. You have agreed to this already. What you feel now has no relevance at all."

"Why, you bastard!" Simon yelled, "You wait, I will have a knife in you before you..." Simon had to stop as the pain level went through the roof.

Looking at the guard, the governor quietly instructed, "Please escort, drag, Mr Tallburg back to his room."

The guard pulled Simon to his feet and pushed him towards his cell's door. Simon heard the bolt settling in place as he walked to the bedroom area. On the bed was a multitude of certificates and bankcards. He looked at them; education qualifications, birth certificate, drivers' licence, video library membership, ATM card. No creditcard. He smiled. They didn't trust him that far. Finally, a small paperback entitled, "The Life and Times of Scott Harold Tallburg".

He sat on the bed for a while, trying to think of ways to escape. He remembered the flimsy door before the gassing. If he didn't do it now, it would be too late. He got up and rushed the door. It was a lot more solid than he remembered. Rubbing his sore shoulder, he went into the kitchen.

Resigned to following IVRRAC's instructions, he made a cup of coffee and sat down to read. "Born on February 6th 1990, I was blessed with a loving mother and father. I was an only child and I admit, I was spoilt as one usually is." The book continued through the school years, detailing dental problems, illnesses, fights and love affairs. He apparently had only two relationships of any substance. He was skilled as a welder, which was the same as Simon. His parents had died in a car crash when he was 19, he had a full time job at that stage so he was supporting himself. Most of the inheritance went towards funeral costs and debts.

The last chapter was entitled "My move to Trentsworth"

"A previously unknown aunt died and left me three million dollars in her will." Simon paused, and walked over to the bed. He checked the bank balance. It was in the low six figures. Puzzled, he sat back down and continued reading. "My thoughts immediately went to Trentsworth, a town I had spent my best ever childhood holiday at. I purchased a house there for a mere two million, five hundred thousand dollars. My childhood dream was finally coming true. With the rest of the money, I purchased a claim up the Trent River, which I plan to occasionally mine to pay for my lifestyle."

Simon put the book down, a simple case of a man with too much money and too little sense. True, such real estate should hold its value, but the interest earned would be little or nothing. Also, only retrievable in the long term. If it was Simon not Scott, it would have been placed in high earning, but guaranteed investment. Simon would have lived off the interest for the rest of his life. The rates alone on that property would be crippling to the common man. He only hoped the money left would support him for the next six months. He didn't want to spoil a great location with working, and that included mining a claim. Simon continued reading.

Prison in a Story

The next morning Simon awoke to knocking on his door. He got up, and had put on his robe by the time he reached the door. Opening it, he found a familiar face on the other side.

"Hello, Simon," the man greeted. "Remember me?" He held out his hand for a shake.

"Andrew, isn't it?" Simon ignored the outstretched hand. "You were one of the two who fooled me into agreeing to this garbage. I should have opted for the week to read it. I would have never signed it then. Where's the lady, doesn't she want to gloat as well?"

"I am not here to gloat; I am going to be your liaison with IVRRAC for the next six months. Our van is about to leave. Get dressed and remember to bring your papers. Your new life is about to begin. From now on you are Scott Tallburg," Andrew announced, his face showing no emotion.

Grunting an affirmation, Simon went off to the bedroom and got dressed. When he came back, Andrew handed him a briefcase for the documentation. Simon gathered up all the papers now lying all over the room and placed them in the case.

Simon followed Andrew out of his room and up the corridor. What Simon noted quickly was the lack of guards now. Were they so confident that their theatre hypnosis would work? He smiled at the gullible. It seemed like he could escape anytime he wanted. He would wait his time. Then suddenly he would be gone. They wouldn't have a chance to do anything. He looked up. Andrew was getting quite far ahead. He was walking quite fast and he sped through the guarded entry without slowing down. Simon had trouble catching up.

The white van he arrived in was waiting outside. Andrew got in the back with Simon and the van started off immediately. "Nice limousine," Simon sarcastically commented. Andrew looked at him with a blank face and then stared at the wall opposite again. About thirty minutes later the van came to a stop and the doors opened. Simon recognised the Domestic Airport of the city. At least they were giving him a chance to say goodbye to the metropolis.

Before he could get his bearings, Andrew ushered Simon into the terminal. An announcement came over the speakers,

"This is the final call for Fight 525 to Christchurch. All remaining passengers, please make your way immediately to Gate 31." They walked past a man in sunglasses and a tan suit. Simon thought he looked like a character out of an American spy movie. As they past, he handed over two boarding passes to Andrew and they continued through the departure gates without a second's hesitation.

A few minutes later they were in the air. Simon realised that if he was to escape now, it would be more difficult to get back home. He hadn't expected such a quick transition from the van to the plane. He looked to his right at Andrew. He had the window seat and the shutter was down. "Could I see out?" Simon asked.

"Sorry, I don't like the view, being so high," was the reply. The hostess came through checking the seats were upright, bags stowed away and seat belts were fastened. Simon noted, as he watched her progress down the cabin, that all the other windows in view were also closed. Most travellers were catching a few minutes sleep.

"You could have given me the window seat then," Simon grumbled. Andrew didn't reply as he had his head in a book. Simon sat there watching Andrew hogging the window seat. Suddenly he felt a great pressure pushing him back into his seat. The plane's engines whined as they powered to top speed. Simon felt the nose lifting and the sudden absence of the juddering from the wheels on the tarmac. Before the plane had a chance to level out, the cabin crew started serving the complimentary hot drinks. They seemed oblivious to the rocking and juddering of the plane as it hit the occasional air pocket. Finally, a hostess reached his row and Andrew had already unfolded the tray from the seat in front. Simon also released his tray. Saying yes to coffee, Simon received a cup on a tray with biscuit and milk tubs. He sat back as Andrew took his and settled down to his drink. After finally working out the complex action of removing the foil from the Ultra Pasteurised Milk Tub, he poured it into the cup, the contents barely changing the coffee's colour.

He sat back and relaxed as he felt the rumble of the engines all around him and the now soothing tiny judder, keeping him informed they were still moving and the journey would be soon over. Simon pulled out the complimentary magazine from the pocket in front of him. He noted that there was an article on Trentsworth's night life, so he started reading all about the twenty bars within two minutes of each other. He wasn't even half way through the article, when he was interrupted by a female voice over the PA system. She explained that Christchurch was a mere two hundred kilometres away. That they had pretty much caught up the few minutes they lost from a late departure. Also, he was informed that the weather was fine, a slight north-westerly wind which apparently had increased the temperature to a wonderful thirty degrees Celsius. It was at that point he realised that he was actually going to go through with this mad scheme. He didn't know why. Perhaps curiosity. Perhaps he was insane, but he almost started looking forward to going.

Then he felt the plane tilt as it repositioned itself for Christchurch. The engines changed tone to sound as though they were stalling but then they stayed constant with the new sound, so he hoped this was them slowing down for landing. His ears told him they were indeed descending as they popped continuously and he felt a slight pressure in his sinuses.

He noticed Andrew putting the tray up in preparation for landing. The cabin crew must have collected his cup while he was engrossed in the article. He, too, returned the tray to its normal position and waited for the sound of the wheels hitting the tarmac. The woman's voice again filled the plane, "On behalf of the airline and the crew, thank you for flying with us, and wish you safe journeys to your final destination. Please remember to stay seated until we stop at the terminal and the seat belt signs are switched off."

Simon felt the wheels touch the ground and the massive deceleration pushed him slightly forward as the plane started taxiing to the terminal. The plane stopped and everyone got up to exit. Andrew, though, stayed seated and motioned Simon to do the same. Simon quickly wondered how far he would get if he jumped up suddenly and made a break for it. He was almost certain he would make it. He ignored the thought. He now wanted to see this trip out to the end. He had never lived in a multi-million dollar house before. He could easily escape parole once he got bored.

Once all the passengers had disembarked, Andrew motioned Simon to leave. Simon stood up and walked with Andrew to the exit. The airport was quite quiet, almost too quiet, as Andrew led Simon out of the terminal building, where another white van was waiting. They got into the back and Simon felt the van move off. Again there were no windows. "Not much for sightseeing, are you?"

"We are relocating you, not giving you the royal tour," Andrew replied in his dead monotone voice, staring at the front wall of the van.

'Smug bastard,' Simon thought, as the van started moving. 'Just because you're not rich doesn't exclude you from my list. Just wait.' Simon stopped as the pain started to emerge.

Around fifteen minutes later the van stopped and the motor was switched off. They waited in the back for another fifteen minutes. The air conditioning had been switched off with the engine. Simon was getting uncomfortably hot when the back doors opened. Andrew motioned Simon out and then followed him. The van was parked in a gravel car park. In front of the van was what seemed to be a deserted train station upon a concrete platform. Andrew walked over to the platform and stepped up.

On the other side of the carpark was a very busy road with several lighted intersections further in the direction Simon guessed was North, judging from the sun. Two guards gently persuaded Simon to follow Andrew, before he even could think of running in the other direction. Andrew had stopped at the western edge of the platform and looked north, then to his watch. "Shouldn't be too long." Simon looked north as well. There was no sign of any train, but something about the tracks caught his eye. He was curious to note that there were three. He knew from the movies that American subways had a third track that powered the trains, but these tracks were outside where, if it was such a thing, surely there would be many deaths of electrocuted children.

To the North the three tracks disappeared into the distance. To the South the tracks split; a normal gauge two track line continued straight, and the three track compilation turned to the right heading west. He looked behind him. An old sign hung from the boarded up waiting room and ticket office. "Rolleston". The name didn't mean much to Simon.

"Rolleston around twenty kilometres from the centre of Christchurch, located on the South & Western train line junction. Around ten years ago people also decided it was a great place to live and commute from. The other use is that it is the last stop on the main highway to board west bound trains. A feature, as you can see from the building, that not many people take advantage of."

At that point the train arrived. The engine was painted metallic gold and had a red and black stripe horizontally across it. What little wasn't glass on the carriages was painted the same. Andrew motioned Simon on board. The two guards went back to the van.

The carriages were larger than Simon was used to. They consisted of mostly thin metal frames and windows. In the first carriage, the seating was arranged in fours around a table. Andrew walked Simon through to the next carriage. Here the seating was more in line with the aeroplane they had left an hour ago.

Contrary to the plane, Simon was happy to note, the seats were much more luxurious; a dark crimson velvet with the letters TRL embroided in gold thread on the head rest. The seat width would have comfortably fit a sumo wrestler. The train started in motion again. Seconds later the clacking of going over the switch was heard and the train diverted, now heading west.

"For the people who boarded at Rolleston, a warm welcome to Trentsworth Rail's lunch time excursion. The buffet car is open and a wide range of snacks are available. You may wish to order a full meal from the menu, which can be found in the pouch in front of your seat. Press the orange button and one of our travelling consultants will be with you to take your order.

"As now all our scheduled passengers are on board, I will take you through a brief history of TRL. Trentsworth Rail Limited was the first railway in the country, originally put into service by the gold mining industry to bring in supplies and export the gold from Trentsworth. The large quantity of gold Trentsworth has mined is from the largest single source in the world. Initially the geography of the area made it totally impossible to full time mine as there was no way to bring in substantial supplies.

"Only the miners who enjoyed eating no more than small hard berries stayed around. Then some intrepid mountaineers decided to make monthly mountain crossings. They bought in supplies and took out the gold. These entrepreneurs charged high handling charges and amassed large profits. Hearing about the transport revolution of steam trains over in Europe, they purchased an engine and track.

"Back here they had commissioned the digging of the country's first transit tunnel. One of ten needed to allow the track access to Trentsworth's valley. It was a long wait for the mountaineers as a couple of the ships were lost. The engine was not fully assembled until more than a year passed. The delay wasn't noticed as the tunnels and viaducts were still being engineered. Finally, New Zealand got its first railway. Being totally imported, it was in European gauge.

"For financial reasons, the government's railway designers chose a narrow gauge. This enabled the engineers to get away with smaller cuttings into the hills. Therefore, the national railway did not comply with TSL's precedent. This of course makes TSL's rolling stock completely incompatible with the rest of the country. But for you, our customer, it provides a larger and more spacious carriage. A more enjoyable journey, as you make your way along the country's original scenic railway. Thank you for your time. This is Chief Consultant Peter Molesworth, wishing you a relaxing trip."

"No wonder Scott bought that claim", Simon mused out loud, "if it is true about it being the worlds largest gold source". Simon looked to his left where Andrew was asleep against the window. Simon looked out of the windows. The Canterbury plains stretched on for miles to the South. Ahead towards the front of the train were the mountains that would form his new prison.

Not for long though, he had plans forming in his mind. He didn't need the actual title deeds to sell the house to some idiot. Then he could sneak aboard the train after he set up a diversion. He would make them think he was still in Trentsworth. He would be back in Auckland before they knew he was missing.

Simon sniggered. He just realised they had made him already a free man. Simon is dead. They made so certain of that. They could not reverse their deception. Scott had not done anything illegal, so they couldn't set the police onto him. Simon decided to go for a wander, and stood up.

"Hold on, Scott," Andrew cautioned.

"Yes?" Simon turned to face Andrew, he was no longer asleep.

"Are you going past the buffet car? I could murder a mince pie, and a beer wouldn't go a miss. I'll pay you back later".

"I suppose," Simon smiled, "I'm a bit peckish, now you mention it, as well." He wandered to the front of the train. As he left the carriage, he looked back and Andrew was back asleep against the window. Andrew was not worried in the least that Simon would escape. Simon was slightly concerned at this. What did Andrew know that he didn't?

It could be that some IVRRAC guards had taken positions as passengers or employees. He realised he couldn't trust anyone on this train. And if they were here, now, what was to stop them being present on all trains in and out of

Trentsworth for the next six months? He knew they had a lot of money riding on him staying in Trentsworth and being a good boy. So he had to strike the train escape off his list and look for another way out of Trentsworth. One they hadn't thought of.

Simon decided to make the most of his walk. As he past the multitudes of rich tourists, he noticed some were looking out at the plains. Others, like Andrew, had fallen asleep. They all thought they owned the world. Nothing could harm them. Well, he would show them. Harm can come to the rich. They too can suffer like the poor.

He felt his stomach lurch a bit. He put his mind towards finding the buffet car. The train seemed longer than he would usually expect in this car orientated world. Finally he came upon a carriage with a counter running along the middle. Along the counter were bar stools. He sat down on one and waited for the waitress to notice him. She was serving a couple next to him. They were still looking at the menu. "Mince Pie?" the man asked, in a broad American accent.

"Classic Kiwi tucker," the waitress answered, smiling. "Ground beef in gravy, sealed in a savoury pastry shell".

"Pies are for dessert ma'am," the man replied. "A couple of cheese burgers." The waitress turned and placed the slip of paper she had been writing on next to the chef. Then she turned and faced Simon.

"And what would you like, sir?"

"Two mince pies and two beers," Simon answered, pointing to a can of beer on the counter. The waitress grabbed two paper bags from the pie warmer and two cans from the fridge. She placed them on a tray in front of Simon.

"That'll be thirty five dollars."

Simon handed over the money and walked back to his seat with the tray. It was at least an hour after he first stood up when he arrived back. Andrew looked up and smiled on his return. "Got my pie?" he asked, not one bit of concern showing about the length of time Simon had been gone.

"On the tray." Simon passed it to Andrew and sat down. Andrew took a pie and beer can and passed the tray with the remaining food back to Simon.

"Have you read all your documents?" Andrew said as the train plunged into darkness.

"Twice," Simon replied. "What happened to outside?"

"As you would have realised, we have now entered the first of the ten tunnels that mark our journey through the Southern

Alps," an announcement came over the speakers. "None of them are shorter than a kilometre, this one is three kilometres long piercing through the foothills.

"This is where the Trentsworth Railway also differs from standard New Zealand railway design. The developers were much more interested in speed of transit than cost. They dug tunnels rather than have reduced speed following the curvature of the hills. This tunnel also marks we are now in the last hour of this scenic journey.

"Digging tunnels also allowed for a constant gradient. Even though Trentsworth is at an altitude of fifteen hundred metres, that is over fourteen hundred metres above Rolleston, having a constant gradient means that the track only needs to rise two metres per one hundred. Being that the heaviest cargo was the trip back to Christchurch, this did not pose a problem to the developer's wish for speed.

"This as well was a great reason to bore tunnels. You try to slow a train down with carloads of gold behind you for a corner ahead. The Christchurch bound trains have a perfectly straight, one hundred and thirty kilometre, track to Rolleston.

"There were no passing bays originally from twenty kilometres out of Christchurch to Trentsworth itself. Now with diesel engines and lighter loads there have been more built across the Canterbury Plains to ease the time tabling..."

Simon let the announcer's voice get absorbed into the many other sounds in the carriage. He couldn't help asking the question to Andrew, "Is there still gold in the valley?"

"There were never 'Carloads of Gold'," Andrew replied. "Gold would be as cheap as brass if there were. Amazing what tourists will believe. But there was a lot of gold in Trentsworth. You have a claim. You can spend your six months trying to get something from the river. If you can access your claim that is." Andrew smiled. "Scott forgot to ask the crucial question of claim location. As you will find out"

"So what else am I supposed to do for the next six months?"

"Live the life of Scott. There are people all over the world who would give their eye teeth to spend one day in Trentsworth. You are spending six months there at the government's expense. You have enough money to party hard every night. You're not here to prove how conscientious you are on getting up in the morning and exercising. You could sleep all day every day as far as we are concerned."

"As long as I don't kill a richie, right?"

"Exactly!" Andrew smiled. "Though I think we would pull you out before the actual deed. It should be obvious if the programming failed. But it won't, definitely it won't"

"Who are you convincing? Me or yourself?" Simon noticed sweat on Andrew's forehead as he thought to himself, 'Fool, you've bitten off more than you can chew this time. You have never had an avenger of the poor, and now you are going to find out what I can really do.'

"You, of course. The programming cannot fail." Andrew weakly smiled, and then whispered to himself, "It would be a massacre if it did."

After those words the two men stayed quiet for a while. Simon knew that what he was going through was experimental and could fail. Which meant he could destroy what the richies hold dearest. Imagine the victory for the poor with the destruction of Trentsworth. No more richies' playground. He would infiltrate their social circles. Find out their weaknesses, then strike. No richie would stand in his way and live. His stomach started knotting up.

He looked out the window and got his mind quickly off the subject, more to stop Andrew knowing what he just was thinking about. If Andrew knew, he would probably pull the plug. His mind drifted back. It was too wonderful not to contemplate.

IVRRAC had handed him the winning ticket in the struggle

against the richies. They didn't even realise it. The joke would be on them. He would use the richies' own weapon against them. They thought they were rehabilitating him. He would rehabilitate them, and with more pain than any hypnotic stomach cramp. Which he realised was emerging with the line of thought. He looked at the valley beneath the train as it crossed the last viaduct.

The train then dove into a tunnel for the tenth and final time. As daylight broke through the window, Simon saw the most fantastic valley ever dreamed of. Pine trees were planted on the edges and cliffs of rock rose above the forests. In the middle was a deep blue lake, on which people were water skiing, paragliding, and just plain boating.

"Trentsworth A," a voice over the intercom announced. "Hot Pools, Trentsworth Towers Hotel, General Store and Ye Oldé Township."

"Wait until Trentsworth E," Andrew commanded as the train slowed down. They moved through a large shunting yard and eventually came to a stop outside a brick station. A few people got off, and the train started again. Simon noted they were presently on the north side of the valley, travelling anti-clockwise around the lake. It was barely mid afternoon and the high mountains had already shaded the sun.

"Trentsworth C, Westville, Trent's Castle, Race Track and

Working Men's Club rooms," The train went into another tunnel. A second later the tunnel ended. Simon realised they were now in the middle of a motor racing track. The train slowed to a stop as it drove into the grandstand building. They were now in an enclosed station.

A few more got off here; quite a few. Simon noted that they weren't wearing the latest clothes and gave more of an impression of average families coming back from a camping holiday. Once the train left the station, they travelled over the motor racing track. The sun was now shining through the window. The track hugged the hills as they rode along the south bank of the lake.

"Trentsworth E, Trentsworth Centre, South End and East Side." The train followed the lake and slowed as it rounded the corner so they were now on the east bank. The train slowly cruised into a white marble building. "Trentsworth E. Please all disembark and collect your luggage from the luggage carousels in the main building. Thank you for travelling Trentsworth Rail Limited.

They left the train. Trentsworth E looked brand new. Everything sparkled. Simon expected nothing less for the gateway to a richies' paradise. This station was also completely enclosed and looked more akin to an airport than a train station. Simon followed Andrew through the platform exit. They ended up in a large spacious lobby. Andrew and Simon followed the crowd and stopped around a black conveyer.

"Do you have a bag?" Simon asked.

"We both do." Andrew smiled. "It would get a bit obvious a person coming here to live and not have a couple of bags accompanying him. Now please remain quiet while we are close to the other travellers."

Simon noted that all the luggage appearing on the conveyor was all brand new. Most of them were adorned with the designer's signature or logo. One by one the tourists lifted their bags onto their luggage trolley and wandered off. The more opulent looking bags were being uplifted by a couple of men in uniform. The real rich wouldn't handle their own bags.

Andrew picked the bags off the conveyor, Simon helped him get them onto a trolley and they headed outside. The sun shone brightly outside and practically blinded Simon. He almost walked into one of the hotel courtesy buses. These were lined up in slanted parking right at the exit. In front of every bus was a uniformed person in the hotel colours. Each with their own clipboarded list of names in their hands.

"They take tourism seriously here," Simon commented.

"That they do," Andrew confirmed. "So far there has been

not one founded complaint about Trentsworth since the turnaround twenty years ago. The hilarious thing though, is that most the hotels are across the road from the station. The buses are more used as large luggage trolleys than people carriers. Get in"

Andrew had opened the door to a taxi, coloured metallic gold with a red and black stripe horizontally down the side. Written on the side in royal blue were the letters 'T T A' and the cab company's phone number. Andrew got in after Simon and the driver loaded the bags in the back. As he got back into his seat the driver asked, "Where to, gentlemen?"

"Thirty six Springfield Rd," Andrew replied. "And don't take any so called shortcuts," Andrew laughed, and the driver chuckled. Simon was puzzled until the taxi stopped again after three minutes and Andrew got out. "Stay here for a few minutes", he told the driver. "I will just help Scott in with the bags. Then you can take me to 155 Uegottabie Kidding Lane."

"We charge extra for insurance on that trip, sir," the driver commented.

"I know, I live there," Andrew smiled.

"Strange name for a road," Simon commented, as they walked down his new path to his new house.

"You wouldn't think so if you saw it. But the housing there is cheap, and I get an excellent view. We all cannot afford lakeside property." At this stage Simon had stopped listening and stood there with his mouth drooped open.

The house was like a mansion. Stone towers were added to the corners, which explained the name over the door 'Springfield Towers'. The stonework was all grey and the similarity to a castle was very unsubtly suggested. They got to the front door and Andrew handed Simon the keys. "Thank you," Simon responded, and after taking them from Andrew inserted one into the lock on the door. Simon twisted and heard a happy clunk as the mechanisms responded to his commands. Extracting the key, he pushed the door open and gazed inside. It was as bright inside as out. He strolled in, then Andrew followed.

The entrance led straight into the living area. Simon gasped. The area was two stories high and fronted by panoramic windows from floor to ceiling. On each side of the room, a staircase rose up towards the windows, then turned onto a u-shaped mezzanine that surrounded the room. A door was placed in the middle of each of the two side walls. "Wow!" was all Simon could say.

"Your kitchen is fully supplied down to fresh milk," Andrew announced. "I won't bother to show you around. You seem slightly preoccupied. I'm sure you can work out which room does what."

"Wow!" Simon repeated, as he gazed out the window. In front of the house was a small well-kept garden, which then merged into grass. The grass then merged with the sand of the lake shore. The grass was bisected by a well-laid footpath that followed the water's edge almost exactly. A couple of scantily dressed girls rode past on double wheeled blades, each listening to their own music stick.

Simon realised he could sit in this room forever. What he would spend his time doing was answered. He would have extreme fun, for the first time in his life. The richies finally don't have it all to themselves. 'And when I am done, Trentsworth is done,' he thought, reminding himself of who he was.

"Well, the taxi's waiting for me," Andrew interrupted Simon's thoughts. He held out his hand. "We'll bump into each other, don't worry."

"I wasn't." Simon smiled and shook Andrew's hand, and walked him to the door.

"Oh, and I'm required to warn you," Andrew continued. 'There is a reason why I have a house with a view of the whole valley. I also have binoculars and telescopes to match. This is a six month probation not a holiday". He paused and smiled. "Well at least not for me, you enjoy yourself."

With those words Andrew walked down the path and into the taxi. The taxi did a U-turn and drove off. Simon closed the door behind him as he started exploring the house.

Escaping Paradise

Once in the large living area, he opened the door on the south side of the room and found it opened into a short hallway. The first door to the left was the laundry with a chute coming through the ceiling. To the right a door opened into the kitchen, with large windows overlooking the lake. Next to the kitchen the hallway opened out onto a porch area with a glass door leading to the lakeside garden. Opposite the porch were two rooms, one had a large glass fronted shower in it and the other a toilet and basin.

The kitchen was what he was really after. He ended his explorations for the time being and made himself coffee. In the fridge he also found a cake topped with fresh cream. He settled down in a large comfortable chair facing the panoramic window. Finishing the cake and coffee, he spent the early evening watching the lake's activities.

It was hard to believe that three days ago he was locked up in a high security prison. The past events had moved so quickly. His grey closed in walls had now turned into one of the most sort after lounges in the country. His thinly padded office stool, into the most comfortable easychair he had ever experienced.

He was really still in shock. He didn't know who IVRRAC really were, but they seemed to be doing everything back to front. Why spend all this money on a guy like himself? Why leave him unattended in a large mansion? Were they so certain their stage show hypnotic suggestions would work? He was totally confused and tired. The thoughts just kept circling his mind as he watched the sun set behind the surrounding mountains.

After a while there were fewer and fewer people out on the lake. Then the valley got darker and the only thing visible was the lights of an old steamer sailing around in circles. He was starting to feel quite tired. He stood up and began to find his bedroom in this maze.

Assuming the bedroom would be upstairs he took the staircase nearest the kitchen up to the mezzanine floor. He tried the door to the hallway on that side and found a few other doors along it. None of the rooms seemed to be ready for him; the beds were all stripped and there were no clothes in the cupboards. Yet each one was twice the size of the room he had in his home back in the city. He wandered around to the other side of the mezzanine and opened that doorway.

It opened out into a small hallway about two metres long with only one door at the end. This door opened onto a large bedroom. It was three times the size of the others with a super kingsized bed in the middle. There were windows that overlooked the lake, the next door house and the street.

He found a switch on the wall by the door which automatically turned the vertical blinds to the closed position. Two doors were on either side of the door he came through. The one streetside was the ensuite. The one lakeside was a walk-in closet filled with clothes. He quickly undressed and slipped under the crisp cotton sheets. Once his head touched the soft pillow he was dead to the world.

The next morning he woke up to a reasonably bright room, as the sun tried to penetrate the vertical blinds above his head. The time of eleven thirty shone in red on the clock to his left. He decided it was time to get out of bed. After a shower to wake himself up, he walked into the wardrobe. The selection of clothes was unbelievable. Half of them he could not even imagine what their purpose was. He managed to find a sports shirt and jeans.

Venturing downstairs to the kitchen, he fixed himself a brunch of cream cake and coffee. 'No point wasting a good cream cake,' he convinced himself. He then sat down on what was fast becoming his favourite chair and watched the various tourist rides on the lake.

Finishing this lavish meal, he thought again about the strangeness of him not only ending up in a two and a half million dollar house, but one in the richest valley of New Zealand. Finally he was being recognised for all his hard work. His struggle against the rich was rewarded. So what if they had put him under hypnosis? That was a mere formality. It wouldn't stop him enjoying this life.

He was finally a richie. The thought came suddenly to his mind. The conniving bastards. They were getting him out of the picture. They were trying to convert him. The hypnosis was there just to stop him while he was being turned into one of them. It would not work. He had to escape. Get out of this valley before he was brainwashed into believing their stupid fairy tale.

But how? The train was easy to keep tabs on. He knew he couldn't get far on that. The mountains made a better prison wall than iron bars. The only other way out was following the river that emptied this lake. He seemed to remember reading about the outlet river. "Surrounded by sheer cliffs, it majestically flowed over huge waterfalls".

He pondered over what he could do to escape when something got his complete attention. An amphibian plane landed on the lake, avoiding the many holidaymakers. He could not take his eyes away from the plane. It slowed down and taxied towards him.

The plane ended up docked at the house next door. The pilot made his way up the wharf. A lady, much younger than the pilot, rushed up and hugged him. He guessed, hoped, that she was his daughter. He instantly found his escape plan, and she was the key. Pretend to fall in love with her, make her love him back so she would do anything for him, including getting him a one way ticket on that plane. Finally, a richie had a purpose.

Thinking of how he would go about seducing this woman, he got up and washed the dishes. He left them to dry on the bench and walked out his front door. He had decided he would spend the afternoon looking around the main centre. He had seen it on the way to his house and it would be a great way to clear his head and think about this new development.

After only five minutes walking south, he found himself in the busy centre of Trentsworth. Tourists were all over the place, ducking from one souvenir shop to another. Occasionally they stopped for a cappuccino or latté, then it was straight back into the shops.

The main area was an outside mall ending in a wharf. Every

shop was either a café or a souvenir shop. He had left Springfield Road as it started rising over the top of the station car park, using the station itself as a bridge support. It rose to hug the southern edges of the valley about twenty metres above the railway line he came in on. Expensive looking houses and hotel complexes were built above and below this road. The north facing slopes were obviously the most sought after and steepest.

He could still see the majestic structures over the top of the shops in the precinct. They would have a grand view of the valley. Above those was a road that twisted and turned up the steep slope. He rightly guessed that this was Andrew's street and he realised there would be no where in the valley that would escape those eyes

Trentsworth was indeed a prison. He looked around the shops at all the richies spending money with no care. He had to start his escape plans now, before he became just another one of them. His mind turned again to the girl with the plane. To successfully woo this woman, he had to make it look as though it was a coincidence that they met. He would have to bump into her here, knocking on her door would be too obvious.

The next day he decided to get the information on the claim. Maybe today he would see the lady next door. She would need to go to the shopping complex sometime. A young lady like her would not stay cooped up inside a house for too long.

The council offices were located on the upper level of the train station. The only obvious way up was by elevator. As the glass elevator rose, it occurred to him that the whole area was based around the station. He found the claims office and sat in the waiting room. The windows overlooked the shopping centre to the north. The bustling area started on the southwest corner of the last intersection across Springfield Road before it rose over the station. To the west the intersecting road curved around a bit but kept in a south-westerly direction. It ended in a wharf on the lake. The eastern side of this road immediately became the station's car park.

The car park was very wide at this point. The car park's southern end was at right angles to the rest. It ran along the northwest wall of the station, and was where all the bus parks were. On the west of Springfield Road, the station turned a slight corner to face due north. This was where Simon was looking out. Immediately beneath him was a grassed area surrounded by shops on three sides. On a southwest angle the grass turned into a sterile concrete wharf.

On the wharf, at the end of each of the two jetties, was a collection of kiosks, each advertising a particular thrill ride on the lake. Docked at the far end of the wharf was the old steamer he had seen sailing the night before.

"Mr Tallburg", the receptionist announced, "Mr Fallsbury will see you now." It took him a few seconds to realise the receptionist was speaking to him. He turned and smiled at her as he entered the door with Mr Fallsbury's name on it.

Simon came out of the station and into the crowd quite dazed. He was still thinking the oddity over and over again. "Inaccessible by boat, road or even walking track." Apparently a climber with three years' experience could just make the trip. So much for the claim; Mr Tallburg was duped quite successfully.

He stopped and looked around him. He was in the middle of the grassed area. He collected his thoughts. 'Now to find the ticket out of here.' It was a long shot finding her in this crowded location. He scanned the grass and did not see anyone familiar. He decided to try the street in the middle of the precinct.

Following the concrete wharf to the north, he found the main mall again. The docked steamer was positioned directly opposite. Again, she was no where to be found. He sat down at one of the cafés and looked at the documentation.

That night he decided he needed to do this methodically. He would get up early and watch her house. When she left, he would follow her into town. Then he would strike. He had wasted two days. He couldn't afford to waste any more. He could feel it; he was becoming one of them. He was starting to enjoy all these luxuries.

The alarm woke him from his deep sleep. Rubbing his eyes, he made his way into the shower. Afterwards he set up a chair in his bedroom overlooking her front door. He was in luck, for not long afterwards she came out and walked up the street.

He waited a few minutes and then walked out of the house, following her at a great distance, making sure she wouldn't think anything of him being behind her. It didn't take long for him to lose her in the bustling crowd. Slowly walking up and down the road, he admitted that she was well and truly hidden. Finally, after an hour and a half, he spotted her at one of the café tables. She was sitting down with a flat white and a book. He located the café that owned that particular set of tables and ordered a cappuccino. He then sat down at her table looking apologetic. "Is it okay if I sit here? There doesn't seem to be any spare tables."

"Sure," she replied not taking her eye off the book. "Just don't try to start a conversation, I am at an interesting part."

"That's okay." Simon looked up at this lady. She was quite beautiful. 'Unfortunately,' he reminded himself, 'she was one of the richies.' He would quite fancy her if she was a normal person like himself. But he had to get to know her, regardless of her status. Trying to get the introduction started, he ventured a simple observation, "Busy here today".

"Please," she growled as she turned to look at him, their gaze locking for a mere second. "I said I am at an interesting part of my book." She then paused, stared at Simon with a flustered expression on her face, then burrowed her head back into the book.

"Sorry!" Simon sarcastically replied before he could catch himself. What right had that rich bitch to silence him. But he did need to be on the right side of this person to escape Trentsworth. It was only that fact that saved her miserable life. He felt a slight twinge in his guts.

Darn that hypnosis, if it weren't for that, he would be able to get a flight with a trusty kitchen knife. Now he had to be nice to the richies to get out of this valley. He changed the subject in his mind to calm his stomach down.

Sitting back, he watched the crowds move along the mall. It was like a seemingly endless swarm of people flowing around him. The waiter came over with his coffee. Picking up the cup, he starting slowly sipping it. He didn't want to finish too soon. He didn't want to leave without starting a conversation with her.

He wondered what the original settlers would have thought of this place now. No eating berries off the odd bush here. All around him was a jungle of shops and cafés. The whole area was obviously designed by the same concrete junkie who created the station. All made of precast concrete walls and aluminium windows. The architect had attempted to hide this with different pioneer facades for each shop, but had failed miserably.

She looked up from the book. How could she have been so rude to this man. She found, since he had spoken to her, she had problems concentrating on the words printed in front of her. She didn't feel like reading any more.

She watched this man who sat opposite her. He was gazing at the awful concrete jungle around them. He was well built, about her own age. His mere greeting had made her feel more alive than ever before. There was something deep within her that had been generated by his smile. How could a complete stranger make her feel this way? With so few words? But he did. She wasn't one to believe in love at first sight, but this man seemed to make her whole past life feel like a dull dream. A dream she had now awoken from.

She pondered his last question. She did not want him to leave before starting a conversation with him. "Actually, it's reasonably quiet for this time of year."

"Huh?" Her answer caught him off guard. He looked at her and saw that he had her full attention. "Oh sorry, I was busy thinking of what the original settlers would have thought, if they were here today, with all these people and buildings."

"Not much, being two centuries dead", she couldn't stop herself. She felt so at ease with him. They both chuckled at her small joke.

"Very clever," Simon replied. "You know what I mean."

"I would say Trent would have been proud."

"Trent?"

"Who the place is named after?" She derided. 'He is new here,' she thought to herself. 'I can show him around. What a great excuse to get to know this guy.' She then, in a more friendly tone, continued. "Apparently he escaped off Tasman's ship, December 1642"

"Tasman?"

"You know, the Dutch guy? The reason the country's called New Zealand? The guy who discovered Australasia?" She pondered to herself, 'Is he having me on, or is he just stupid?'

"Oh him". Simon smiled. He knew who Tasman was, every

New Zealander did. "Trent isn't a very Dutch name, though."

"Neither is it Spanish"

"What's Spain got to do with this?"

"Trent was a Spanish spy on Tasman's ship. He felt he was just about to be found out. So he jumped ship while Tasman sailed past the West Coast. Rumour has it that he was the one that persuaded the Maori to attack Tasman's ship. But I think that is going too far, myself". She looked across at him; he seemed puzzled. "You know they attacked him just north of the South Island?"

"Yes! I knew that," Simon lied. "You are a fountain of knowledge, aren't you". 'Richies! Always showing off. Do I really have to get to know this woman?' he asked himself.

"Got it hammered into us at High School. Part of a tourism scheme, all the locals are to know all about Trentsworth's history". 'Easy, don't over do it,' she thought, 'No one likes a know it all.' She had already destroyed a few prospective relationships with her excessive talking. But this guy just made her want to keep going. His grey eyes staring straight at her. His dark hair, hard to tell the exact colour in the bright sunlight, framing his handsome face.

"So, you're a local then?" Simon asked, trying to keep the

pretence of it being a coincidence they met. Trying to keep a liking for this richie.

"Mostly, moved here when I was thirteen." She looked at him and smiled. "Though some here would consider me a long term tourist."

"I guess you could call me that as well," Simon stated. "Moved in two days ago. I was going to mine a claim, but I found out where it was yesterday."

"You're not Scott Tallburg, are you?" she asked, thinking to herself, 'Wow! My luck has changed. He's my next door neighbour.'

"Yes I am", Simon answered, 'Shit, she is quick on the uptake'. "What made you come to that conclusion?"

"I knew, well everyone knew, that you purchased the 'Fools Claim' as it is known. Changed hands more often than any of the other claims put together. It is also common knowledge that you moved in day before yesterday. Trentsworth is quite a small town, really". She smiled, "I'm Kyndrea, I live next door to you."

"Hi," Simon responded. "Which side?"

"North, you know the one with the amphibian docked on

the wharf"

"Oh right, that side." Simon feigned ignorance, thinking, 'Not even fully introduced and she is already showing off her treasures. Richies!'

"Pretty obvious isn't it. I have asked dad hundreds of times to get a shed for it. I feel it's so pretentious, it being the only one in Trentsworth."

"Why don't others have them, must be a godsend not having to rely on the train system," Simon asked. He smiled from cheek to cheek. 'She said "dad"! I was right.'

"We don't use it much for actual travel. The train is cheaper than the airport fees at the other end. Dad just likes flying. So what did you do before coming here? The local rag was pretty unspecific on that."

"I was a messenger," Simon answered, then thinking to himself, 'Made sure everyone got the message.' A slight twinge in his stomach forced him to look into Kyndrea's eyes, trying to keep his thoughts off the violence. Her eyes were green but also slightly hazel. They matched her light brown, sun streaked hair perfectly. She had it tied back in a pony tail, but he imagined her with it flowing over her shoulders.

"A bit different than lying around Trentsworth doing nothing", she observed. She looked at him. He wasn't telling her the full truth. He was hiding something, but just made her want to know him more.

"You can say that again. But I am not just going to lie around, believe me", Simon stated, continuing to himself, 'You and your richie friends will find that out soon enough.' He looked at her, trying to keep a pleasant look on his face, which was easier than he first thought. Just looking at Kyndrea made him feel strangely fulfilled. "And yourself?"

"Lie around Trentsworth doing nothing", she smiled, half laughing. "No, seriously. I mostly look after my father; that itself is almost a full time job."

"What about your mum?"

"Died around ten years ago." Kyndrea immediately started getting teary eyed.

"Sorry to hear that", Simon comforted. A fleeting thought went through his head. 'Do the rich have feelings? But then what can a richie know of suffering. You wait Missy. Just wait. You will know the real meaning of suffering when I am finished.' He passed her a serviette from the table, trying to ignore the cramps in his stomach.

"That was why dad and I moved here", Kyndrea continued,

"Start life anew". She wiped her eye with the serviette. She didn't know why but she was still very upset about it. It was as though it happened yesterday, rather than a decade ago. Perhaps it was the way her mum died.

Simon decided to change the subject. "It would have been nice if someone had told me about the location of the claim. Before I handed over the money."

"Maybe you'll be the one to find a way to mine it". Kyndrea laughed, obviously not having much confidence in her words.

"Laugh all you want, I will find a way," Simon retorted, thinking to himself, 'Either that or find a way to escape. Which is why I am even talking to you in the first place, Miss Kyndrea.' Just then there was the sound of a steam whistle. Simon looked over at the steamer. There was a lot more smoke coming out of the funnels.

"Lunch time cruise on the Yohanne", Kyndrea explained.

"Do you want to go?" Simon asked. He needed to quickly get to know this girl intimately. There was no time to muck around with being careful.

"No, I have a lunch date with some friends."

"Oh." Simon didn't hide his disappointment.

"But", Kyndrea added, "I am free for lunch tomorrow. As you're the new one here, I'll shout."

"You're on"

"Meet you at the wharf this time tomorrow, then." Kyndrea got up and smiled as she left the table, quickly being absorbed into the crowd.

Simon just sat there pondering his surprising success, until his thoughts were broken by a waiter asking if he wanted anything else. Realising he had nothing else to do he ordered lunch.

Just the Ticket

Standing on the wharf, Simon waited. The whistle had just blown and there was no sign of Kyndrea. Was she standing him up? Then, to his relief, he saw her running through the crowds.

"Sorry for being late", she apologised as she caught her breath. They joined the queue at the ticket office. "Everyone leaves their tickets to the last minute. No good if the weather is bad. "

"Outside decks?" Simon blurted out before realising he could see the answer. Most of the decks were sheltered.

"Some, but believe it or not the lake can get quite choppy". Kyndrea paused, thoughtfully. "You know I don't invite every strange man I meet to a cruise. It's just that, you know, neighbours and all."

"What's the world coming to that you can't invite your next

door neighbour to lunch."

"Exactly," Kyndrea laughed. Why was she shouting this stranger to lunch? There was something about him. She had met handsome men before. It was part and parcel of her leisure job. This Scott, he was turning her heart inside out. Worst of all, she didn't know why. It was as though they were meant to be together. She couldn't believe herself. It was just like being in one of those awful romance novels. 'Their eyes locked together. Both of them knowing they could never be apart, ever again.' She giggled to herself.

"It wasn't that funny. You can stop now." Simon nervously laughed. 'Is she having me on? Is this just a game to her? How could she know I am poor? It would just be like the rich, though, to lead a poor man on, then when he is at ease, laugh him out the door.'

"Sorry", Kyndrea looked up at Simon. "You made me think of an old joke I heard."

"What was the joke?" Before Kyndrea could to answer, they were interrupted by the lady behind the ticket counter.

"How many, please?"

"Two, thank you Susan," Kyndrea answered.

"Oh", a look of recognition came onto Susan's face, "Kyndrea, having a good day?"

"Very much so", Kyndrea looked straight into Simon's eyes. "And yourself?"

"Just the normal", Susan replied, handing over two tickets. "Though Reg is home with the flu again."

"Wish him well for me," Kyndrea said as they walked towards the steamer.

They boarded the small steamboat docked nearby. There was a reasonably sized dining room situated on the lower deck and a café on the upper. Kyndrea showed Simon to a table in the dining room and a waiter came over with two menus. He handed one first to Kyndrea then Simon. Simon☐fs face dropped as he read down the list.

"I will definitely need to access that claim at these prices," Simon grumbled, but trying to be light about it.

"This is one of the cheapest places to dine, Scott", advised Kyndrea. She looked at him with a smile on her face. "You should get in touch with reality. Haven't you eaten out in the last ten years?"

"Not for a while, no"

"Oh?"

Simon looked at Kyndrea, 'She wants an explanation,' he thought. 'Time to see if my study of Scott Tallburg was successful.' He put down the menu and gazed into her eyes. "Until a couple of months ago, I had just enough money to survive. So there was no way I could afford luxuries like this. My aunt never gave us any money while we were alive. She hoarded it all to herself. I guess if my mum was still alive, all the inheritance would have gone to the cat. Dad's family never got on with mum's. Especially after he left."

"Your dad left?"

"For another woman. He never bothered to keep in contact. The first I heard from his family was the cheque in the mail. I guess my aunty still had a soft spot for me. Blood thicker than water, etc. Water will do me though. If dad was a still around, I wouldn't cross the footpath to save his life."

"You feel betrayed," Kyndrea confirmed. "I feel full of anger for my mum dying. But at least she didn't leave me consciously. How could a man be so callous as to break off from his son."

"Believe me, it is possible". Simon sighed. "This conversation is getting a bit too deep for me. I am not used to spilling out my life story". Simon looked back at the menu, then up at

Kyndrea. "It's interesting, I have just met you and already I'm telling you things I couldn't even tell my mum."

"When did your mum die?" Kyndrea asked, though it was getting a bit close to home again.

"She died of a broken heart ten and a half years ago. She basically starved to death. Then I was officially labelled an orphan and put into care."

"I suppose at least I have my dad. You should meet him. Though once he hears I shouted you a lunch on this boat, he'll think we're serious. He jumps to conclusions like that often," she laughed.

"Are you ready to order?" the waiter asked. Neither of them noticed his approach. Simon ordered a steak and Kyndrea some fish and a bottle of Sauvignon Blanc. They looked at each other's eyes as the waiter went off towards the kitchen. No one spoke for a while as they just sat there.

Kyndrea just soaked in Simon's features. She could not find fault in any of them, Simon busy thinking what to do next in the conversation. He kept reminding himself who this person opposite actually was. 'A richie, nothing more, nothing less. What pretence do I have to act out to get on that plane,' he pondered.

"So", Simon said, breaking the spell, "Who would be the guy you would immediately fall in love with then?"

"Me?" Kyndrea laughed. "Me fall in love? Now that's funny!" But she felt that it was already a fait accompli and she didn't know why. He was a rouge. He grew up on the wrong side of the lake, so to speak. Yet there was something about him that made her feel so alive.

The waiter came and placed their respective meals in front of them. Kyndrea smiled at Simon while she seasoned her food. They ate in almost silence, Simon wondering how far he would have to go to gain Kyndrea's confidence; Kyndrea pondering how come Scott made her feel that her whole past life was just a dream, from which she now had awoken as though she was sleeping beauty and Scott was the handsome prince. He was handsome, no debate there.

She felt safe around Scott. She knew he could never hurt her. There was no logical reason for her to think this way, but since when had love been logical? An old saying came to her mind, 'This is the first day of the rest of your life.' This was the life she wanted, no holding back this time. She was going for the chance of being with Scott and blow the consequences. She had always been careful, tiptoeing around on egg shells. All that did was destroy any chance of being truly related. Scott was worth the risk; he was whom she was waiting for. She just knew it, with every bone in her body.

Simon had surprised himself being so open with her. Sure a lot of the story was just that, made up by the IVRRAC team. His father leaving, though, was true as was the part about his mother. He never told anyone before, let alone allow the emotion to show as well. He had obviously immersed himself in the part too well. If it got him out of this prison it would be worth it. After all, if he did break this heart of Kyndrea's, who cares; she is just a richie.

"I suppose I am just a plain romantic," Kyndrea answered, after the waiter had collected the plates. "I suppose I would want someone who isn't scared to tell the whole world of his love for me. Someone who would write in mile high letters 'I Love You, Kyndrea.' Someone who makes mistakes. I don't want a perfect person, for I am not. One who will admit to being wrong and ask for forgiveness. Someone who is strong but knows when to be weak. A man who is handsome of course; must keep up my standards." Kyndrea laughed.

"What about financial status?" Simon queried. 'There she is,' he thought, 'making light of keeping up standards.' Yet he knew how much standards meant to the rich.

"Oh, to me intelligence is the most important aptitude". Kyndrea looked at Simon, 'He's worried about his chances. Be careful,' she warned herself. Even that morning, money would have been the major concern for considering a possible companion, but now, yes now it didn't matter. "Money comes to those who think, and work, plus my dad needs someone to bounce his views and theories off. I quite enjoy having the odd intellectual discussion as well. A man like yourself, really." She laughed, and Simon could not help joining in. "What about you?" She continued, "Who would be your perfect woman?"

"Oh, I take people as they are, no prejudice there."

Kyndrea smiled, thinking to herself, 'Everyone has a prejudice, what is yours Mr Tallburg?' She looked him straight in the eyes. "Really, you treat everyone the same?"

"Of course, everyone the same," Simon answered. 'Except,' he thought, 'richie scum like you, but they don't count.' The whistle sounded and Simon noted that they were coming into dock. He didn't want to lose this chance he had to organise their next meeting. "So what are your plans this afternoon?"

"Meeting my friends again. We've planned to have a morning shopping tomorrow in Christchurch. So we have decided to stay the night. We're taking the late afternoon train, having an evening meal out on the town. Sometimes it's good to get out of the valley."

"Oh I agree with that." Then continuing to himself, 'More than you know.'

"But I have to be back early. I have a Black Tie dinner on tomorrow night. In fact I purchased two tickets," she lied. "One for me and one for dad. But dad has decided, in his wisdom, that he needs to stay home. He gets easily bored at these functions. So if you want I can take you instead. I know it is quite short notice". She knew the organiser, should be easy getting the extra ticket.

"Sounds good to me," Simon smiled. "You know, I should be the one asking you out."

"Chauvinist!" She laughed. "I'm sure you will have your turn. But make the most of me paying the bill. I warn you, I have expensive tastes."

"You? No, you wouldn't, would you?" Simon replied back trying to make light of her comment, thinking, 'You would buy the world if you could, you rich bitch.' But the hate wasn't there as it should be. The thought didn't give him the satisfaction it used to. He wondered what was happening, was it the hypnosis? Perhaps he was being more careful now to avoid the pain. Yes, that was the reason. "Where shall we meet tomorrow?"

"I'll pick you up from your place at seven thirty tomorrow

evening. Remember it is black tie." Then the boat docked and they went their separate ways.

Kyndrea went straight to see Janine about the black tie. Once Janine heard what it was for she managed to find another ticket. She was a great organiser, but she went after anyone in trousers. Especially men Kyndrea liked. Time was getting on. Kyndrea had to rush home to pack for the trip. On the way, Kyndrea thought about the next night. Concern built up whether inviting Scott to the dinner was a safe thing to do. He was different to Martin; he would stay true to her.

Simon spent the rest of the day looking at all the tourist activities available. There was plenty of brochures on display, scattered throughout the shopping centre. Trentsworth was not short of adventure, if you had the money. He wondered if he would have time to experience any of them before the escape.

The clouds started gathering around the mountains and the temperature dropped. He decided it was time to get back to his house. He found some frozen meals in the freezer. He reheated one for tea. Afterwards he sat down in what was becoming his favourite chair with a cup of coffee. Drinking the warm liquid, he looked out the window. Beyond the cloud covered walls which made his new prison, he noticed a pinkish tinge.

He watched the clouds slowly clearing away from the majestic mountains, revealing the artistry of their afternoon's work. The snow covered the entire top of the mountain range surrounding the valley, the gleaming white layer clinging to the rock cliffs as easily as the chocolate coating remains on a freshly dipped strawberry.

The sun was gently sliding behind the mountains to the west highlighting the top ridges, making them resemble a cardboard cut out against the pale blue-pink background of the sky. The taller peaks developing white fur as the snow on the other side evaporated, a final effort from the dying sun's heat. The valley had gone silent, almost in awe of the dramatic scene unfolding. The valley once more bid farewell to the sun. Simon watched as the giant peaks became silhouettes and then blended into the black of the night sky.

He thought about the day's events. He couldn't believe his luck that Kyndrea opened up like that, that she was so infatuated with him. It was as though it was meant to be. She was there to be used for his escape. Use her and dump her, or kill her. He smiled, then winced with the pain. Something was not quite right. Nothing ever was this easy for him. But then, he was due for a change in luck. He decided it was best not to think about it. A yawn forced its way through his mouth. Time for bed, busy night tomorrow evening. What on earth was a black tie dinner?

The Refugee from Misery

Simon awoke the next day at ten o'clock. After breakfast he looked around the house some more. He opened the door to the lower level of the north wing. It opened onto a large room which took up all of that wing. The floor was about a metre lower than the rest of the house, making the room about four metres high. He walked down the ramp on the other side of the door flanked by two waist height glass brick walls.

At the northern end, going east-west, was a small swimming pool with three marked lanes. On the western side between the pool and the lounge was a spa. On the eastern side was a full size snooker table. Simon set up the pool balls and started a game with himself.

It was almost lunch time when the door bell rang. Simon walked back into the lounge and headed to the central front door. He opened it and found Andrew on the other side. "Oh it's you," he observed.

"Settling in are we?" Came the obvious question, as Andrew walked into the lounge.

"Pretty much. Come in." Simon had not expected to see Andrew so soon. Then he realised he should have, being that he was still in a prison of sorts. In prison you do see the guards quite often.

"So, how are you?" Andrew queried as he sat down in Simon's favourite chair.

"Better if the claim you gave me was worth something," Simon answered in a disapproving tone. He chose to sit on Andrew's left. The view of Kyndrea's was blocked by a tree growing on the boundary. "As you can see I am still here. Is there anything else?" Simon felt ill at ease with Andrew around. He didn't like guards poking their nose in, especially when an escape plan was being implemented.

"Oh I thought I'd just pop in and see how you are going. I'm amazed you went to the claim office so soon after arriving. We couldn't afford a proper claim as this house put us back quite a bit. Our budget is limited."

"I was quite curious". Simon watched a water skier on the lake, then turned back to Andrew. "So has anyone been able to reach this claim?"

"Oh, it was well excavated in the nineteenth century. So before you think it would be worth spending money getting there, it is doubtful." Andrew smiled at Simon, "Someone would have done it long before you if there was a chance of getting the investment back."

"Thanks," Simon sarcastically replied. He noted there was almost a laugh in that smile. He was enjoying having the control over him. 'Well, enjoy it while you can. You will be laughing on the other side of your face soon enough,' he thought as he played along with the conversation. "So I have only the money in the bank."

"That's right. Enough to last you the six months, including the occasional meal out and paid adventure. Though if you want to save the money for when you leave, you would be best to get a job. Either that or find a rich girl and marry her." Andrew laughed. "I think a job would be easier. Besides, you now have a clean slate. You are Scott now. You have not broken any laws, not even a parking ticket. And to be honest, I think there are rules about leaving this valley with no attachments. Parole board have no romance in their souls."

"Me? Marry a richie?" Simon laughed. He looked carefully at Andrew's eyes. Then he dismissed the thought. There would be no way Andrew would know his plans. Then it occurred to him, Andrew might know something else. "I must admit, I have been invited out. What is a black tie dinner?"

"You have already been invited to a Black Tie? My gosh, you do work quick. Perhaps you won't need to get a job after all." Andrew slapped Simon on the shoulder as he got up from his chair. He motioned Simon to follow.

"Ha ha." Simon could not help smile, though. He got up and followed Andrew up the stairs. "Well, she's the quick one. One lunch meeting and she invites me to this black tie thingy."

"Well, well. I suppose you had better look the part. I am sure we provided you with the right clothes. After all, Scott is meant to be a guy who wants all the things of the rich."

Simon followed Andrew into the master bedroom. Andrew looked through the wardrobe and found the Black Tie attire. "There you go, Scott. One white shirt, black bow tie, black trousers and jacket. You will be one of the crowd this evening. Remember the Italian shoes as well. I expect it's a charity function. They usually are, an excuse for the rich to meet friends. Have a great meal and feel good that they are helping the more unfortunates."

Andrew stayed for lunch and left Simon the afternoon to get ready. During lunch he had continued on about the dinners. Warning him about the ploy of feeding the guests copious amounts of alcohol, then having an auction once their defences were down. Andrew finished off by reminding him of his limited funds.

Simon shook Andrew's hand as they said their farewells at the door. Now that Andrew was talking more, Simon realised he was quite a likable guy. He seemed down to earth and obviously didn't think much of the rich society. Well, he was going to spend the next six months with Andrew being his only outside contact. He supposed it was good that he enjoyed his company.

Then he remembered the purpose of going out with Kyndrea. It wouldn't be six months. Hopefully it wouldn't even be a month. In which case he had to impress Kyndrea. He had a long session in the bathroom. Something that was completely against his nature, but then so was going out with a richie. Feeling that his hair was a bit untidy he even went off to a hair salon, unable to find a local barber, to get his hair cut. Now that was an experience he found very unique, and hoped it would stay that way.

The train arrived back at six o'clock. There was barely enough time to get ready. Why did she decide to go to the city, today of all days? She did have a great time with her friends, and she also found the perfect dress for the evening, plus she had her hair styled in the most exclusive salon in Christchurch.

She had thought the trip would be long and drawn out. She was so excited about that evening. Now she had returned it seemed all a blur, as though it was just a dream. She got a taxi home, so as not to upset the hair styling. Her father greeted her at the door with his standard comment about her stunning looks. She smiled and returned a short hello as she rushed up the stairs to her room.

Simon watched from his bedroom window. Richies, spend all that money in the big city, then waste more on a taxi. Tonight he would be entering their den. He would be at the mercy of them. But not for long, and then... He started getting cramps again. He concentrated on getting his shirt done up. At least the bow was pre tied on an elastic band.

Seven thirty came around and the doorbell rang. Simon opened the door. "Wow! You look fantastic!" Was all he could mutter at the sight.

Kyndrea looked at his shocked expression and smiled. She portrayed a definite likeness to a fairy tale heroine. She wore a large ball gown flowing out from all sides. Her hair was tied up with little white flowers through it. He looked at her face. It was so beautiful. The taxi on the street gave a quick hoot on its horn. Simon quickly grabbed his jacket and walked Kyndrea up the path.

He felt so proud. He had made it. He was now a richie. He caught himself, 'No I'm not! I am still Simon Tallsbury. I am the avenger for the poor. I am a spy now, nothing more.' What was happening to him? 'Blasted hypnosis! Messing around with my mind.' He had to watch himself. He was now his own enemy. 'Concentrate! Open the door for her. Behave like a gentleman.' His hand went under the chrome handle of the car door. Pulling it open, he stood aside and let her get in. Closing it again, he went around and got in on the street side. She said a hotel's name to the driver. The taxi made a U-turn and drove up over the station into the collection of hotels behind.

It didn't take long. The taxi stopped underneath a covered entranceway. The porters rushed up and opened their doors. Simon and Kyndrea got out. He was reminded of watching the Academy Awards on television and how the movie stars were helped out of the limousines.

The large glass doors opened automatically as they approached. An enormous foyer greeted them once they were through the threshold. Scattered throughout this extensive three storied space were clusters of chairs and potted plants. To their left was a large marble counter stretching along one wall. Behind the counter, five uniformed staff were standing, silently waiting. The surrounding walls were all a textured cream. Large highly polished brass chandeliers hung from the ceiling. Kyndrea lead Simon through the maze of leather and greenery towards a grand staircase. It had a wide welcoming base that got narrower as it curved up to the mezzanine floor at the back of the foyer.

As they approached the top, Simon saw an impressive three metre high doorway. The doors were wide open. There was a lot of chatter coming from within. At the top of the stairs a man dressed in a dinner suit welcomed them and politely requested the tickets. Kyndrea showed them to him and he moved slightly aside to let them pass. Near the entrance to the room there was a line of waiters holding forth a tray of drinks, from beer to champagne. Kyndrea stopped at the first waiter. She turned and smiled at Simon. He looked back at her, then at the waiters. He was at the threshold to the richies' world. Once he stepped past these guards, he would be one of them.

Suddenly it hit Simon at full force; he was a fraud! He couldn't go through with this. Here he was, standing at the top of some stairs. People were offering him a range of drinks, like he was royalty. He wasn't royalty. He wasn't rich. He didn't belong. He should have been the man on the other side of the tray.

He looked around. There was no one noticing him. What would they do when they found out he was just a poor man, a despised piece of garbage. He was surrounded by richies. He wouldn't get out of there alive; he was trapped. He couldn't even raise a finger to them as the hypnosis would stop him defending himself. He felt like Trent on a ship full of Dutchmen.

"Scott!" Kyndrea brought him back. "For the third time. Do you want a drink? The decor isn't that amazing. It is good, granted, but it needn't take your breath away."

"Huh?" Simon smiled. 'Keep up the pretence.' "Beer, I think." He took a glass and followed Kyndrea into the crowd, taking a deep breath. 'Fraternising with the enemy,' he thought, but then so was going out with a richie. He needed that plane, he told himself.

The room on the other side of the large doorway was two stories high. Smaller brass and crystal chandeliers gave the room light. The ceiling was plastered with so many patterns that it looked like an upside down wedding cake. The wall was also textured with large rectangular plaster boarders. The outside of the large rectangles were a dark crimson, the inside a dark cream. Simon felt as though he was in the main ballroom of a royal palace. Directly in front of them and to the right were a multitude of round tables set for dinner. To their left was a dance floor of polished wood, Simon didn't have a clue what type. At the end of the dance floor was a podium. On either side were sets of large straight tables, on which were various items. Kyndrea lead him straight to the nearest set of tables covered in expensive items. "Tom bola, you buy a ticket for ," she paused, looking for a notice, "Two hundred dollars. During the meal they announce that it is time. Then there is a rush for the tables. First in gets the best products and so on."

"Seems a waste of money, some of these aren't worth a hundred." He picked up a metal object with retractable legs. For the life of him he couldn't work out what it was used for.

"It is," she giggled, "It all goes towards a good cause."

He looked further down the table. "Look at this, a certificate for a decorating consultant. I guess that means you are spending two hundred dollars. Then have someone to tell you how to spend thousands on paint and wallpaper."

"I usually charge at least five hundred a room," a lady said behind Simon. "But I throw in advice on how to spend tens of thousands purchasing furniture."

"Hi Janine!" Kyndrea laughed and Simon turned around to face Janine. She was dressed in a tight red velvet dress showing off her voluptuous figure, low cleavage and curved hips. A sparkling diamond necklace was around her neck. Her short golden hair offset the matching earrings which almost touched her shoulders. Her face was hidden under a layer of thick make up.

"I see you put your extra ticket to good use," she commented, smiling. She turned to Simon, her eyes searching every part of his body. "Hi, I'm Janine Gousing." She held out her right hand to Simon. He shook it, feeling the weight of the silver looking bangle banging against her slim wrist. It, too, was covered in diamonds.

"Janine, this is Scott Tallburg," Kyndrea introduced. "He lives next door. Scott, Janine has been busy these past few weeks getting everything together for tonight."

"So you organised this evening?" Scott queried as he released Janine's hand. "Must be quite a skill. You do this often?"

"Certainly. I am quite involved in the charity scene in my spare time". Her brown eyes stayed permanently fixed on Simon. "So how come I've never seen you before? However, Kyndrea, did you manage to keep him secret."

"Not hard, Janine. We just met a couple of days ago. Scott is my new next door neighbour." Kyndrea attempted a smile, thinking, 'Impossible to keep any man a secret from you, Janine. Just keep you hands off this one, bitch.'

"Oh, the one that bought the fools claim!" Janine's smile enlarged even more. "Everyone has heard of your purchase. It is definitely a good idea coming tonight. This is a great way to get to know your neighbours. And of course, all the right people."

"Janine's Black Ties are well known for their entertainment.

They are a great networking opportunity for any New Zealand businessman", Kyndrea explained.

"And the word is spreading, Kyndrea. In fact I have a few guests from America tonight. The auction should be quite interesting. So, Kyndrea thought you needed to meet some interesting people?" Janine surmised, her gaze lowering to his belt. "You needn't go any further than me. I can show you a very interesting time."

"I am sure you can. Thanks for the offer", Simon responded, holding Kyndrea close. "But I already have a great guide for the valley".

"Well, must mingle," Janine announced, her eyes back on Simon's. "Nice meeting you, perhaps Scott we'll met again. I assure you, you won't regret it." She winked and smiled. Turning, she saw a group of men in the distance and made a beeline towards them. "Jack, David and John! How wonderful to see you three here, how's the brokerage business these days?"

"I'm sorry Scott", Kyndrea apologised. "Will she ever change? She has been after anyone I date. Anyone would think she can't get a man herself."

"Sorry for what?" Simon laughed. "I must admit, she was not backward at seeing if I could be enticed. Don't worry, she is not my type at all." He completing to himself, 'She doesn't have a dad with an amphibian.' He felt more at ease now. Janine made him lose his original feelings of being a fraud. He realised how much better he was than anyone else here.

"Let's go and look at the auction tables," Kyndrea said, pulling Simon towards the tables alongside the lectern. Spread over the tables were many assorted items. Some were quite ordinary but with signatures on them. The others were very expensive pieces of equipment.

"Interesting collection of items", Simon commented, "But who would buy a lot of second hand items just because they're signed by someone who used to be famous?"

"Collectors. Oh my!" Kyndrea gasped as she held up a tattered poorly bound book. "It's the original bound copy of Sula. My all time favourite book. I've heard of this in magazines. This author always binds his completed text in a book for his final proofing. This copy will have all the text that almost made it to publishing but was cut for various reasons."

"How much do you think it will go for?"

"Not as much as his first story's proofing book. That was given to his girlfriend the night he proposed. She edited that story as his wife, but this one will still fetch more than I can afford.

There's a lot of collectors in this place tonight", Kyndrea said in a disappointed tone. She carefully placed it back on the table. "I could not justify spending that amount of money, even for that."

An announcement over the speakers interrupted them. "Ladies and gentlemen. Welcome to the fourth annual Trentsworth dinner for Refugees, sadly needed once more. Please take your seats for the aperitif and entrée."

Kyndrea found the seating plans along with everyone else. Finally getting the chance to view them she directed Simon to their table. The other eight at the table were older couples. The ladies were obviously kept quite adequately by their husbands. They all had travelled from Auckland just for this event. Their conversation was primarily about the last black tie they had attended and how this one compared.

"Of course", one of them started, "The aperitif is the drink we had when we entered. The announcer should have just said entrée."

"Are you sure Deirdre?" another responded. "I thought it was a drink to stimulate the palate, and this drink here definitely is stimulating." She laughed and they all joined in.

After the entrée, the tom bola was announced. Simon took great pleasure in watching these richies rush for the prizes.

They were like little children at a lolly scramble. Straightening their clothes, they came back to the table. Placing their trophies on the table, they continued from where they left off.

As the evening wore on, Simon realised why he hated the rich so much. Here they were, raising funds for refugees displaced by a recent civil war, yet all they talked about was how slow a waiter seemed or how the food could have been cooked slightly longer.

This small talk continued throughout the main course. He just looked at Kyndrea and she looked back; neither of them wished to join in the conversation. Then a representative of the project receiving the funds made a small speech on what they would be spent on. They totally ignored the speech content and refused to discuss anything not directly concerning themselves. Simon would have stabbed all eight there and then, if it wasn't for the giant knot in his stomach threatening to double him over. 'Selfish rich pricks,' he thought to himself. He mightn't have a job. He might be poor, but he was one hundred per cent more human than these wind bags. Though it was these wind bags who ran the country.

They didn't speak too much about their work, no doubt scared of espionage by the others. Again, through dessert, Kyndrea and Simon looked at each other's eyes, trying to read each other's thoughts. He realised that was the difference. Kyndrea saw the inner self. All the other rich bitches just saw the outside. He wondered if she would be the same if he didn't live in the house next door. If he was poor and lived in the workers' cottages. Probably not when, all said and done, she was rich. But then, for the moment, so was he.

Kyndrea wondered what he was thinking. It was embarrassing. Janine had put them at this table on purpose. She knew it would stop them from having a decent conversation. Everyone avoided being anywhere near these snobs. So up themselves, what would Scott think? This is probably the first time he has been anywhere near this sort of function. And these eight are his first impression?

The announcer introduced the auctioneer. He came up and started telling a few jokes. Once the whole ballroom was in tears of laughter, he started talking about the items up for auction. Throughout the auction, Simon noted that the people at his table would never go over the actual price an item was worth. Except Kyndrea who keenly bid for several items. Each time, though, she was outbidded.

Then the auctioneer held up the copy of Sula. Kyndrea started the bidding, but soon the value went well into the thousands. Simon looked at her face. 'Well,' he thought, 'I won't need the money. I'm not going to be here for long, am I.' "Six Thousand!"

Kyndrea heard the shout. She was so disappointed in losing out to some really high bidders that she didn't realise who actually shouted. The auctioneer closed the bidding at six thousand. 'Nice dream,' she consoled herself. It wasn't until the assistants came up and wrote down Scott's name that she figured it out.

"Don't think about it. Just accept it," Simon said as he handed her the book. The look on her face was worth twelve thousand. 'There you go, richies!' he thought 'That is how you give money to a needy cause.' He showed them! He could play their game even better.

Kyndrea wasn't interested in the rest of the auction. She looked at the book, her book. She should be angry at Scott, spending all that money. Money she knew he couldn't afford to waste. She knew it wasn't the money. He knew she wanted it. It could have been sold for five cents or a million dollars, it would have been the same. Scott had bought her something she held dear. There was no going back now. It suddenly hit her, she had fallen in love with this man.

The band then started up and they got up to dance. Kyndrea was very patient with his fumbling feet. In fact she seemed to enjoy that she had to teach him something. What he had to do to escape this valley, he told himself, but in reality, he knew he was enjoying it. As the evening wore on, he was surprised to see that the crowd was thinning out, so much so, that in the end they were the only ones left in the large hall. The band was still playing, seemly appreciating that the two of them were enjoying their music so much.

"I cannot remember an evening that I have enjoyed as much, Scott."

"Neither can I and that is the truth". Through all his campaigns and fights against the rich he had never allowed himself the luxury of a girlfriend, nor a true friend for that matter.

"Is it just me, or is there something here more than just friendship?" Kyndrea looked into Simon's eyes, "I know we only just met, but I feel you and I were destined to be together. It sounds awfully corny."

"I feel the same, as though I have met you before." Simon decided to play this out. He could see the amphibian getting very close. "I have never connected this well before. Well, except for a girl I knew back when I was only eleven. We spent so much time together the others teased that we would marry. We went to different high schools and she ended up marrying an ambulance officer."

"An ambulance officer? Interesting choice of husband, someone that I wouldn't consider."

"She was only of average means, you forget I inherited the money. I am not from the society you are from." Simon started seeing the gap between Kyndrea and himself again.

"I wasn't thinking of money." Kyndrea noted the slight edge on his voice. An inkling that Scott may have a slight chip on his shoulder. She decided to clarify her statement. "Just they wouldn't be able to have a life together; him out at emergency calls all night. Well, I think this evening is practically over. Can I invite you over to dinner tomorrow night?"

"Sounds good," he smiled.

"Don't speak too soon, that also means you have to meet my dad. He is very protective of me. You will have to win him over. He's suspicious of any male friends I bring over."

"No worries there. I'm sure we'll get on like a house on fire," he stated, feeling totally unsure. It was vital though, to get his escape plan to work. He hadn't expected it to come so quickly, but he had to go with the pace. It would be good to get out of the valley as soon as possible.

"You know, I think you might, you are different to the others. You might just be the man he approves of." Kyndrea smiled and they stopped talking. Finally, the band leader completed the evening, bringing their dance to an end.

Kyndrea left the hotel hand in hand with Simon. Not a word was spoken from then to when they got out of the taxi in front of their houses. Kyndrea looked again into his eyes. Simon moved closer. Kyndrea kissed him full on the lips. He didn't resist and felt a warm rush flow gently all over his body as the kiss became more intimate.

They said goodbye. "See you here at seven, then," Kyndrea confirmed as she walked down her path. He went down his and walked into the house. Half in a daze he went straight to bed. How could he feel so light, why did she do this to him? Amazing what a little kiss can do. Once his head hit the pillow, he immediately fell asleep.

Kyndrea watched the lights on the lake. Her father had already gone to bed. She supposed she should as well, but she sat there for a bit, running the evening's events through her mind. She had never felt this way about anyone before. No wonder her last relationship failed. Her friends kept saying that there was this spark whenever they were together with their boyfriend. Now she knew what the spark felt like.

She could never go back. She had tasted love, and she needed more. Well, it would be a long wait, but seven tomorrow evening she would see him again. She went up to bed, knowing that she would just lie there. With all these thoughts rushing through her mind it was going to be a long night.

Bob the Pilot

Kyndrea, after getting up early the next morning, immediately started cleaning the house. Her father came down as she was polishing one of the many sideboards. "The place is looking great. What's the occasion?"

"There doesn't have to be an occasion", Kyndrea growled back, "for me to clean the house."

"No, but you never polish the wood, unless?" He smiled at her. He was wellbuilt with grey hair. A person would easily mistake him as being a retired body guard. He walked up to Kyndrea and put his hand lovingly on her shoulder. "Who is our guest tonight?"

"Scott from next door." Kyndrea turned around and faced her dad, "I took him to the black tie yesterday."

"That explains a lot. You don't usually get that dressed up for one of Janine's functions."

"I must admit, he is quite good looking," Kyndrea blushed. "I must get on with this polishing. Sometimes I wonder why we have so many damn sideboards."

"To store all your porcelain dolls," her father chuckled. "Have you had breakfast?"

"No time."

"Well, make time. I'll fix you some toast. You finish that sideboard off and then sit down at the kitchen table. There is always time for breakfast. Besides, I want to hear all about this Scott fellow."

It was well past noon when Simon woke up. Putting on some casual clothes, he walked down to the kitchen. There he fixed himself pancakes. He loved making pancakes. It was the only thing his mum let him cook in the kitchen when he was young. Taking his favourite chair, he sat and watched the activities on the lake, thinking about the evening to come. He had to make a good impression on Kyndrea's dad. After all, it would be him who decides who flies in his plane. This was the crucial meeting. He started feeling queasy in his stomach. It wasn't the hypnosis. It was just plain nerves. It was like all those failed interviews for employment. This time it was life or death. The only saving grace was that Kyndrea's dad did not know his past history. He decided the best way to start on the right foot was to bring over a bottle of wine. He had seen this many times on television. He spent the rest of the afternoon wandering the shops asking shop assistant after shop assistant their advice on the best local wine.

That evening, making sure he was presentable, he walked out the lake side door and over to Kyndrea's house. Kyndrea and her dad were out on the patio. Kyndrea saw him and got up. "Hi", she greeted him as he entered their property. "This is my father, Robert, though everybody calls him Bob. Sit down. Do you want some coffee? The brew is still fresh."

"Yes", Simon answered, placing the bottle of wine on the patio table.

Bob stood up and held out his hand. "Hello, Scott."

"Hello Bob, nice to meet you", Simon replied as he shook Bob's hand. He was so nervous; it seemed he was reciting from a script. "Kyndrea has told me only good things about you."

"Well, you must have been doing most of the talking then," Bob laughed. Simon laughed back as they both sat down on the cane furniture. "Thank you for the wine. Good choice, I know the vineyard owners well."

"I must admit I had help. I don't know much about the local

wines at all."

"You will have plenty of opportunities to change that." Bob laughed again, "Enjoying this small valley?"

"Yes! Very much so. I'm glad I made the choice to move here. This place is so relaxing." Simon started letting his guard down. It was not the interrogation that he thought it would be.

"Well, that is why so many of us live here. So why did you choose Trentsworth?"

"I always wanted to come back here. And with the inheritance I could afford to."

"Which, I hear, you spent all on the house." Bob challenged, "Ever heard of investments?" Bob watched Simon's expression, thinking, 'No one is going after my daughter for her money.'

"I bought a claim up the gorge," Simon defended. It wasn't his fault that IVRRAC decided to spend all the money. "That's investment enough."

"Wait until you see where the claim is before you say that. You actually planned to work the claim?"

"Of course, how else do you think I would get enough money to live on?" Simon looked at Bob straight in the face. 'Now the interrogation starts.' Continuing he asserted, "I still have rates and utilities to consider. As well as food and living expenses. True, the claim is presently inaccessible, but I can wait. Technology will catch up, then it will be worth a bundle. But for the present time I will be looking for part-time work to supplement the meagre return on what is left of the inheritance."

"Sounds sensible", Bob smiled. He was enjoying this conversation. He decided to change tack, "so what are your other plans in Trentsworth?"

"Relaxing, what else?" Simon smiled. Bob looked back at him sternly. His face changed slowly to a smile then he laughed.

"Well, you picked the right town for that!"

"And I can show you the best places to wind down", Kyndrea added, as she returned with the coffee. "So how do you like to spend your time? When you're not living the high life at charity functions."

"For here, I don't actually know." Simon smiled sheepishly. "Until now television has been my interest. But I have been told there is no reception in this valley."

"That's correct, but we do have satellite. Have you thought of getting that, Scott?" Kyndrea asked.

"I am looking into it, but I need to rework all my finances first. Luxuries are low on my list of priorities." Simon noted an approving look on Bob's face. Another good mark; this was easier than he had first thought. He continued, "but first I have to find out how much it actually costs to live here."

"Yes", Kyndrea agreed. "We had to rework all our finances moving here after my mum died. Not that I minded shifting to Trentsworth. Dad was so much happier and there is an endless supply of things to do here."

"Is there?" Simon teased. "Haven't we done everything? It is a small place."

"One trip on the Yohanne and you think you've done it all?" Kyndrea smiled. "Before you go any farther Scott, may I remind you that I consider myself a local. So by insulting Trentsworth, you insult me."

"And if you insult Kyndrea, you insult me", Bob added. Simon felt the undertones of a warning in Bob's voice. He knew what Bob was actually saying, 'Don't hurt my little girl in any way if you want to live.' Bob's body was well toned with an ample supply of muscle. He was definitely not a person to be on the wrong side of. At least, not without a trusty knife.

"I could never insult such beauty, Bob." Simon replied. Bob seemed to relax. Kyndrea smiled, acknowledging the compliment. Simon could not help himself and added, "And I wouldn't insult Kyndrea either."

"Well!" Kyndrea growled, "If that is the way you feel, I will just leave." Kyndrea got up and left the table. "Besides the roast won't cook itself".

"That's one black mark you've given yourself," Bob chuckled.

Simon smiled. The conversation lulled so he decided to bite the bullet. "Kyndrea has been telling me of your hobby. You fly often?"

"Every day," Bob smiled. "I used to fly tourists around the mountains, but now I just fly myself. I find it very calming, plus I do a bit of photography for the local geologists and even meteorologists. The shifting of the glaciers is of interest to them."

"I thought they did that all with satellite these days."

"They wish! No, budget restraints don't allow such luxuries. They are government based, so they have to cut corners, which is a godsend for myself. One day, if you're lucky, I might just give you a chance to see the real Southern Alps."

"Thanks, I would appreciate that." Simon tried to hide his excitement. 'This is easier than I ever dreamed,' he thought. 'Now I have a flight out of here. All I need to do is train myself to ignore the stomach cramps.' In the meantime he needed a distraction.

"Well, the roast is basically cooking itself," Kyndrea said as she returned to the table. "It looks fantastic, if I say so myself."

"It smells delicious," Simon confirmed. A richie that can cook, will wonders ever cease?

"You like roast lamb, then?" Kyndrea asked.

"Love it, Kyndrea," Simon smiled. Silence enveloped them as their eyes made contact. Simon felt awkward. 'How could I find such a person attractive. She spends money as though it was sand running through her fingers. There were people out there living on stale bread, and she just thinks of herself.'

"So Scott, what did you do before the win?" Bob asked, breaking the spell.

"I was a messenger for a local group helping the poor." Scott replied truthfully, "They didn't pay much, but then I mainly did it for the love of man, not for the money."

"All the poor need to do is get off their lazy backsides and start working," Bob grumbled.

"They would if the people in power would let them", Simon replied.

"They aren't stopping them." Bob looked straight at Simon.

"Oh yeah?" Simon sneered, "I know these people, they want to work, but no one would employ them."

"Do they make an effort to get employed?"

"They go to interviews"

"Dressed like?"

"They can't afford to get dressed up."

"Well, perhaps your charity should concentrate on getting them dressed up and showered. Instead of giving them money to gamble away at the casino"

"They don't gamble their money."

"No? Well, those that don't, spend it on booze instead."

"Oh", Simon growled, "That's the exact comment I would

expect from a person in your position!"

"Hey you two! Shut Up!" Kyndrea yelled. "Scott is our guest here, dad."

"Sorry dear", Bob calmed down

"And Scott!" Kyndrea firmly stated. "Might I remind you that you are a guest here as well."

"Just a discussion, Kyndrea", Bob started.

"I know your discussions dad," Kyndrea smiled. "Any more discussion and your face would explode. Besides, I think it is time we adjourn to the dining room. And I will prepare the final touches to the meal as you lay the table."

"All right. Sometimes I wonder if you are my daughter or my mother." Bob succumbed and stood up. He looked at Simon, thinking to himself, 'Nice guy. Hearts in the right place. Needs a bit of education though. Kyndrea could do worse, a lot worse.'

"Show me where the cutlery is Bob, I'll do that", Simon offered as he got up from his chair.

As they set out the table, Simon commented to Bob. "Kyndrea is a wonderful lady. You must be proud to call her your daughter."

"I am," Bob smiled, his pride showing on his worn face. "She's grown up too fast, though. She took the place of her mother once we moved here and really missed out in all the later teenage life that everyone should experience. Because of that, she usually doesn't get on with us mere males. I am surprised how much a shine she's taken to you. I hope you won't abuse that feeling. I won't see her getting hurt."

"No, I won't Bob", Simon replied. Yet another warning. He found it strange to have this conversation with her father as they had just met that evening. Obviously her father cared a lot about his only daughter. This complicated matters as far as his escape was concerned. After the discussion with Bob, he realised that this life was not for him. Escape was all he could do. He had to keep reminding himself that Kyndrea was a Richie, not a human being. They were worlds apart. This feeling for her could not be love; it was too soon and they were totally different people from totally different worlds.

Kyndrea came out with steaming bowls of food and placed them on the table. Simon and Bob were sitting waiting. Bob had already poured out some of the red wine into the three glasses. They each dished out their own meat and vegetables. While light jazz music played in the background they slowly and quietly emptied their plates.

Over the after dinner drinks the conversation moved to the less controversial topics involving how useless the national teams were in the latest international games. Both agreed that if either Bob or Simon were the coaches they would be world champions. Finally, around one in the morning, Simon got up and walked to the door saying farewell to Bob. Kyndrea got up and saw him off via the patio.

"Well, it has been a great evening!" Simon commented smiling.

"What are you doing tomorrow Scott?" Kyndrea asked as she walked him to his lakeside garden.

"Something important, like lazing around home all day."

"I was going to invite you on a tour of Trentsworth, but if you are so busy?"

"I suppose I could reschedule it for Tuesday." Simon quietly laughed.

"I'll pick you up at ten then and show you the actual Trentsworth."

"Sounds wonderful." He lent over and kissed Kyndrea. It was short but very passionate. He then turned and walked off towards his house.

Kyndrea smiled as Simon walked away and she wandered back wishing it was already ten o'clock.

Trentsworth

He awoke to the sound of knocking. He looked at the clock on the bed side cabinet and saw it was ten o'clock. "Shit!" He exclaimed and shot out of bed. A dressing gown hanging on a stand before the door reminded him he was naked. He quickly put it on as he rushed down the stairs to the front door.

He tried to open it but found it locked. The keys were still in the clothes he was wearing the night before. He shouted through the door. "Just getting the keys." He rushed back upstairs to the bedroom. After a frantic search of his pockets, he saw the keys on the bedside table. Picking them up, he ran back down the stairs. Totally out of breath, he opened the front door. Kyndrea was on the other side smiling.

"You slept in?"

"Ummm." Simon smiled. "Yes, it seems that way."

"Well, you get upstairs and get showered, etc., and I will fix you a breakfast you've never experienced before in your life."

"You're on."

It was twenty minutes later that Simon came down the stairs to a wonderful smell of bacon and eggs. Kyndrea was sitting at a small round table in the family area under the southern staircase. Smiling, she watched him approach, occasionally taking another sip of her coffee. The breakfast was waiting for him in front of the empty seat to her left. "Bacon and Eggs Kyndrea style, I hope you like them. And a cup of coffee to get you going. It's going to be a long day."

Simon ate up. It was even better than the meal the night before. Kyndrea was a great chef. The coffee was just as he liked it, she remembered how he took it. Strange, he thought, that he noticed this. After he finished she took the plates and went into the kitchen. He followed. "You don't need to clean up as well," he commented.

"It's all right. You have a dishwasher."

"I do?" Simon mentally kicked himself. All that time he had wasted washing the dishes the last few days.

"It's only a simple matter of putting the dishes in the drawer."

She smiled again. "I enjoy the kitchen, and you have a wonderful one here. The guy who designed this place was a great architect. I wish we had enough money to get him to do our house, but dad had his priorities. The plane was on the top of the list." She paused and smiled. "Well, after me that is."

Five minutes later they were out of the house and walking up to the station. "We will take the train to the old town first. We can explore Trentsworth Centre anytime."

"You're the tour guide," Simon commented and followed Kyndrea up the street. "I will just listen and obey your every instruction, lest I get lost."

"Lost?" Kyndrea laughed, "Here? Oh well. Quick the train will be here soon." She tugged at his hand and pulled him towards the station.

Just as they got to the platform a train arrived. Its carriages were open like the trams Simon had seen in the movies. Kyndrea just hopped on board. Simon followed suit and the train moved off. "This train is free. It continuously goes anticlockwise around the lake." The train continued down the east side of the lake. Just before a bridge, the train stopped at a small platform with sheltered seating.

"Trentsworth F", an automatic announcement came over

the speakers. The train moved off again and then crossed what seemed to be the lake's outlet, which went through a deep gorge to the east. The rocks on either side were sheer cliffs. Simon was reminded that the railway was the only transport out of the valley. Except one amphibian. Which, he reminded himself, was the reason why he was riding a train with this richie beside him.

Shortly afterwards the train, turning to the west, joined the track on which he arrived. The train slowed down into the brick station. An automatic announcement stated, "Trentsworth A". Kyndrea got off and Simon followed suit.

He looked at the platform. It seemed quite old and worn. The paving stones along the track edge were individually embossed with faded writing. It seemed to be an old stylised TRL. The bottom section of the logo was now covered by a new white stripe denoting the platform's edge.

He looked ahead of him. The building was not as old as the platform. He figured late fifties architecture, recognising the similarity between the station and his grandmother's state house. This time he had a chance to study the lack of fine detailing of the building. Kyndrea noticed his gaze.

"It's okay, but it's nothing to what used to be on this site. A fire destabilised the original station in the sixties. So they demolished it and built this one. Trentsworth was in a bad way that decade. They didn't attempt anything fancy. In fact there is a campaign to rebuild to the original plans. But with today's prices, such an attempt would be more expensive than Trentsworth E."

She then walked through the large gap in the station building that took them through to the street side. The stones of the platform gave way to lino tiles, then to concrete ending in three wide steps down to the pavement. The sun was shining as they emerged out of the station.

Directly ahead of them was a church. It was at the other end of a three hundred metre long cobbled stone street. This old-fashioned street was surrounded by shops with stone or wooden facades taken straight from the nineteenth century. They were a major improvement on the concrete jungle where Simon had first met Kyndrea.

"Dad used to quote my granddad," Kyndrea announced. "'Trentsworth. You arrive by train. You leave with Jesus.' Meaning once you got here, the only way you leave is by dying."

"I understand that feeling," Simon grumbled.

"Beautiful place, isn't it," Kyndrea said, not noticing the sarcasm. "The actual name for this street is a predictable 'Main Street', but it's come to be known as 'Life's Journey'.

Though, I'm not saying life is full of tourist shops that are trying to get every last cent from your pocket."

"Sometimes I feel that's what life is all about."

"Well, I would expect that from someone willing to spend their entire inheritance on a house." Kyndrea smiled to show she was not being too serious.

As they left the station, Simon saw that behind the shops to his right was an eight storied brick hotel. An old sign on the top, half faded, announced that it was the 'Trentsworth Hotel'. It looked quite sad, like an old forgotten toy on a high shelf gathering dust.

Kyndrea saw where he was looking. "It used to be the place to stay. Royalty has stayed there, but now it is a backpackers. This area is a time capsule; nothing away from this road has been touched for the last forty years. The tourist industry decided there was better reason to build all the expensive hotels on the sunny side of the valley.

"Well, except for the hot pools, and they are worth a visit. Say one day we bring togs?"

"Seems a good idea to me", Simon agreed. He looked at the shops as they got closer. Kyndrea had continued walking along the west side of the street.

"This street itself was put under restoration thirty years ago. Then a bylaw was slapped down that all buildings had to be in the style of the gold mining days", Kyndrea continued. Simon realised he was with a walking encyclopaedia, but he liked her voice. She seemed happy telling him all these little facts. He adored her smile when she was happy. "The tourists love it. Now there is a new ban on vehicles from 9 am until 11 pm on Main Street. So it's just like the old days and it does create a unique photo opportunity."

"I see a horse and carriage here though," Simon argued, with a slight playfulness in his voice.

"Well, of course vehicles that fit the gold mining time period are exempt." Kyndrea lightly pushed Simon on the shoulder, laughing. "I'm sure even your small excuse for a brain could work that one out."

"I don't know," Simon laughed back. Did a richie just call him an idiot? 'Oh, if it wasn't for this hypnosis she would be.' His thoughts stopped. He realised it wasn't the hypnosis stopping him this time. Truthfully, it wasn't even the need to escape. His mind was finally catching up with his feelings.

As he pondered these new realisations he looked at the street. Apart from his brain size, Kyndrea was correct. It was a picture perfect scene. It was as though they were no longer in the valley. The old shops blocked the view of the lake and its mass tourism thrill rides. Through all the bustling of tourists he heard a sound he could not place. It seemed to be getting louder as they walked towards a gap in the shops. The shops stopped as the road crossed a small humped back bridge over a stream. A footpath followed the stream in both directions on the other bank. The noise was from upstream.

"Spring Waterfall," Kyndrea announced, "Is the noise you hear. It is a drop of 100 metres into a deep pond over there." Simon looked to his right where she was pointing and saw though the trees a small stream of water falling from the top of the huge cliffs above. "At the base, the mountain water is supplemented by fresh water springs, thus the name. Also, it makes delicious drinking water and why the original township was built here and not around Trent's River."

Simon looked towards a café that was on the other side of the stream. It had tables outside on the stream's grassy banks. Kyndrea followed his gaze, Do you want to eat lunch here?

"It seems such an idyllic setting to waste it." Simon answered, "I'll shout you this time. What do you prefer?"

"Flat white and a chicken panini," Kyndrea stated as she sat down at one of the sturdy wooden tables. The sun was bright, though foiled by a large green umbrella positioned over the table's centre. The sound of the waterfall still filled the air, accompanied by the soft babbling of the stream. She watched Simon disappear into the café. She was still amazed at how quickly she had fallen in love with this man. It was only seven days since they met, but it seemed like she had known him all of her life. It was as if she was specifically created to be with Scott. The heat of the sun and soft babbling almost sent her to sleep. She didn't notice Scott coming out of the café, until he was placing the two coffees and plates on the table. He sat down opposite her.

"Not to belittle your information on 'Ye Oldé Township', which I found very interesting, but what about yourself?" He asked, passing a coffee over to Kyndrea. "What do you do? When you're not guiding VIP parties, or for that matter next door neighbours through the area."

Kyndrea blushed slightly, "Oh I'm not worth talking about."

"Believe me you are," Simon smiled. Against all his old prejudices, he was falling in love with this woman. Perhaps it was her way of not putting on airs or graces. She cooked her own food, when a house servant would be well within their means. She even cooked him breakfast without any fuss. She was not like the other rich people he knew. Perhaps all rich people were like that? No, he put that thought out of his mind. Kyndrea was special.

"Well, I don't do much actually," she started. "Dad's got enough money in investment that we can both comfortably live off the interest. I sometimes take special VIP tours around the valley, but mostly I spend my time looking after dad, really. He's got a medical condition, though you'd never know it. He can't overtax himself too much. It's a blessing someone came up with an auto pilot capable of landing the plane in the lake, or he wouldn't be able to fly. That would have killed him."

"What is the matter with him?" Simon asked. "If it's not too personal."

"His heart is a bit faulty. It isn't life threatening, if he can get to his medicine within an hour. He used to take tourists but then his heart started playing up. He was grounded for what seemed like life, so he put me through flying classes.

I got my pilot's licence, put up my flying hours enough that he was able to get a special licence to allow him to fly if another pilot was on board. Then technology caught up and we got a landing-capable autopilot. Of course, this limits him to a forty minute radius around the lake. The autopilot is programmed only for the Lake of Worth, and cannot land anywhere else."

"The lake of what?" Simon asked.

"You didn't know the name of the lake?" Kyndrea asked, with a look of disbelief on her face. "You buy a lakeside house and don't even know what the lake's called? Sheesh! You are one in a million."

"Okay. Okay!" Simon said, his hands waving to stop Kyndrea's laughing. "So why is it called the Lake of Worth?"

"One of the world's richest rivers flows straight into it. They say there is millions of dollars worth of gold at the bottom of that lake."

"So why don't they just dredge it out?"

"It's more than two thousand metres deep." Kyndrea started to explain, "There is no actual proof that the gold has settled there. Only speculation and the cost of getting the equipment needed to get to it would itself be in the millions. But whether it is there or not the lake is still called The Lake of Worth." Kyndrea placed her empty cup on the saucer. "Shall we continue on now? Scott?"

Simon was staring into Kyndrea's green eyes. His mind lost in her beauty. It took him a while to respond to his new name. "What? Sorry, I was just thinking of all that gold," he lied.

"Shall we continue our walk?" Kyndrea repeated standing up from her chair.

"Of course", Simon answered. "Nice coffee, I will remember this café."

They continued walking down the main street towards the church. Kyndrea stopped at each shop to view the various souvenirs on display. Simon followed slowly behind walking on the road, looking at the surrounding mountains visible above the shop's facades. The bright morning sun was still reflecting off the white snow capped peaks. It was a beautiful day. He could see that this street he was walking down must be one of the most photographed and painted. The contrast of the old wooden structures and the imposing peaks was incredible.

"Scott! Look at this!" Not hearing any answer, Kyndrea turned around and saw him on the road. "What on earth are you doing over there?"

"Where else can man feel so insignificant?" Simon replied.

"Sorry?" Kyndrea pondered and then looked at where he was gazing. She walked over to him and placed her hand around his waist. "Yes, it is magnificent, a true wonder of God's creation. Probably another reason why the street ends in a church. After marvelling at his work, you can thank him personally."

"True", Simon smiled. "True, after buying the souvenirs of

course."

"Well, what is money for, if not to spend", Kyndrea observed.

"Now that is a female comment", Simon teased.

"I was not the one to spend all my inheritance on one house," Kyndrea laughed. "You should have bought one of the workers' houses down the way and invested the rest."

"Workers' Houses?"

"This side of the lake. The west side's where all the cheaper housing is. No sun in the late afternoon you see. So all the people who earn an average wage working in this valley, live on this side."

"And that is what every one calls them?"

"Everyone I know", Kyndrea replied, "I don't know what they would call themselves."

"But if I bought over here, would I have meet you?"

"No. Definitely not."

"Well then, I think I did well." Simon smiled, but his smile was mostly pretend. His mind was going in circles. This woman he fell in love with, was talking like a true richie. Us and them, separating society by the bank balances. Even admitting she would have nothing to do with him if he lived on the wrong side of the railway tracks, or in this case, the lake.

He did not like this side of her. Could he just ignore it, and pretend it didn't exist? But then why bother? She was a means to an end, a way to escape, nothing else. 'I can't afford to fall in love with this woman!' he told himself, as he continued the conversation, "How could someone discover this valley, one so inaccessible, without the aid of an aeroplane?"

"Its amazing what a person can do when he is being chased by a tribe of angry natives and the only escape is upwards."

"Sorry?" Simon laughed in spite of his inner turmoil.

"Oh, the story of Trent," Kyndrea answered. "And it's most probably just a story. There's been no actual historical evidence to prove what the valley's second discoverers said they read in his diary. Remember I spoke of him before? Well, these two climbers came upon this valley in the late nineteenth century. On their return they announced they had found a castle and a hand written journal theoretically written by Trent. Apparently Trent upset the Maori once he escaped Tasman's ship. They had tracked him to the western base of the Southern Alps. Trent, though probably English with that name, was used to the mountains in Europe. He knew his way around sheer cliffs. He lost the Maori warriors after managing to cross a few dangerous passes and slowly found his way here.

"Apparently he followed the Trent River though the gorges and caves to end up here. I know it sounds impossible and probably never happened, but there is still a half ruined castle to explain, and why a couple of enthusiastic mountaineers would make up such a far fetched story."

"Wow!" Simon looked at Kyndrea, then quickly looked back at the mountains. "This half ruined castle is still here today?"

"Trent's Castle?" Kyndrea stopped in even more amazement. "Yes of course it is. Are you blind? You would have seen it from your house. Why don't we have a picnic lunch there tomorrow?

"Sounds a good plan to me", Simon agreed.

"Good. Now I'll show you this waterfall. It'll pass the time before tea."

She led him around a corner and walked through a side street on their right. This street joined another street running parallel to the main street, which she walked up. It ended just after the multi-storeyed hotel at the stream they had coffee beside.

Kyndrea took Simon by the hand and led him up the gravel path. As they made their way through the thick native bush, the sound grew louder and louder, until finally the waterfall was in full view. It was the same type of waterfall Simon had seen in many movies. Particularly the romantic sections where the hero and heroine would skinny dip and then fall in each other's arms afterwards. Unfortunately, being in the north-west corner of the valley and now well into the afternoon, the sun was hidden behind the majestic cliffs. There was a slight cool breeze and Simon did not feel the tiniest inclination to skinny dip. They sat on a rock beside the small pond in front of the waterfall. Simon looked at Kyndrea, straight into her eyes. There was a stillness in the atmosphere, waiting for something to happen. Neither of them spoke as they listened to the deafening sound of the waterfall. Kyndrea moved closer to Simon and laid her head on his shoulder. He felt the warmth of her body close to his.

There was no way he could deny his feelings now. He was in love with Kyndrea. He moved his arm around her waist and held her close. He smelt the sweetness of her hair as her head snuggled in even closer. He gently moved her head back, so he could see her face. He kissed her sweet mouth, not taking his eyes off hers. Slowly she parted her lips and Simon felt a surge of passion flow through his body. They stayed in the embrace for what seemed an eternity.

Kyndrea's stomach grumbled. Simon couldn't stop himself laughing. The spell was broken. He looked at her, "Hungry?"

"I guess I must be," Kyndrea replied, laughing. "I suppose we should head back to the main street anyway." She got up and led the way back through the bush to the old township. A new level of relationship seemed to have been reached. Kyndrea fell quite silent, and didn't utter a word as they walked back. Simon knew it was that she felt love for him, but didn't want to approach the subject. She also obviously felt it was too soon to have these feelings. All it made Simon feel was that she was as human as he was. Not at all what he understood richies to be like. She seemed to break all the rules.

They had early tea at an unassuming restaurant on Main Street. The food was good but nothing special. Kyndrea suggested they work off the meal by walking back along the lake shore. Kyndrea showed the way around the hot pool complex and onto the sand. As they walked they eventually met up with the concrete path that followed the beach past both their houses.

"Pick you up at eleven this time," Kyndrea suggested as they parted between their houses. Simon noticed Bob at the window, so he gave Kyndrea a slight kiss on the check and wandered home.

"For lovers, you aren't being very passionate today," Bob commented as Kyndrea opened the patio doors.

"Not with you spying on us, dad." Kyndrea laughed and gave her dad a hug. "Have you had any tea?"

"I made something quick and easy."

Kyndrea went to the kitchen and cleaned up the dishes. Bob's idea of a quick and easy tea somehow managed to use every kitchen utensil in the place. She smiled as she needed something to occupy herself while waiting for bedtime. She couldn't wait until the picnic tomorrow.

The next day arrived with another glorious sky. The absence of clouds allowed the sun to reflect off the snow capped mountains, making them seem more majestic than ever. Leaving Trentsworth B, an empty platform except for a couple of sheltered seats, Kyndrea and Simon walked past houses built in the late fifties to early seventies. There were no airs or graces here. This was normal New Zealand suburbia. In the front yards kids were playing a mixture of tennis and cricket. Some were spending the hot day under a sprinkler or hose.

After walking for about half an hour they reached a river.

Across the river Simon saw the racing track rise above the railway tracks to his left. Kyndrea turned to the right and Simon followed. On a small island in the river was a five storied stone tower. The tower was in disrepair and connected to the ruins of what could have been a castle. A small pedestrian bridge crossed the river from a gravel car park. They walked across and managed to find a soft piece of grass in the middle of a ruined courtyard. As Kyndrea removed the picnic gear from her backpack, Simon looked at the sight in awe. "One man built all this?"

"There is a theory that Trent was actually an Englishman. He was hired by the Spanish to lead a team of spies. But, not many people want to explore this theory. If you believe all the stories that this valley holds, Trent was a super hero," Kyndrea commented. "I wouldn't be surprised if they find the remains of an aeroplane that he made. He just about invented everything else."

"According to the true and correct stories of two madmen?"

"Exactly," Kyndrea laughed. "History has a way of becoming grander than reality. I reckon if a person created a time machine, they would be very disappointed in what they found out about the past."

"It is all in the story telling," Simon agreed. "Something I have never managed to do."

"Not many can, though I had a friend who could make cleaning her teeth sound like the world's most exciting thrill ride. I wish I had that skill."

"You do in a way, I have been enthralled by all you have said these past days."

"Thank you." Kyndrea started dishing out a lunch of fried chicken and fresh bread rolls. Afterwards they laid on the soft ground looking up at the lone tower. They both just soaked up being so close to each other, talking about what each would do if they were Trent, alone in such a romantic valley. After a while as the sun got lower behind them, Kyndrea looked at her watch. Her face took on being slightly serious. "Unfortunately, I am to partner my dad in bridge this evening. So I better head my way back to Trentsworth B. I wish I could get out of it. I love spending time with you."

"No, you go and play bridge. We have still got tomorrow."

"Yes and I am tending towards a nice soak in the hot pools"

"Sounds wonderful."

"I'll pick you up in the afternoon. I have a tour party in the morning."

Simon watched Kyndrea rush back to the station. He

decided to stay and have a wander through the streets of the west side. He had a lot to think about. He was falling in love with Kyndrea, that was obvious.

He walked through the school grounds which started opposite the castle's car park. A whole new row of terraced housing was along the school boundary. It was obviously new. In one of the back yards a man was busy levelling out the ground while his wife was plastering the newly laid concrete verges.

That was the house Simon should have. He wasn't made for the luxury he found himself in across the lake. The whole house he was looking at could fit in his lounge; roof and all. How long could he really stay sane in his present situation?

He had to keep his mind on the plan ahead. He had to escape this valley. He had to keep focused, until the day he was invited onto that plane, until finally he could escape.

Always Book Ahead

A week passed. Every day he spent time with Kyndrea, each day waiting for the invitation; each day subtly hinting that he had never been flying before. And each day Kyndrea left him with no hint of when Bob was going to finally agree to a flight. After all, Bob was definitely interested in taking him up.

Simon and Kyndrea had just finished a great meal cooked in a restaurant based within an old house on the north side. "I'm sorry, I can't see you for a few days," Kyndrea apologised. "It's dad. He has an appointment tomorrow at Christchurch hospital for his condition."

"Oh, is it serious?"

"No more than the condition. It's just a routine check up. It will take a few days of observation. We will return on the afternoon train on Wednesday." Kyndrea paused in thought, then continued, "Do you have plans for tea Wednesday?"

"You know I haven't."

"I know, that is why I have booked a table at Peak View Restaurant. I was very lucky. Sometimes it is booked out for months in advance."

"Sounds very exclusive. Is it that good?"

"Good?" Kyndrea laughed. "It not only has views of the whole valley, but you can see quite a bit of the coasts as well."

"Sounds nice"

"Nice is an insult to this place; it's amazing."

"Just like you," Simon complimented, making Kyndrea blush. Simon paid the bill and walked Kyndrea home.

At Simon's gate Kyndrea kissed him. The embrace was even more passionate than Simon had ever experienced. Kyndrea was obviously going to miss him. "Oh, I almost forgot", Kyndrea announced suddenly. "Dad said he's going out for a flight on Thursday. He's keen to have you come along as well."

"Sounds great! Just try to stop me," Simon confirmed. "See you Wednesday night then."

"Bye!" Kyndrea walked down her path as Simon entered his house. He went to his favourite chair and sat down. Many things started encircling his mind as he watched the Yohanne circle the lake.

Only two days away and he would be free. It was a pity in some ways, as he had never met anyone like Kyndrea, but then what would happen after six months. IVRRAC wouldn't let him keep the house. He didn't want to, either. He would be poor again. Kyndrea would have nothing to do with him. She was just another richie after all. It was better this way; a quick full on relationship then just the memories. He had to think of the long term. He had to keep the escape plan in mind. Six months would be unbearable in this place, even with Kyndrea to speak to. He could never be free if he stayed here. This was his only opportunity to escape, plus he would disappear from their sight before they even knew he had gone. He knew they were lying by telling him after six months he was a free man. No way would a man as dangerous as himself be allowed to be free. Truth was, he hadn't been rehabilitated. It wouldn't take long for them to find out. Then it would be back into jail forever with no way out. They must know the hypnosis wouldn't hold. He had remembered several people he would love to teach a lesson to that morning and only a slight twinge from his stomach. No, he would not stand for six more months of this torture. Not being able to perform his self appointed duty. He could not give in to emotions. He had to remain clear on his mission.

The task now was to organise his escape once he managed to get away from Bob and Kyndrea. He knew a few people in Auckland that might be able to help. He quickly picked up the phone. Dialling his best mate he received a disconnected tone. He was reminded of the time he tried to call an overseas number from a toll barred office phone. The tone sounded the same, 'Fool!' He cursed himself. 'His house phone would be toll barred; they would also be monitoring the calls made from the house.'

The next day he got up and after breakfast he left his house. Heading towards the mall, he walked quickly, hoping Andrew wasn't keeping too much of an eye on him. A false hope, he knew, as the phone call from his house would have tipped them off. He had tried to make contact with the outside world. They would be watching him very carefully today. He had to lose them in the crowds around the busy mall.

After an hour of ducking in and out of shops, playing the casual tourist, he decided enough time had passed for him to try a pay phone. The next shop he ducked into, he purchased a phone card.

"What value, sir?" The man behind the counter asked.

"Enough to make a call to Auckland," Simon answered.

"How long a call, sir?"

"What?" Simon looked at the man with impatience, "Doesn't matter."

"Yes it does, sir. The calls are charged per minute."

"Just get me the middle sized one", Simon commanded exasperated.

"They are all the same size, sir?" The salesman answered, slightly puzzled.

"I mean the middle valued one." Simon looked at the salesman. He looked intelligent. Was this guy pulling his leg? It was amazing this store did any business if this was the attitude of all the staff. Simon paid for the card and quickly took it as he exited the shop.

Making certain there was no one watching, an almost impossible task, he snuck into a phone cubicle and started to dial. Again he got the disconnected tone of a forbidden call. Did they have a toll bar on the whole valley? IVRRAC had more control than he first thought. He realised he dialled the same number as he did at his house the night before. They probably had a search out for that number. Would the phone card be now marked?

He purchased another phone card, this time specifying the value and tried a different phone. He dialled another acquaintance. Another disconnected tone. He tried yet another acquaintance just in case the phone was disconnected, that too returned the tone. They must be watching him. There was only one other option, a cell phone. He decided to be ultra careful and got cash out of an ATM. He then bought a cheap disposable prepaid phone from a street cart. He dialled his fourth and final acquaintance. The phone rang then someone picked it up.

"John Brown?" Simon asked.

"You signed an agreement you would not contact the outside world", was the reply.

"Andrew?" Simon recognised the voice.

"I will call around tomorrow morning, Mr Tallburg. Please do not try and call out of the valley again." Andrew hung up and left Simon with the now familiar beeping in his ear. How on earth did he do that? Did they know all his contacts in Auckland? They could not have known that last person. Simon had not spoken to them for the past five years. He went straight home. Suddenly he found he was not in the mood to stay around the Trentsworth populace. One thing though, this made him even more eager to get out of the valley. A slight concern entered his mind as he walked down

Springfield Road. If they could track his actions in the mall so easily, could they also know what his escape plan was? What could they do if they did? Apart from stop him doing it. He would just have to go through with it, be extra careful and see what happens. True, he had signed an agreement, but that was as Simon Tallsbury, not Scott Tallburg. They could no longer take him to court. Once out of the valley, once out of their control, they were powerless to do anything.

Awaking the next morning, Simon still felt tired. He did not get a good night's sleep. The feeling of being watched every second by IVRRAC played on his nerves. He was just getting dressed when the doorbell rang. He walked slowly down the stairs. He wasn't looking forward to this meeting with Andrew.

He opened the door and let him in. Andrew smiled as he crossed the threshold. "Had a good sleep?"

"Not really," Simon replied abruptly. "Can we get this reprimand over and done with. I have a lot planned today."

"Reprimand? There is no need to reprimand. Did you contact anyone outside the valley?"

"No, you know I didn't."

"Then you didn't break the contract, did you." Andrew

stated. "I thought I would just check on you to see how things are going."

'Sure,' Simon thought. 'You purposefully got me worrying about today. That was obviously enough for you, you smug sadist. You are no different from the prison guards I left behind.' Simon wandered over to the window, "Things are going well. Got to know the next-door neighbour well. You know she is a tourist guide?"

"Yes, I have current data on everyone in this block. They pose no threat to your stay here."

Simon decided to bite the bullet. Andrew wasn't stupid. He would have thought of the amphibian scenario. "You're not concerned that they have a plane?"

"Oh, that!" Andrew smiled. "We were concerned for a while, almost canned the whole parole. Then we got his licence details. Her father isn't permitted to take passengers. He used to fly tourists all the time. You know he has a medical condition."

"Kyndrea has mentioned it."

"Well, he would be grounded forever if he ever took a passenger, even a family member, let alone a practical stranger. The plane is his life. He would die before he risked his licence. You can take that route off your escape list. Believe me. You are stuck here for the next six months."

"Well, I suppose it is good that I have made such good friends with Kyndrea then." He looked at Andrew carefully. He didn't seem to be lying.

"Well, must be off", Andrew suddenly announced. "I can see you are coming to terms with your stay here. Have a good couple of days. I'll call back on Friday." With that, Andrew left, closing the door behind him.

Janine

Simon looked back out the window. Was Andrew just playing him along? It didn't seem to be the way Andrew operated. One thing with Andrew, he had always been open. Hadn't he told him at the start they were keeping an eye on him? So why should he be surprised about the night before? What would be the point for Andrew to lie about not knowing that Kyndrea had a pilot's licence? It would be to their advantage to tell him now that they knew his plan. Stop him before anyone got hurt. Andrew was quite confident that the plane was a no go. Besides, Kyndrea having a licence would be easily missed if they weren't looking for it.

He was brought back from his internal thoughts by the sound of the doorbell ringing. He knew it was foolish to hope that it was Kyndrea so early in the week. As he opened the door he discovered he was right. Standing on the doorstep was a lady donned in jewellery and make up. Simon looked at her, puzzled. "Yes?"

"Don't you remember me, Scott?"

"No," he honestly replied.

"Janine? From the black tie?"

"Oh hi," Simon said in welcome. "Why don't you come in." He was surrounded by richies, so he had to be polite. For the next day anyway, then after his escape he could once again be the avenger.

"Thank you." Janine stepped into the lounge and had a good look around her. She looked pleased with the layout. A dining area, a group of couches in the middle of the room and a few easy chairs facing the window. "I have been wanting to come over since the dinner, but things kept cropping up last minute. How are you settling in?"

"Good! Have a seat by the window." Simon studied her as she wandered over to the window. Now she said who she was, he recognised her. She was dressed in more casual clothes this time, but still managed to show off her legs and bust. "Kyndrea's been busy showing me around these past few days."

"So I hear," she said taking the seat next to Simon's favourite. "She is an excellent tour guide. My father's business employs her for all the major clients. She charges the earth for it as well. Think yourself lucky you need not pay going rates."

"I am glad you think I'm well looked after." Simon walked over and sat in his chair.

"I didn't say that, Scott," gently sliding closer to him, she continued, "I reckon there's a big difference between being a tour guide and being looked after. Though, so I hear, Kyndrea can mix the two up."

"Well, I have no complaints. She is very knowledgeable about this small valley." Simon ignored the innuendo and decided to keep being civil. 'Only a day to go,' he told himself. "Do you want a cup of coffee?"

"Do you have an espresso?"

"No", Simon started, then he remembered seeing an appliance in one of the cupboards. "Well, there is a machine but I wouldn't know where to start."

"Here, let me show you how." Janine got up and led the way to the kitchen.

"You know your way around the kitchen?" he asked, thinking to himself, 'I thought you would have paid help for all those menial jobs.' He walked past her and opened the kitchen door.

"I know my way around plenty of rooms in the house Scott,

believe me." She smiled as she walked past Simon, too closely for Simon's liking.

Once in the kitchen, Simon got the machine out of its cupboard and placed it on the marble topped island in the middle.

"Now stand in front of it and I will show you how to operate it." She took a jug and filled it with water. Walking up behind him she reached around him with both arms. He felt her breasts pressing against his back as she directed him to unscrew the pressure cap on the top. "Now pour in the water to the level marked on the side."

Simon followed her instructions, trying to keep his mind off her obvious advances. As he screwed the cap back on, she continued. "Then wait for the pressure to build up. Don't release too soon. We don't want to be premature." She moved her mouth right up against his right ear and whispered, "You aren't normally premature, are you Scott?"

"Not as far as I know." This was getting beyond his experience. He had never had a lady be so up front with him and he felt at a loss. Mentally separating himself from the scene, he just blindly followed her instructions. She continued to sensually direct him around making the coffee and then heating the milk.

"Now slip the nozzle in gently, not to quick; gently release the steam, now move the jug in and out. Gently now, we don't want the milk too excited. She moved her mouth to his ear, "Just imagine the jug is me and that powerful steam filled nozzle is you." The jug fell to the bench, milk splashed all over them. Luckily, it didn't have much chance to heat up first.

"Sorry," Simon lied. He hadn't meant to drop the jug, but it released a lot of tension, for which he was not sorry.

"Oh, you clumsy idiot!" she yelled, and then she regained her composure. "I hope that isn't the way you treat all your lady friends." She laughed, "Do you have a dressing gown or something I could borrow?"

"I'm sure I have", Simon replied, leaving the kitchen to head upstairs. "I'll go and find something."

"I will meet you in the laundry", Janine replied, following Simon out into the hallway.

"Okay", Simon stopped and looked at her slightly puzzled. "Do you know where it is?"

"That door behind you," she pointed to the laundry door. "I know the layout of most these houses. I am an interior designer, after all."

"I will go and get the dressing gown." Simon excused himself as he went through into the lounge area.

It was not too long that he was back at the laundry door. He knocked carefully on the wood. "Are you decent?"

"Come in", was the reply.

Simon walked in and saw Janine at the washer. She had already taken off her wet clothes and was standing in her underwear. Simon felt slightly embarrassed. "Sorry, I thought I heard you say come in."

"I did. You know, you should get out of your wet things as well." She smiled as she took off the last remaining vesture of decency and placed them in the machine. Then she took the gown from him and wrapped it around herself. She didn't do it quickly, giving Simon enough time to see all her womanly features. Seeing her naked body he realised that under all that makeup was a beautiful lady. The skin, now hidden by his dressing gown, was smooth and luxurious. She looked a lot younger and he wondered what her face actually looked like.

"I'm glad I didn't wear my red lingerie, then I would have needed to do two washes."

To Simon's surprise she pressed the buttons on the machine

like a touch typist would use a keyboard. It was not what he would expect of a richie. "You know how to operate one of those? You amaze me," he blurted out before he could stop himself.

"Why?" Janine asked in puzzlement. "You are amazed a woman knows how to wash clothes?"

"How do you know so much". Simon paused, thinking of a polite way to put it. He failed. "Well, how can I say it, menial work?"

"Oh", she smiled, "You expect me to have servants doing everything for me?"

"To be honest, yes."

"Well mostly I do. Why work when you can pay someone to do it for you? But my mum and dad were not always wealthy. So mum was able to teach me the basics. When we went to one of the baches, we didn't bring staff with us. They stayed back and looked after the main house. We liked to spend the time as a family, no other interruptions, or people. It was sort of a holiday from being rich."

"So your family kept their roots."

"A lot of our friends did the same. Otherwise you can grow

up with a real warped view of the universe. Besides, it's nice to know if push came to shove you can survive by yourself. You never know what is around the corner."

"True." Simon was in puzzlement. Here was a woman. The epitomy of richness, yet she was washing her own clothes and didn't think twice about it. Were the richies that lived in Auckland different to these Trentsworth families? Or was it that he never got to know them?

Was Janine trying to fool him? Yes, she was a true richie. She was hiding things from him. She was being too open, too soon. She was putting up a front to get him in bed, but she was very good at pretending; too good really.

"Can I borrow your shower?" she interrupted his thoughts.

"Sure," Simon affirmed. "I suppose you know where it is"

"Yes I do", she made a gentle laugh. "Could you get me a towel?"

She walked down to the hall and into the room opposite the back door. He heard the shower start and looked around the laundry for where a cupboard was. He found it and plenty of towels were stocked there. Taking two he walked down the hall to the bathroom. This time he didn't bother to knock and walked in, placing the towels on the heated rail.

"I got you two, in case you wish to wash your hair." He remembered his mum always came out of the bathroom with two towels. He couldn't help taking a look at the shower; Janine was busy scrubbing her face. The glass door did not obstruct the view at all and he looked at her fine body features. Her body was obviously a product of the dieting sect. Her muscles were almost non existent, yet there was no flab. Though she hadn't gone too much overboard, Simon would have preferred to see less of her skeleton. Simon realised he couldn't really pass judgement. He was too far the other way, especially since moving to Trentsworth.

Simon's thoughts moved onto Kyndrea. She knew how to eat, but she also walked a lot. And it showed, even under her clothes. He knew she would be slim but well built. He realised, to his relief, that all it did, seeing Janine nude, was to make him hungrier for Kyndrea. Perhaps after tonight she might stay for coffee. 'So I can further my escape of course,' he told himself, but even he didn't believe it now.

He went up and quickly used his ensuite shower. After changing into cleaner clothes he adjourned to the lounge. He had been scared of Janine's advances; worried that he would succumb to his male weakness. Now that he knew his love was completely Kyndrea's, he felt he had a suit of armour on.

He heard the shower stop and a hair drier start. Fifteen

minutes later Janine walked in and sat down beside him in the two towels. He looked at her as she sat down, and then towards the window. A slight awkwardness had grown between them.

Looking at Simon, Janine broke the silence. "I put my clothes in the dryer. I shouldn't really, but tongues would waggle if I'd hung them up. I wouldn't mind so much if it was true. Kyndrea is a lucky woman to have you."

"I wish that could be true," Simon honestly replied. "Believe me, you are the lucky one." Simon looked back at Janine. Now her makeup was off she looked quite human. "Even if I did take you up, it wouldn't be fair to you. I would be just using you for your body."

"Every other man does, why should you be different?"

"Have you ever wondered why?" Simon studied Janine's eyes. What was he doing, being so nice to this woman? She tried to steal him away. She was just another piece of richie scum. Yet he could not help but see something more than that in her. She was not just a beautiful body. No one was. Everyone had their own thoughts, their own emotions. It would be a crime to take another human for granted in that way. Were the rich also human then? No, when push came to shove, they weren't worth thinking about. He just had to talk about something while her clothes dried. And why not be honest? Show her what the rich miss out on with all their airs and graces.

"All those diamonds and forwardness attracts the wrong types of guy", he continued. "You look much nicer now without that war paint on. Your pretence hides your natural beauty."

"Pretence?"

"That is what it is. Pretending you are a wealthy lady. In reality, you are no different from the people on the west bank. Be the young carefree woman you really are. Flaunt your natural beauty, not a lie."

"Unlike Kyndrea, I don't have 'natural beauty'. I need assistance."

"Well, I disagree, but then what do I know? I'm just a man. And really I'm not much of that. Kyndrea's the first real relationship I have had, I don't want to jeopardise it."

"Well, you passed the test big time today."

"Really, I shouldn't have even looked. I got a C at the most."

"B minus," Janine laughed. "No, I saw your eyes in the shower. They were looking, but your mind was elsewhere. You are truly committed to Kyndrea. If she does to you, what she did with Martin, she's more a fool than I first thought. Well, you always have me." Smiling, she tried to make light of what she had said, but Simon could see anger in her face.

"Martin?"

"Kyndrea's first and only boyfriend."

"Oh! The one you stole," Simon stated, before he could stop himself.

"She told you that?" Janine turned away from Simon for a few seconds and then turned back. "I suppose she was technically correct. He wasn't as committed as you were, but she was not entirely blameless herself. True, I do, end up fishing in other people's ponds. I have to."

"Only when you hide behind the makeup and jewellery", Simon interrupted.

"You've made your point." Janine looked deeply into Simon's eyes. "You really are telling me the truth aren't you. I can't imagine that you would ever lie. Well, I will return the favour. I will tell you the truth. Martin was madly in love with Kyndrea. I was madly in love with Martin. It was the great love triangle. Martin wanted Kyndrea to move in with him. I saw Martin slipping away from my grasp. As Kyndrea's best friend, I wanted to see her happy. Kyndrea came first, so I bowed out of the equation. Then it came time for Kyndrea to move out. Everything was planned to the smallest detail. The moving truck came and then without any reason she sent it away before the men even got out of the cab. Suddenly she realised that it would mean leaving her father. I don't think any man, even you, would measure up to her father. Obviously Martin was immensely disappointed. I was there to pick up the pieces. One thing led to another and the rest is history."

"And what happened to Martin?" Simon looked at Janine. Her eyes were filling up with tears. She turned away and watched the action on the lake. A few minutes went by. No one spoke.

"Here's the most important advice I could ever give anyone," Janine suddenly stated, still looking away from Simon. "Never be the rebound lover. Martin left the valley a month later. I don't know where he is now."

"Here", Simon said, handing Janine a paper tissue. This was something beyond his comprehension. A richie bawling her eyes out over a man. A man she stole from Kyndrea, though. He had to remember that. She was all he hated about richies, but he still let her sit in his house. It was like picking at a wound. He found this conversation very painful, but he could not help wanting to have more. "Do you still want that coffee?"

"Yes!" She went to get up but Simon directed her to stay sitting.

"I think I can go solo this time", he said, as he walked towards the kitchen. A few minutes later he came back with the coffee. It was quite noticeable that Janine had spent the time composing herself.

"I'm surprised you haven't chucked me out. I was so obvious," she said, as she took the coffee from Simon. "I need to be obvious. What I mean is that you, well, you didn't take on my advances, and yet you make it easy for me to talk to you. You are one in a million."

"No", he said, thinking, 'Just not rich.' He sat down and took his cup from the table. "I just find it easy to talk to you, because you're now being honest about who you actually are. Do your advances ever work?"

"Sometimes they do. Mostly by men here on business holidays. I crave the attention I suppose. You wouldn't think I am a very successful person, would you? But I am, I'm the second wealthiest resident of Trentsworth."

"You must charge a lot for your design work."

"No." For the first time since the shower, Janine smiled. "Investments, I own half the hotels here and have a major stake in Peak View. And yet I always feel empty. All I want is someone to spend the evenings with, someone to tell my worries to. I have found out the hard way, money is not the be all and end all."

"Really?" Simon looked at Janine. Something just crumbled in his mind. This icon of richness. This Richie of the Richies just said money's not the solution. He no longer had a Richie opposite him. He had a human being. A poor disillusioned person who had no confidence in herself.

She had opened her heart to him. He had to help her. "Look, go and put on some leisure clothes. Not designer, just plain cheap touristy clothes. Leave your face alone and sit in the main mall with a coffee. In seconds you will have men sitting at your table, believe me. I will bet you a favour." He looked at Janine's hopeful face, "Anything that doesn't involve intimacy."

"I might just take you up on that, in fact I will, morning tea on Thursday." She looked at her watch. "Is that the time? I have a meeting in an hour and I need to get ready. I haven't even had lunch yet." Janine stood up and walked to the laundry. She came back five minutes later fully dressed. "I can't change my appearance too soon. I'll give everyone a heart attack. I must say I didn't expect a morning like this, but it was worth it." She went to hug Simon but then thought better of it. She left and closed the door behind her.

Simon just stood there. Janine moved like a whirlwind when she needed to. He went to the kitchen to fix himself some lunch. He thought about how Janine had come to the realisation that money couldn't buy happiness. Had he converted her from a richie to a human being? Or was she always one to begin with?

He started thinking of Kyndrea. She was a human being, no doubt there. In fact he wondered what he would do without her around. Sitting down in his chair with a plate of sandwiches, he looked out at the amphibian. Perhaps escaping wasn't such a great idea after all. He could escape via that plane anytime he wanted to. Why not leave it until the six months were over. Perhaps IVRRAC would allow him to stay in the valley - not in the house of course, but he could use the excuse of moving in with Kyndrea as a reason to sell. He loved Kyndrea, loved her enough that spending a lifetime in this valley no longer terrified him. He couldn't wait until the next evening when he would see her again. This time he would not hold back. He knew he loved Kyndrea. He knew she loved him. Why deny it any longer?

Reality with a View

Now he had finally realised his inner feelings, he was impatient for Wednesday night to come around. He spent the rest of Tuesday and Wednesday morning playing pool and swimming. He had to do something while he passed the time. It may have been only two weeks since they first met, but he had never experienced this feeling before. For once he knew what his life was all about. It was to be with Kyndrea. That evening he would pledge his undying love for her. Begin life anew.

Kyndrea walked into her house with her dad. The doctor had said that Bob seemed to be improving. The whole episode seemed like a distant memory now she was back in the valley.

She looked at the clock in the hallway. It was getting late. She rushed upstairs to her room as Bob slumped into an easy chair in front of the television. Thirty minutes later she came downstairs. She had purchased another dress in Christchurch. This time it was more towards the casual end of the designer market. It caressed her body, accentuating all her womanly curves.

Bob turned around. His eyes almost popped out of their sockets. "Scott's very special to you, isn't he?"

"He's the one for me, dad. I know it."

"You know, I think you might be right. You two seem perfect together. If nothing else, he has got you looking the best you have been, ever."

"Why, thank you dad", Kyndrea kissed her dad on the cheek and then went out the front door.

Simon was coming down his staircase when he heard the knock on the door. He opened the door to reveal Kyndrea. He stopped still. He was amazed how wonderful Kyndrea looked. She had outdone herself again. He kissed her in greeting, not able to stop himself. "I have never seen anyone as beautiful as you Kyndrea"

"Thank you." She looked at him, feeling slightly awkward. She wasn't one for compliments. "Do you want to take a taxi or walk?"

"It seems to be quite a still evening. I say we attempt a walk."

"Okay, let's go, or we'll be late." Kyndrea physically grabbed his arm, leading him towards the road. Simon was just able to hold off enough to close and lock the front door. They walked up the footpath towards the new Trentsworth centre.

They continued along Springfield Road as it became a flyover above the station. Simon looked down over the waist high railing. "We must be at least ten stories high here. Aren't they worried about jumpers?"

"If anyone was planning on suicide, they'd go where we're headed. No one would even look twice at such a paltry excuse for a jump. By the way, if you're interested, this is where Springfield Road ends. Once we are on land again it becomes Southern Heights Road."

"Can you stop being a tour guide for one evening?" Simon smiled; he wasn't really complaining.

They passed all the large hotel buildings built along the side of the steep hills that surrounded this area of the valley. As Southern Heights Road turned west there was a side street heading south-east, right into the corner of the huge cliff-like hills surrounding this area. Kyndrea turned down this road and Simon followed, noting the name was Cable Street.

As they continued walking, a strange humming sound

became apparent. It got louder as they approached the end of the road. The humming seemed to be coming from a small well lit building. The walls were mostly made of glass and he could see a queue of people inside. They walked through the large glass doors and joined the queue. The queue ended at a ticket booth beside another glass door in a glass wall on the far side. While waiting in the queue, Simon looked through the glass wall now on his right. On the other side he saw some carriages hanging off a large chain rounding an enormous pulley. The carriages were made of white fibreglass, and to Simon looked very flimsy. The fibreglass shell was punctuated by various windows on all four sides. The top was connected to a large metal plate by four large bolts at each of the plate's corners. Welded to the plate in the centre was a thick arm. It was the top of this arm that was hanging off the slow moving chain. As they rounded the corner, the closest fibreglass wall split in two and became doors sliding apart for the patrons to quickly hop inside. The carriage did not stop, so it was quite an exercise in dexterity.

"Trentsworth Gondolas," Kyndrea announced, as they slowly got nearer. "If you want to know how it all works, ask dad. He's the one who is into all these mechanical things. All I care about is that they don't fall off the cable once we get going."

"Cable?"

"You'll see." Eventually they reached the ticket booth. Kyndrea handed over some money. She then went through the door. The humming that Simon had heard out on the road was now deafening. A carriage rounded the pulley, its doors wide open. Kyndrea hopped in, pulling Simon after her.

As the carriage continued along the chain its doors automatically closed. He then felt the carriage suddenly accelerate. After a few bumps they exited the building and they started climbing, following the steep cliffs of the southern hills.

He realised they were basically in a small cable car dangling over certain death. A small lump developed in his throat. "Has there ever been any accidents?"

"Only a man who climbed out a window then fell off."

Simon didn't say another word as he saw Trentsworth spread out beneath him getting smaller and smaller; the ground beneath them getting further and further away. Kyndrea just sat and smiled. Finally, as Simon thought they must almost be in space by now, the ride levelled out. Ahead of them was a lighted entrance for the cable car. After a few more bumps the carriage entered the building and slowed down. The doors opened and they stepped out. Simon had to concentrate on standing, as his legs were like jelly. Following the arrows on the floor, they walked into the warmth of the foyer. Kyndrea seemed to know exactly where she wanted to go. Simon just followed as she led him through a labyrinth of hallways and stairs. Finally they reached the reception desk of what looked like a five star restaurant. Kyndrea said her name and the waiter took two menus and led them to a table right against the large panoramic windows. The view was amazing. The valley stretched out beneath them, slowly disappearing into darkness as the sun sunk in the west. Directly ahead of them were hundreds of mountain peaks stretching out into the distance. "Peak View", Simon quoted, in realisation of what the name actually meant.

"Now you understand," Kyndrea bragged. She always liked the look of awe on the person's face when they saw this for the first time. "Can you make out your house, Scott?"

"Almost, we're quite high up here, aren't we?"

"Reasonably, wait until sunset, and then you will really understand the name."

They had just ordered when the sun started to fully descend into the western ocean. Suddenly in front of Simon, peak after peak turned orange with the setting sun. The number of mountain peaks seemed to double in front of him as the dying sun made each one shine out singularly.

"Isn't it an amazing sight?"

"Not as amazing as the sight across the table from me." Simon could not help himself. She was indeed a wonderful sight to behold.

"Why, thank you," Kyndrea smiled. "Corny but appreciated. Speaking of sights, are you still keen to fly with us tomorrow? We will make a day of it, you, me and dad. Then you'll know what the Southern Alps is all about."

"Most certainly." Simon smiled, watching the view as slowly the peaks disappeared into the dark and all that was left was the small twinkling lights of the town below and the stars above. He no longer wanted to escape, but he couldn't imagine anything finer than to spend a day in the middle of nowhere with Kyndrea.

The waiter came with the soups. Kyndrea started telling Simon all about her trip to Christchurch. Simon decided it would be more politic not to mention his day, and just listened to all the details of Bob's check-up and how trendy all the shops had got. He didn't feel like talking, anyway. All he wanted was to hear that sweet voice and watch those eyes so full of excitement and wonder.

"Oh my", Kyndrea exclaimed, as the coffee's arrived. "We are at the end of the meal and I haven't let you say a thing. You must be bored stiff. I mean it's not as though my Christchurch visits are that exciting. Even I feel as though I dreamt it all when I come back. Sort of like a distant memory."

After the coffee they boarded the gondola and headed back home. Simon invited Kyndrea back for a "quiet port or something" and to his relief she agreed. He didn't want this evening to stop. Now he had fully accepted the fact he was in love with Kyndrea, she was even more wonderful to be around than before.

They were sitting looking out at the lake sipping brandy when Kyndrea noticed a photo of a lady on one of the wall units. She stood up and went over to it. Simon had forgotten he had put it there. It was one of the few personal possessions he had managed to keep on his journey, albeit without any glass on the front.

"This your mum?" Kyndrea asked.

"Yes, beautiful isn't she." Simon looked down at his feet. "She didn't deserve to die like she did. Starved to death by remorse. Remorse and guilt my father ladled onto her relentlessly."

"I know my mum definitely didn't." Kyndrea put the photo back on the cabinet and wandered back to Simon.

"How did your mum die?" Something deep in Simon's heart warned him not to ask. But something else told him he had to know, the answer was important.

"I suppose you have to know sometime," Kyndrea stated. "But I will need a cuddle if I tell you, I cannot help but get emotional. It was when I was about thirteen. Mum was picking me up from the Grammar School." She sat down right beside Simon. "Please hold me Scott, otherwise I will not be able to continue."

Simon put his arms around her, looked into her face. Then he suddenly realised. He knew exactly what Kyndrea was about to say. 'No!' He screamed in his head, 'No!' How could it be? How could fate be so cruel to him? As Kyndrea continued, he remembered the incident. He remembered every detail clearer than Kyndrea could ever recall that day. How when her mum got out of the car to help Kyndrea with getting her science project into the boot.

"A young boy about my age wandered past. He stopped and looked at my mum. He seemed to take an interest in my science project. I started to explain to him that it was on microscopical views of everyday items. I was mid sentence through how blunt knives actually were, when before I knew what was happening, he wrenched a knife from the display board." She paused as tears welled up in her eyes, "He. He then stabbed my mother. For some reason I couldn't avert my eyes from his as he did it again and again. All I can remember about him was the look of hatred in his face. I froze. I might have been able to save her life, but I froze." Kyndrea looked into Simon's own tearful eyes. Simon was looking firmly at his feet, deep in thought. "Suddenly, the boy ran away. I couldn't give them a description, only how his eyes were so full of hate. It happened so fast.

"They found him around the corner, thirty minutes later, hiding in a hedge. Apparently he was sitting shaking, with the knife still clasped tightly in his hands. He got sent to a boarding institution. He was not jailed as he apparently was too young. He used my knife, my own knife to murder my mum. Do you know how that made me feel?"

"You must hate him with every bone in your body," Simon commented, holding her tight, not exactly knowing why. She would never forgive him. Why should she?

"I should, you know, Dad does. For him, if he ever found that boy," she paused. "I guess he's a man now. If he ever found that guy he would kill him without a second thought. As for me? I'm not sure. Yes, he took my mum away from me, but he also gave me my father back. I hate myself for thinking like that, but ever since that day, dad has been at my side.

"Dad was into the stock market. He didn't have much time for mum or me. He came home late every night exhausted from all the hard decisions he made during the day. Even though he had more money than we could ever spend, in his thinking, he never had enough money. He would have had a heart attack by now if he had stayed that way.

"So in a sense there was a positive side to it. That it made dad think about life, so we moved to Trentsworth. A place where he could appreciate his wealth and spend time with me. But I'm sure we could have come to this result without mum having to die.

"Mum was the nicest person you could ever imagine. She didn't deserve to die, let alone be stabbed in that way. And the language he used! The things he called my mum while he murdered her. If I hate him I hate him for that. Yes, I hate him, of course I hate him. I would gouge out those eyes. Those eyes so filled with hate.

'Then, as mum slumped away, he turned and looked directly into my eyes. Oh my god!" She suddenly realised something. Talking to Scott, she now understood. "I was going to be next. He was going to stab me, too. Our screams had finally been heard by the teachers and they had just rushed out the gate. He ran away, but first he whispered something in my ear. Something I would never forget. An insult. I found it hard enough to repeat it for the nice lady police officer. Please don't ask me what it was."

"I wouldn't, Kyndrea. I don't need to." Simon paused for a second. "Know." He looked into her eyes; yes if he had time he would have killed her, too. But when he saw the teachers, he knew he would be caught. He didn't know why he killed her mum at that point. He was confused then, it wasn't until after a couple of years in the institution he had worked out how the world actually was.

"I would love to see him suffer, the way I suffered. I would like him to feel the pain of losing a loved one. I wish he could see how he wrecked my life. And yes, I would love to see him dead." With that she burst into tears. Simon left her crying into his shoulder, rubbing her back in comfort.

In his mind the turmoil had started. How could he expect Kyndrea to forgive him? He would never forgive the rich for killing his mother. So why should Kyndrea be any different? There was no way the love he felt for her could ever be realised. He prevented that from happening ten years ago.

Why should he need to be forgiven in the first place? She was just a richie. He did nothing wrong. Kyndrea's mum deserved to die, just as Kyndrea deserved to die. He should celebrate! Tomorrow he will get the chance to finish what he started. And not only Kyndrea but the dad as well. 'Freedom and completion, what else could a man want?'

He was back in charge. He had awoken from his hypnotic

trance, for that is what it must have been. How could he love a richie? The proposal was laughable. IVRRAC had played around with his mind, but he had won through. The idea he could love a richie was as ridiculous as expecting Kyndrea to love him; her mother's avenger.

All he needed to do now was to see out this cry baby's episode tonight. Then keep up the pretence tomorrow. Well, until they were in mid air anyway. Then he would strike. He would once again avenge the poor and bring the richies to their knees.

It was not long after that Kyndrea decided bed was in order. Simon saw her to the door. She looked tearfully into his face, "Sorry, Scott. I'll be all right after a good night's sleep."

"That's okay, Kyndrea. I'll see you in the morning."

"Nine thirty?"

"Sounds perfect", Simon responded, as Kyndrea walked down the path to the street. Kyndrea was glad it was quite late. Her father would be in bed. She didn't feel like talking to anyone else. Once in the house she went straight up to her bed and fell asleep on her tear soaked pillow.

Simon closed the front door and went straight to the kitchen. He rummaged through the draws, opening and closing each one. Then his eye caught something on the windowsill. He grabbed the knife block and placed it on the bench. His fingers slowly moved from handle to handle, until finally they rested on one of the lower ones. Slowly, he pulled the knife out of the block. The blade glinted in the kitchen spotlights. He stabbed the thin air a couple of times. Smiling, he placed it on the bench beside the espresso machine.

Lying in bed, he tried to get to sleep. His mind was racing about how exactly he would go about it. It was then that he realised not once that evening did he feel the slightest stomach cramp. Tomorrow would be the day his new life actually begins.

Back to Normality

Simon awoke to the sound of his alarm. 'My last day in Trentsworth,' he thought. He was feeling a bit groggy, partly from the wine, partly because it was only four in the morning and still dark outside. It occurred to him just before he went to bed that he had to somehow avoid IVRRAC's all-seeing eyes. Using a small torch he got dressed and showered. He couldn't risk turning on any lights. This would alert IVRRAC he was awake. He picked up a small backpack from the dressing room and packed a few items in it. He couldn't pack too much for fear of making Kyndrea or Bob suspicious.

He worked out most of the fine details. He made sure the kitchen knife was in his pack. He was definitely going to need that. He would get them to land somewhere there were roads back to the main centres. Kill them and hide the bodies so he would get a good head start. First, though, he had to fool Andrew in thinking he was still in his house. Once the sun came up, he presumed his house would be under complete observation. They would know he went to Peak View last night. They wouldn't expect him to be up at this hour of the morning.

He made for the front door. Just before he opened it, he remembered something. Slapping his forehead in disgust he went and grabbed the handset to his portable phone. He tucked it into the pack, then stepped out the front door. The outside air was fresh and cool. His mind started working even better as he walked down Springfield Road towards the lake's outlet.

The hypnosis had worn off just at the right time. All concern about Kyndrea was miles from his mind. He was now back to his own good self again, a crusader for the poor. Pity he didn't have time to deal with all the other richies around here, but he was happy with what he had. He could always come back at a later stage. Finish the rest off then.

As he walked down the street in the dark, the silence enveloped him. It was as though Trentsworth had become a ghost town. Suddenly there was a noise behind him. He turned around defensively. It was just a plastic cup bouncing its way across the road in the breeze. He relaxed and continued down the street. He reached a small park beside the outlet and there was a bench hidden in amongst the trees. He decided that would be a great place to keep out of IVRRAC's watchful eye. He sat down and slowly the quiet of the dawn and lack of sleep overtook him. He shut his eyes.

Kyndrea woke up at the sound of her father in the kitchen putting the dishes away. She got out of bed. Looking at herself in the mirror, she thought she looked a mess. She hadn't undressed properly and was still in her underwear. Her makeup was all over the place and she had the worst panda eyes she had seen. She decided a shower was required before she greeted her father.

She felt more refreshed as she walked down the stairs in her dressing gown. Her father was still mucking around in the kitchen when she entered. "The blasted thing hasn't cleaned the lasagne off properly again," he said, hearing her bare feet on the floor.

"Did you rinse them first?"

"What's the point of spending all this money on a machine if I need to do its work for it?"

"Rinsing only takes a couple of seconds." Kyndrea smiled as she took the plate off her dad. "Here, let me finish this off. You go and get the coffee brewing."

"Scott and you are still okay?" Bob asked suddenly. Kyndrea turned around with a guilty look on her face. "I heard you crying last night", Bob explained.

"Oh. No, it wasn't over Scott. It was over mum. I explained

to Scott how she died and of course it brought it all back to me. He was great, gave me comfort, though I wouldn't blame him if he didn't want to see me again. Not a great way to finish a romantic evening."

"Romantic? Ah, now the truth comes out." Bob went over and gave Kyndrea a hug. "If he's as smart as I think he is, he will appreciate you even more now. He's still keen to come on the flight today?"

"Yes, he's coming over at nine thirty."

"Well, you better get changed, unless that's the new trend in travelling wear." Bob pointed to the kitchen clock. It was nine twenty.

Simon woke up with a start. The birds were chirping quite loudly. It took him a few seconds to remember where he was. He looked at his watch. It was nine thirty. He was already late. Late for the most important flight of his life. He quickly picked up his pack and started walking back up to Kyndrea's house. This time he followed a stream that hugged the bottom of the steep hills to his left. 'The trees growing here should give me some protection from prying eyes,' he convinced himself. Eventually he came upon the small side street just north of Kyndrea's house. It crossed the stream and ended abruptly at the hill. 'One day,' Simon thought to himself, 'Some idiot would continue it up the hillside and probably charge the earth for a piece of land suitable only for rock climbing.'

He followed the side street and ended back onto Springfield Road. He quickly crossed it and through Kyndrea's gate. He knocked on the door. To his relief it opened quite quickly. Bob was on the other side. "Hi, Bob."

"Good morning, Scott. I hope you are ready for the grandest sights you'll ever see."

"Ready and willing, Bob." Simon looked furtively behind him as he entered. He greeted Kyndrea as she was coming down the stairs. "Feeling better Kyndrea?"

"Much, thanks," Kyndrea answered as she reached the bottom. "Sorry about last night. Didn't mean to have it end on such a sad note."

"That's all right. I'm glad you're a lot happier this morning, though."

Kyndrea came over and gave Simon a cuddle. "A lot happier, especially now you're here."

"Same", Simon lied. "I know I should have, before I came over, but could I use your toilet?"

"Men!" Kyndrea laughed. "Through that door there." She pointed to a door in the north wall. "Second on the right."

Simon walked into the toilet and closed the door behind him. He opened up his pack and got out his phone. "Now to make sure they think I'm still at home," he muttered to himself. He pushed the pre-programmed key for Andrew.

"Hello, Andrew speaking", came the answer.

"Andrew, it's Simon", Simon said very quietly so Kyndrea or Bob would not hear.

"Ah Scott, what is it?"

"I was just getting breakfast and I thought about tomorrow."

"Yes?"

"Well, I thought, since we're in this great valley, we should have lunch at a café or something."

"Ah! Now you're sounding like a true local. Sure, I'll meet you on the wharf and we can go from there."

"Good. Eleven thirty?"

"Sounds fine to me. You're starting to enjoy Trentsworth now?"

"Definitely. You will have problems after the six months is over as I won't want to leave."

"There's nothing in the contract saying you have to."

"Oh right. Great! See you tomorrow." Simon hung up. Well, that seemed to work. Now they would think that call came from his house. So their eyes should be on his front and back doors, allowing him to board the plane undetected. He was about to exit when he realised he did actually need the toilet.

When he emerged, Kyndrea was waiting for him. "And they say women take ages in the bathroom. Are you ready now? Dad's checking the plane over."

Bob was busy at the plane when Kyndrea and Simon reached the end of the dock. He seemed quite quiet, inspecting the plane's engines. Bob obviously took flying quite seriously. Simon helped Kyndrea get their packs on board. Kyndrea had worked hard on a large lunch to have while in flight. 'Or,' he thought to himself, 'Had she just paid someone to make it for her, after all, she was just a richie.'

Simon looked around for any sign of IVRRAC spies. Not

that he had managed to spot any before. He had to do something to calm himself down. He quickly got into the plane. Kyndrea followed and sat next to him. Bob finished the checks not long after that. He untied the ropes and got into the pilot's seat and then started the engine. Simon half expected a gang of men to run down the dock and stop them. He looked out of his window on the right. The plane taxied to the centre of the lake. There was no sign of any other craft on the water. Once positioned, Bob pulled the throttle, and the plane roared into the air.

Bob pulled back on the stick making the plane rise very steeply. Even with that they barely avoided the mountainous cliffs all around Trentsworth. Simon couldn't believe it. He had managed to avoid IVRRAC's forever watchful eye. He was now a free man and he was determined to keep it that way.

Through Simon's panoramic windows Andrew watched the plane disappearing over the mountains. "Crunch time, Mr Tallsbury," he said to himself. "Now we find out whether we've succeeded or not. I love this job!"

The mountains unfolded beneath them as the plane flew on "See why I fly most days, Scott?" Bob yelled over the engine noise. Simon gasped at the view. It was even more majestic than that of the restaurant.

"Most definitely, Bob", Simon yelled back. When should he strike? 'Patience,' he told himself. 'Plenty of time, so enjoy the ride for a while. Relax, it will be your last chance."

"Mt Cook is over there, Scott," Kyndrea pointed south. The tallest mountain in the country did not stand out as much as he thought it would. It lay gently amongst the other peaks of the ranges. "Bob thought it might be nice to have lunch on the glacier"

"The glacier?"

"Tasman, the largest non-polar glacier in the world", Kyndrea proudly announced.

"Sounds cold," Simon stated.

"Not at noon in the summer, Scott. There is no wind so it will be quite warm."

"Though I would recommend a jersey, we are at a high altitude," Bob interrupted.

"I brought an extra one if you didn't bring one," Kyndrea added.

"Thanks", Simon answered, his eyes firmly fixed on the scenery outside. His mind though, was still on other things.

When should he make his move? Before or after this lunch? Curiosity pushed him to wait. He had never been on a glacier before. There was plenty of time. He might as well relax and soak up the view. This was the realm of the rich. No normal person could afford to view this. He was glad that he was almost rid of these foul people. To think he was fooled into liking these folk. That hypnosis was quite strong. He should have stabbed Janine as soon as she had walked through the door. It was laughable that she was even remotely human. She would go to the café today, but her richieness would put a stop to any possible romance.

What is Reality Anyway?

The swaying music floated over the babble of voices as Janine sat at an outside table with her coffee. She had taken Scott's advice and just wore enough foundation and lipstick to avoid feeling naked. Wearing an "I've been to Trentsworth" T-shirt and some unassuming jeans, she just relaxed and watched the world go by.

She pondered on the mix of sounds entering her ear. The many conversations of friends meeting over a cappuccino. The clash of dishes as the café staff ran around trying in vain to end the queue of customers at the counter. The gentle splash of a fountain nearby and the flute.

He stood there as the chaos flowed around him, playing his flute to some pre-recorded accompanist. Proudly displaying his CDs for sale and hoping that one of these hundreds passing him by would stop and purchase.

She briefly wondered if there was some mail order firm

sending out CD production sets, generating a mass of buskers, then sending them into the cruel world of reality. She noticed that the tourists seemed more interested in buying an overpriced woollen jersey than a cheap CD. They all seemed to pass him by.

She took another sip of coffee. The music stopped. She looked up and saw that a man was purchasing one of the CDs. Her eyes followed him as he walked towards the café entrance. He had quite a few shopping bags hanging from his hand. As he entered the café, he took a quick glance at her.

Several minutes later, he re-emerged with a cup. Glancing at her a second time, he then looked around at the other full tables. Suddenly he walked over to her table. "May I share this table?" he asked, a slight English accent showing through.

"Definitely", Janine answered, "New in town?"

"Arrived last night", was the reply. He put his bags on the empty chair to his left and placed the cup on the table. He then sat down opposite her and looked straight into her eyes "Yourself?"

"Been here all my life", Janine answered. She felt slightly violated by this man. It was as though he could read her mind with that stare. She turned slightly away.

"I'm not really a tourist," he stated, misreading her slight evasiveness. "Though it may seem it. I'm planning to live here. Once I've found a good property."

"I could help you there," Janine offered. This man intrigued her. It was mostly that he decided to choose her table. She wasn't putting on any falsehoods and yet she was still attractive.

"That sounds great." He smiled, "I'm Richard Coster." He held out his hand in greeting.

"Janine Gousing", she replied, gently shaking his hand. She felt the rough skin of his fingers. He obviously had done his fair share of physical work. He might have an interesting past. She realised that she didn't need to fall in love with the first man ever to show an interest in her. But he seemed to be someone she could have a few good conversations with.

"Great to meet you, Janine. What do you do here?"

The drone of the engine changed slightly as Bob circled Mount Cook, preparing for a landing.

"There, Scott", Kyndrea pointed, "See the river of ice flowing down the side of Mount Tasman?"

"Looks like a giant ski slope."

"A lot of people use it as such. They get a helicopter to drop them off at the top and then ski down to a pickup point lower down."

"Couldn't they ski right to the bottom?"

"No, not only is the bottom covered in shingle, which would be hard to ski on, but..." Suddenly, there was silence.

Everything was black. Simon wondered what had happened, he felt as though his consciousness had wandered off on its own. He thought he heard a faint voice mentioning some gas. Was there a gas leak on the plane? Had he passed out from it? Then something about mountains and an extra person overtaxing something. Had the plane crashed? Is this what death was like?

"Scott?" A voice spoke to him. "Scott, are you all right?" He opened his eyes. He was still on the plane. The constant rumbling of the engine started coming back to him. Kyndrea was staring into his face. A smile replaced her serious look as she saw his eyes move. "Scott, you had us worried, dad has changed course and we are on our way to the Mount Cook airfield."

"Huh?"

"You passed out," Kyndrea continued. "We were rushing you to the airfield in case you didn't wake up. Some people just can't handle high altitude in these unpressurised planes. It seems like you are one."

"It was so strange. Like I was in a different room with the lights out."

"You've never fainted before, Scott?" Bob asked, as the plane continued on the descent. "It's quite a shock the first time."

"No, never," Simon replied. 'Perfect,' he thought. 'It is as though I planned it all along.' He wouldn't need to threaten them to land. That would have been messy anyway. All that needless screaming and yelling. All he would need to do now was to get rid of them once they left the plane. A quick stab and get rid of the bodies. The airport staff would presume they were spending the day, even nights, at Mount Cook village. The alarm wouldn't be sent out for days. He would be well on the way home by then.

"We could stay a couple of nights at the Hermitage, give you a chance to rest," Kyndrea winked.

"Sounds like a brilliant idea," Simon smiled. Even better, 'a Do Not Disturb' sign on the door. Bodies not found for ages.

"I'll fly back solo if need be." Bob laughed, "Threes a crowd, you know."

"Thanks dad," Kyndrea smiled.

"That's nice of you Bob." Simon commented. 'Oh well,' he thought, 'Escape is the important part.' It would probably be easier without Bob anyway. He is quite a strong guy. He would have put up a big fight. 'In fact,' Simon realised, 'he probably would not have got away with Bob around.'

Have a night with Kyndrea, then kill her in the morning. Why not have some fun first? What else are richies good for? Take her cash and get a ticket on a bus. 'And I am gone.'

The plane started descending steeply, "Dad!" Kyndrea shouted. Simon looked to where Bob was. He was slumped over the controls. A loud beeping suddenly started. The beeps gradually got quicker and quicker. Then as suddenly as it started, the beeping stopped.

The plane then corrected its descent and started banking back towards the mountains. "Emergency Autopilot," Kyndrea explained, as she climbed over the seats in the front. "Could you help me get dad in a position for him to breathe easier?"

"Is he all right?" Simon asked following Kyndrea's instructions as they both moved Bob into a more relaxed position.

"No, of course he isn't!" Kyndrea yelled back. "But he will be if the plane lands back home within an hour so I can inject him with his medication."

"Why not bring it with you?"

"Doesn't like high altitude; like yourself." she smiled weakly. She loosened Bob's collar and belt. Simon sank back into the seat and saw his pack. For a brief moment he felt something for Bob, but just as quick, he remembered why he was on this plane. He grabbed the pack and moved it to his side.

"Wouldn't they have the medication at Mount Cook, it is a lot closer."

"No, it's very specific. The nearest supply would be Timaru; two hours away. His only hope is the syringe back home."

Simon's hand reached for the knife handle. 'Well, you're going to land at Mt Cook any way,' he thought. Pity he would now have to threaten her. He needed her to turn the plane around and land at Mount Cook. True, it was not as nice a plan as previously.

Drastic measures called for drastic actions. She was just a richie after all. His hand moved the knife, but he couldn't bring himself to unsheathe it. 'Why? The hypnosis has gone, there is no reason not to,' he pondered to himself.

'Get a grip on reality. She is just a richie,' he told himself. 'She deserves to die. She deserved to lose her mother when she was only thirteen. She deserves to lose her father now.' He pulled the knife further from the pack.

'Why? Because she had more money than he did?' Simon thought as he slipped the knife back into the bag.

'No because the rich are heartless souls.' He started to extract the knife again. He stared at Kyndrea, this heartless richie, her face full of concern. Concern for her father's life.

'But if she was heartless, why the concern? Why did she cry remembering her mother's death?' Simon released the knife handle, letting it fall back into the pack. He looked at her again. She was so worried about her father she had not seen the knife.

'So what if she cared for her dad? He is just a richie,' he convinced himself again. 'So what if she cared for her mum? She was just richie scum. So what if she cared for him? She was still just another richie. Someone to despise.

'Get control of yourself, Simon. You are the avenger, the champion of the poor. You do not hesitate. You do not falter. Take the knife and get her to land the plane. She is the enemy! She's a richie scum.' He pulled the knife from the pack and held it in his right hand. He carefully kept it obscured from her view so he would keep the element of surprise. He watched her face intently, waiting for the right moment. Tears were flowing from her cheeks.

"Dad! Dad! Scott, he's worse than ever", she stated. Her eyes still fixed on her father's motionless body. Tears ran down her cheeks. "Dad, don't die. Only ten minutes to go and then we are home. Only ten minutes, Dad."

'Only ten minutes,' Simon repeated in his head. 'I have to strike now.' He sat up and began to reveal the knife. Then he stopped. 'The rich are heartless souls? Those tears are not fake. Would a heartless soul cry like this? What about last night? No richie could be skilled enough to fake that. Her sorrow. Her terror.

'Kyndrea is not a heartless soul! She doesn't deserve to die.' Simon dropped the knife. No, Kyndrea didn't deserve to die. Yes, she was a richie, but she was also human. Simon picked the knife up and placed it back in the pack. He looked at Kyndrea caring for her father. He tried to avoid thinking about what he had just realised, for deep down, he knew what the conclusion would be. But despite his best efforts, his thoughts kept on racing inside his head, racing like a runaway train speeding down the track, to finally end at the obvious and terrible conclusion.

'And if Kyndrea doesn't deserve to die, did her mother? Bob said Kyndrea was very much like her mum. Her mum would have also been caring, emotional and, most of all, human.'

The plane landed on the deserted lake. The autopilot had obviously alerted the lake authorities. The thoughts kept on flowing through Simon's mind as they taxied to the dock. 'If her mother didn't deserve to die then did my second victim? Was my second victim human also? Did all the rich have feelings?'

At the dock was the Trentsworth ambulance. Simon watched in a trance-like state as they pulled Bob from the plane. Once on a stretcher the ambulance workers gave him an injection. Then they started fussing around him, like bees around a hive. "Please don't die, dad," Kyndrea pleaded over and over.

'And what about my third? Fourth? Fifth? Sixth?' Simon's legs gave way under him as the full realisation hit him. "Even the seventh?" he asked out loud.

"Sorry, Scott, what did you say?" Kyndrea turned around and saw him on the ground. "You look awful. Go up to the house and get a drink. I'm okay here. Don't worry. Dad's going to be all right. He doesn't even need to go to hospital.

We'll be up there soon to put him in bed."

Simon walked from the kitchen after fixing himself a drink to the lounge and up to the windows. On the nearest sideboard was a photo he had previously missed seeing. It was of Kyndrea aged twelve, Bob, and a beautiful woman. A woman that Simon could remember very well.

Was it a coincidence he had a house next door to the daughter of his first victim. Somehow IVRRAC had planned this. It was nasty. It was despicable. It worked. He knew he could never kill again. There was no longer a reason to do so.

That wasn't enough, though. How could he bring these seven people back to life? He couldn't. No one can undo such a crime. He sat in a chair with the photo and cried. He spent the last ten years of his life living a lie. His whole life was worthless. He was just a nasty murderer, nothing more. The scum of the earth.

Somehow he had to make amends, but how? He threw the picture at the window. The glass of the frame shattered as it fell to the floor.

Firstly, he had to come clean. He could no longer live a lie, even IVRRAC's. He just sat there waiting. Waiting for the hardest thing he had ever done in his life. Then, after that he would do the easiest.

With a bang, the ambulance workers charged into the lounge with the stretcher and followed Kyndrea up the stairs. Five minutes later they bounded back down the stairs and out to the waiting vehicle on the dock.

It wasn't long after, that Kyndrea came down the stairs. "He's fine, we got him back in time." She smiled weakly. "He just needs a long rest now." She looked at the window and saw the picture frame. "Scott? Why is that picture there?"

"Look at me, Kyndrea," Simon commanded, grabbing her shoulders roughly, holding tight. "Look at my face."

"What, Scott?" She looked worried. "You're scaring me." She had never known Scott to be so blunt. What was he doing? Her father had almost died and now Scott was yelling at her.

"So I should be," Simon replied in a softer voice. He stared straight at her. "I am not a nice person. You know me Kyndrea, you've seen me before."

"Yes, at the café", Kyndrea agreed, thinking, 'What on earth is he on about? Why did he smash my family photo?'

"No, I mean before that." Simon took a deep breath. "I mean ten years before that. Look deeply into my eyes Kyndrea and tell me you don't recognise me."

"I already know you. You are Scott Tallburg. You live next door." She looked at Simon's eyes. Something flashed up from her memories. She started feeling uneasy. Something inside was telling her to stop this conversation immediately. "It isn't really time to play around. Dad's upstairs recuperating. It will take him weeks to get back to his normal self. We've both had a hard day. I think it's time for you to go Scott."

"My name isn't Scott. My name is Simon Harold Tallsbury."

"You have two names?" Kyndrea asked, as another uneasy feeling flashed up from the past. "I said goodbye, Scott!"

"That name is not mine, Kyndrea. I was given that name by a criminal rehabilitation programme." He had crossed the line and there was no going back. Kyndrea knew enough to eventually work it out. He had to be there when she did. He had to speed up the process.

"You are a criminal?" Kyndrea knew what type of criminal too, but she refused to admit it. "You are a thief rehabilitating in a two and a half million dollar mansion?"

"No! A murderer rehabilitating in a two and a half million dollar mansion. A murderer, Kyndrea! Do you not recognise me yet?"

"No!" She lied, keeping the hope alive. "Are you trying to tease me, Scott? You are Scott Tallburg. You live next door. You love me. Don't you?"

"Yes I love you. If I didn't love you, you would be dead by now. I love you more deeply than I have ever loved anyone in my life. Which is why I need you to know who I am. I can't have you loving a lie. Sorry Kyndrea, but I need to say it. I need you to know for sure who I really am."

"No, Scott. Don't! You are Scott Tallburg, that is all I need to know."

"Rich Whore's Excrement!"

"NO!" Kyndrea screamed. "No! It can't be! You can't be! Get Out!" She pushed him away. Then she marched up to him at full height. "Get out, Simon! How could I ever love you? Get out now, you bastard! Before I kill you!"

"I wouldn't mind if you did!" Simon answered as he walked to the door. "Except then you would have the guilt I have. You would have the remorse. I couldn't live with that. You don't deserve the anguish of a murderer. Don't worry, I'll do it myself and save you the trouble." He quickly marched to the front door and opened it. He turned back for a second and looked straight into Kyndrea's hate-filled face. "I only wish I could kill myself seven times over. Once for every life I took." He closed the door behind him as he walked up the road.

Kyndrea collapsed on the closest chair and burst into tears. After her mum had died, she had made a promise to herself. A promise that she would not lose another loved one. She had kept everyone at an arm's distance.

She finally relented and fully loved another and what happened? She lost him. And the same person had taken her love away. What had she done? What had she done in the past that she deserved this fate? She promised herself she would never love again.

IVRRAC

Simon looked at the valley spread out beneath him. 'Interesting the thoughts you have before suicide,' he pondered. He also wondered whether he was the first to jump from this viewing platform. Would he pass out before he reached the bottom? Would it hurt? He hoped it would; he needed to pay back as much as he could. All the pain he had caused others, he needed it to be visited upon himself tenfold. He wondered why none of the Peak View staff had yet come up and ask him why he was so high up on the railing. You would think suicide attempts would be a high priority of concern from the staff. Perhaps they knew him. Perhaps Kyndrea had told everyone and they all thought, 'Well he should kill himself, do the world a favour, I won't stop him.' Right, he was ready. He would jump. One Two Three, would he feel the breeze pass by him? Would it feel more like flying than falling? Would he get so high on the feeling he would just hallucinate on the way down? Would there be anything at the bottom to autopsy? Police like an autopsy. He knew that: even with 20 knife wounds in the back, still need an autopsy. Maybe she died from a heart attack instead of the blade? Well, he would disappoint them this time, unless they want to autopsy lumps of meat. Right, this time jump on the count of three: one two, would he hit a rock halfway down? Now that would be painful! Tumbling down the side of the cliff instead of just falling, hitting a rock now and then. Just like the man who fell off the end of the ship in Titanic and hits the propeller blade. Ouch, that would have hurt. Though if he hit his head on a rock he would definitely fall unconscious before he actually died. Why isn't any of the staff stopping him yet? Okay, on the count of three: "one two three!" His foot got stuck in the railing and he couldn't climb over the edge. 'How embarrassing, he thought, if anyone saw that.' Then out loud, "Right, get my foot out and then."

"If you're going to jump Simon, jump!" a voice said behind him. Simon almost fell off the railing in fright. It had been so quiet until then. He then realised the person had called him Simon. There was only one man who knew him as Simon.

"I'm going to jump, Andrew, don't worry. I don't deserve to live."

"Okay, that's fine by me. We still get the money from the government whether you live or die."

"Oh don't use reverse psychology on me. I know all that garbage!" Simon yelled, not turning, staying ready to jump. "You would care if I died."

"Care? Why would I, Simon? You killed seven defenceless women for a reason even you don't believe in any more. Why would I care if you died?"

"You wouldn't have put me through all this rehabilitation if you didn't believe in me."

"Believe in you, how?"

"Believe that within the heartless exterior beats a warm heart of understanding."

"Well that's deep, Simon." Andrew smiled and walked closer to the railing, "But then you have been having some deep realisations lately, haven't you Simon?"

"What do you mean by that?"

"I mean, why didn't you threaten Kyndrea with the knife to make your escape? Freedom was within your grasp, all you had to do was sacrifice the life of two richies. But you didn't, did you."

"How do you know?" Simon turned around and looked into Andrew's face. Again it showed no real emotion.

"Well, you are here and not racing down the highway in a tourist bus."

"No, how did you know about the knife? You have cameras in my apartment?"

'Nothing so crude Simon." Andrew looked down into the valley. "You don't think we would let you loose in a village of rich socialites without some surveillance?"

"Spies? Agents hiding in the bushes? What?"

"Come down off that railing and I will explain all."

'Trying to stop me with curiosity?"

"Well, it's a basic ploy, but it works most of the time." Andrew pointed to a table on the balcony. "I have coffee for both of us over there."

"It worked this time as well." Simon tried to smile as he started to get down. He felt he needed someone to talk to. He could always continue from where he left off later that night.

Andrew helped Simon down and they walked back to the table. Simon couldn't remember that table being there when he arrived. He realised how much he must have been out of it before he got to the railing. He had made his way to the balcony outside the main restaurant. It was a trapezoid in shape, coming to a point overlooking the gondola cable. Andrew offered Simon the chair facing the point. There was a window to Simon's right, but the curtains had been drawn for some reason.

Simon was trying to look behind him to the restaurant doors when Andrew interrupted. "Drink up, before it gets cold." Andrew sat down opposite and looked at Simon. "Do you actually know what IVRRAC stands for?"

"I never really gave it much thought," Simon answered. He waited for Andrew to continue. There was silence. Then it occurred to Simon that there actually was too much silence. It was even quieter than the early hours of that morning. That seemed days ago now, so much had happened in the last ten hours, and he had a feeling the roller coaster ride was only half way through. The complete silence was getting to him. Part of the reason, he just noticed, was that the gondolas were not operating. There was no subduing hum from the pulleys.

Andrew broke the spell by continuing. "You weren't meant to; knowing what the acronym stands for would lessen the effect of the whole exercise. "IVRRAC, Simon. That acronym is the key to it all. And now you're ready to understand what it is all about."

"Okay, Andrew," Simon said, pushing his coffee aside. "You're dying to tell me. What does it stand for?"

"Institute of Virtual Reality for Rehabilitating Active Criminals," Andrew proclaimed.

"Okay." Simon looked blankly at Andrew. "And that's meant to mean something to me?"

"Oh?" Andrew stared straight into Simon's eyes. He stared for almost a minute until he felt Simon getting agitated, then he continued. "It means you have never left the complex, Simon."

"I flew down to Christchurch! I travelled in a train to Trentsworth. You were even with me. How can you say I never left the complex?"

"It was, is, all in your mind. Well, almost. Your mind and an array of thousands of hextracore processors." Andrew paused and then added, "Which, might I say was not enough when it comes to simulating flying over mountains. You'd think that would be easy with all the flight simulator programs there are, but not with the ultra-realistic framework we use. All those air currents and temperature ranges, all the various thermals. Plus that we added a fourth 3D, that didn't help."

"Pardon?" Simon looked at Andrew, 'Was he going mad?'

"Sorry, too much, too soon. Basically, this valley is fake, generated by computer. Have you heard of Virtual Reality?"

"You mean those computer games?"

"Well, if you can liken a Wendy house to a mansion, yes. Unlike the games, to make the whole thing work, we had to copy the basic fundamental physics of the real universe. Then we placed them in a sophisticated computer model. Otherwise you would see straight through it. If you dropped a stone on the ground and it stopped at the level of the concrete only, subconsciously you would know it is fake. When the stone lands it needs to displace other tiny pieces of dirt and bounce slightly and roll. It needs to follow all the physical laws for your mind to say to yourself it is real."

"Sorry?" Simon thought he realised what Andrew was saying, though he didn't believe it. "In short, you are saying I am in a great big computer program?"

"We both are, but to you it is totally real. All your senses are plugged in. Myself, I am wearing gloves and eye goggles. It is not so real to me. But I can still be part of the world we have created."

"So if I did kill myself I would not die?"

"You would, sorry. I wouldn't, as I am fully aware that this is fake. I can take off my goggles and I can see the computer room around me. I can smell the computer room. I can feel and taste the air conditioning of the complex. Your body is fully merged into this world via physical connections to your brain from the computer. You actually think you are here. If you die here, the resulting pain and realism would certainly give you a real and serious heart attack, if not a stroke. You may survive, but you would definitely be paralysed, or worse a vegetable."

"So you have made a computer game of Trentsworth and placed me here." Simon was stunned, this was getting weirder by the minute.

'There is no Trentsworth to make a computer model of." Andrew laughed. "You don't really think such a valley exists? It goes against the social grain in so many ways."

"But I remember knowing it from my youth." Simon smiled, 'Now I know he's lying.'

"We mixed up your memories slightly with hypnosis. A more solid type than the one we used to make you ill. Trentsworth is a children's book, a book about child detectives who live in a small mountain community where many adventures take place. These are the memories you have. All kids your age know of them, grew up with their adventures. I did as well. To be honest, I enjoyed the excuse to build a computer model of Trentsworth. I always wanted to see the Lake of Worth; to climb the castle tower." Andrew pointed to the restaurant doors, "To dine at Peak View."

"You're mad." Simon got up. "If you think saying all this garbage would make me feel better, save your energy. No matter what this place is, it doesn't change what happened one iota. I killed seven innocent women!"

"Sit down, Simon," Andrew requested in a low voice.

"No, I won't sit down. I am going back to my house. When you feel you have had enough of making up fantasies, come and see me."

Simon walked to the restaurant doors and opened them. Inside the restaurant, the tables were, as usual, packed with tourists, though none of the people were moving. Some were in mid chew. It was as though he had walked into a wax museum.

"Come back and sit down," Andrew politely requested. "I stopped the simulation so we wouldn't be disturbed."

Simon looked at the horrific sight carefully, trying to detect a flaw. There was a glass knocked off a table in mid fall. Wine being poured from a bottle, stopped in mid flow. He walked over to a frozen tourist and touched the skin. It was solid like hard plastic. He put his finger in a glass of wine and found it, too, was solid.

Simon smiled. "You can't fool me with your plastic

mannequins. They don't even feel like real people!"

"I am not fooling you, Simon," Andrew said standing in the doorway. "They feel like that because the simulation is not reacting with your presence. Come out and sit down."

"If this is a simulation and I am under computer control, just make me sit down."

"I can't do that! It would play havoc with your mind." Andrew walked back out of the deck and spoke to mid air. "Turn it back on, Kevin."

Simon walked through the still restaurant towards the exit doors. IVRRAC definitely had money. Booking out this entire restaurant would have cost thousands.

Andrew looked exasperated, "Okay, okay Kevin. Yes, it would play havoc. Switch it on when he goes through a doorway. Then the 2Ds won't notice his appearance."

Simon walked through to the foyer. On the other side there were people waiting at the reception desk, some more ordering drinks from the bar. Simon breathed a sigh of relief. He was in a normal world. He made his way through the maze of corridors to the gondolas. He was surprised that there was no queue of people. The gondolas not operating for the past fifteen minutes should have caused quite a backlog. Perhaps IVRRAC had paid people to stay on later, given them a free meal or something to avoid one. Simon hopped on the next gondola coming round and started the descent back to reality.

Simon didn't know what to do with himself now. Not only would Andrew stop him each time he tried to pay back his crimes, he was feeling less and less convinced that suicide was the answer. There must be another way to make reparation to the world.

As soon as he got home, he locked the door and went straight to bed. There was no way he could rationally think feeling this tired. Tomorrow had to be a much better day. Anything would be better than the day he just had.

The Seed of Doubt

Upon waking up the next morning, he decided he needed to do something. He walked to the new town centre and milled around the main street. Deciding on a cup of coffee, he chose a random café. The man behind the counter smiled nicely. "You would like to order?"

"Flat white, please"

"Certainly, sir. That will be five dollars." Simon handed over some money. "Please take this number and your coffee will be delivered to your table."

Simon took the rectangular piece of plastic and found that it slipped nicely into a stand on the table. While waiting for the coffee to arrive he absentmindedly listened in on a neighbouring table's conversation.

"After placing the disc in the tray you press the open button again to close", the man said.

"The player will then start immediately, allowing you to choose, on screen, what options you desire", replied the lady.

"If this is the first use, it is recommended you select the set up option first", responded the man.

"Your flat white, sir", a female voice interrupted him. He looked up into the eyes of Janine. "Mind if I join you?"

"Not at all", Simon affirmed. "I need a decent conversation. Are those two behind me sharing an instruction manual?"

"Sorry?"

"Don't worry. How did it go yesterday?" Simon asked, remembering she was going to try out the no frills approach to life. It was then he noticed her T-shirt and jeans. "That well?"

"Yes, very productive thanks." Janine sat down and waved at a waiter holding another coffee. "The guy's name is Richard. There's no chemistry, but he is a great friend. Just like you."

"Thanks." Simon stopped for a bit and thought. Then he asked, "Janine? You are a born local, aren't you?"

"Yes, born and bred Trentsworthian. Why?"

"Tell me about your childhood. What playgrounds you frequented, interesting stories."

"Sorry?"

"I'll shout you lunch," Simon offered.

"Now there's an offer. Okay." Janine looked around, "What about Kyndrea?"

"Well, to be honest we've had a little discrepancy. It turns out we knew each other in Auckland and, well, I did some things I'm not proud of."

"Oh, skeletons in the closet. Don't worry, I've seen the love you two share. Nothing's insurmountable."

"You would be surprised. But anyway, I want to hear about you."

"Well, my father's a specialised tourist facilitator. That's a fancy way of saying he organises customised tour packages for very wealthy people. My mum's the manager of Peak View. It has got to be a rule in our house to leave work at work. Otherwise they would be at each other's throats all day and night."

"I thought a tourist attraction manager and a tour organiser would fit like hand and glove."

"You would be correct, but." Janine stopped. "Are we talking about my parents or me?"

"Okay, sorry."

"Well, with two parents like that, of course our family was not one to want. Well, at least want for money. So I've been to boarding school since I was four years old. I grew up only knowing my parents in the school holidays. Apart from the occasional weekend they would visit me in Christchurch. That made it worse, really. I always wished I was able to board the train with them each time I saw them off. Each time I ended up bussing alone back to the school without them.

"I don't begrudge them my education. I mean, that is why I'm such a successful lady. Why I can keep living in the manor to which I am accustomed. So you see I didn't spend that much time of my youth in Trentsworth. My best friend here was called Tiffany. She ended up going to the same high school as me. You have to board at high school, as Trentsworth is not big enough to support one. Though when we were back here she would quite often be busy with her other friends, Susan and the boys. I never got on with them much, too mischievous for me."

Simon let Janine's voice float over him as she brought back memories of days at the hot pools. Selling juice to tourists outside her parent's place, until they found out, of course. This was not the memories of a computer program. This was real life.

With every memory, Andrew's preposterous tale was being shot away. He was totally satisfied even before the lunch arrived, but he noticed Janine was enjoying herself so much he just kept on listening. Besides, it took his mind off Kyndrea and his crimes.

When it came time for coffee, Janine was still going on about her later years. "I suppose I am the direct result of having a capitalist father and a mother tending towards the communistic end of capitalism. If there's such a thing."

"What do you mean by that?"

"Mum agrees that money is the way of the world, but feels that people shouldn't be able to use it to disadvantage others. Like for instance. Dad would love to pay a sizeable amount to book out the entire Peak View Restaurant for his clients, but mum looks at that as disadvantaging a person, who has the same money per head, having a chance of dining there.

"She has a strict policy never to close the main dining areas to general public. Dad's always cursing that policy."

"Not even for a government function?"

"Especially not for the government. Mum hates having to pay taxes."

"Interesting." Simon pondered on this. He was getting contradictions from every direction. 'If Andrew was right, Janine could just be an actress. But if this was so, why keep up the facade? Especially when they want me to believe it is fake.'

"Well, I must be off." Janine picked up her bag and stood up. "I do have work to do. Though this lunch has been wonderful. It has been a while since anyone has been interested in my life."

"Thank you, Janine. You have given me a great gift in what you have told me. I appreciate it immensely."

"You're welcome." Janine merged into the bustling crowd. How could all this be a computer program? But then why would Andrew make up such a fantastical lie? He must be insane, all this time alone in a house on the hill. Makes people a bit strange, solitary living. Just then, Andrew emerged out of the crowd and sat down on the chair opposite.

"Are you ready to concede?"

"After what Janine has told me?" Simon sighed in resignation. Andrew just didn't give in. "Just because you pay two tourists to quote an instruction manual to me?"

"I thought that was a cute touch. Had you thinking for a bit though, didn't I."

"For only a split second."

"We usually have the basic 2D units quoting from romance novels. I scanned in a manual I had next to my computer just for fun."

"Look, Andrew, I will not be taken in by any of your fantasies. Does IVRRAC know you've gone mad?"

"IVRRAC knows everything. We are in IVRRAC."

"I don't know what you're in but I'm in Trentsworth. Look at all these people around us. Does this seem fake to you?"

Simon looked around, smug in knowing he was right. Then in a single breath the world stopped. The clattering of dishes. The steam on the Yohanne. An escaped kid's balloon. All stopped instantly as though someone had pressed pause on the world's remote control.

"Yes, Simon. It looks to me exactly like a computer program."

"What the...?"

"I couldn't do this straight away. The shock may have given you a serious stroke. But the doubts had been forming in your mind. You were giving it serious consideration, though you didn't know it yourself."

"How the?"

"I think it would be best if we went to your house and sat down. You probably have a lot of questions and sitting in a wax museum is not really the best place to have them answered."

Andrew snapped his fingers and the world started again. He got up and Simon followed, his mind going around in circles.

Kyndrea's Reality

Kyndrea slept in that morning. She had gone straight back to bed after getting her dad a light breakfast and checked he was okay. She didn't feel like greeting the world at all. She wished yesterday had never happened. Perhaps it didn't. Perhaps it was all a nightmare.

Finally, at lunch time she made her way downstairs. After fixing a tray and taking it up to her father, she then sat down with her own lunch in front of the windows. As she took her first bite, her eyes fell on the broken glass still all over the floor.

No, it wasn't a nightmare. It was real. "Why!" She screamed to no one in particular. Tears welled up in her eyes. She put aside the plate and just sat there.

Andrew opened the door and they both walked into the house. In a daze, Simon sat in his favourite chair. Andrew looked seriously at Simon. Did he go too far too soon? "I'll fix you a cold drink."

"Uh ha", Simon muttered in response, staring out the window. There was no denying it now. He was in a computer program. That could not have happened in real life. People just don't freeze in an instant. He didn't know what to do next.

"Here you go," Andrew said, placing an orange juice on the coffee table. Andrew sat down next to Simon. "Drink up."

"Why bother, it isn't actually there, is it."

"Not really, but to you it is as real as anything can get. If you spill it you will get wet. You will feel the cold, sticky liquid seeping through your clothes."

"But it isn't the truth!"

"What actually is the truth, Simon? You spent your whole adult life believing a lie. Everyone lives in their own reality. Does it matter if it is computer generated or not?"

"But I didn't choose this reality!"

"You didn't consciously choose your previous one either, but you lived it. You believed it was real. You believed it was the truth."

"But it wasn't, was it. The truth was, I murdered seven

innocent people. What is the truth? Tell me. Did Kyndrea move to another town? Was she successful in life, like the Kyndrea here?"

Simon paused, waiting for an answer. Andrew did not speak, but looked at the ground. Simon continued. "Or was that too, just a hypnotic memory implanted in my mind?"

"No, you are right. There was a thirteen year old girl present when you killed your first victim. You did call her a 'Rich Whore's Excrement.' You did almost kill her as well."

"Then what is the truth? Did she and her dad move away and start a new life?"

"I wish I could say that. I wish for your sake, Simon, I could say everything turned out okay in the end." Andrew sighed. "Her dad blamed himself for the murder. He was in a business meeting instead of picking Kyndrea up. It was actually his turn that week. He had pleaded with his wife to forego an afternoon social meeting, and she had reluctantly agreed.

"Kyndrea also put the blame on herself. She thought she should have been able to save her mother. She thought she should not have included the knife in the project. Finally, regardless of a few weeks of counselling, the guilt got too much and she committed suicide. "That sent her father over the wall. He stopped work; refused to leave the house;

and only opened the door for delivery men, predominately from liquor stores. Eventually the house was sold from under him by the bank. He spent the rest of his life sleeping in a cardboard box under a bridge. He died of malnutrition and alcohol poisoning a year later."

"So where did the Bob and Kyndrea I met come from? Were they just actors playing made up parts. Kyndrea, or whatever her real name is, knew I was a murderer all along? Though," Simon confessed, "She is a brilliant one. She deserves an award for that last scene alone."

"No." Andrew answered pointedly. "There are no actors, I do not cheat. Well, except for the governor. Apart from him, once in IVRRAC, everything you experience is computer generated. I am the only other real person here. The Kyndrea and Bob you know are mere data in a memory bank."

"So you mean, when I am not around they don't exist?"

"We wouldn't get the continuity if that was the case. No, they are always present as is the whole valley always present in the simulation. I can show you if you like."

Simon nodded, "Whatever". The realisation of where he was, what he was connected to, was pushing him into information overload. He wasn't sure what was real and what was fake any more. How much of this could he believe?

In front of them a lighted rectangle appeared. "It's only a trick of the light", Andrew explained. "Due to the nature of the simulation it is very difficult to manipulate solid objects. It causes a lot of instability, bending the laws of physics too much. However, playing around with light refraction is slightly easier."

Suddenly, within the lighted rectangle a view of Kyndrea's lounge appeared. Sitting in a chair crying was Kyndrea. Simon noted she was still in her dressing gown. In her hand she was holding the photo that had been thrown at the window.

"At least I now know how you managed to keep tabs on what I was doing." Simon commented off handedly as he watched the rectangle studying Kyndrea's actions. She just sat there holding the picture.

Andrew got up while Simon hypnotically stared into the translucent screen and walked over to the southern hallway. Simon heard the clank of dishes in the kitchen.

Simon desperately tried to get to grips with all this information suddenly thrusted at him. He was definitely in information overload, but he had to know everything now. Something was bothering him. Something needed to be realised and it had to be done before Andrew left.

2D or not 2D

After a few minutes he came back with two coffees. "I don't know why I bother, I can never taste the coffee in this world. It's become a habit now, makes the subject feel more at ease."

"So you are saying," Simon stated in a tone of disbelief, "That all that emotion is only a computer program?"

"Yes, realistic isn't it", Andrew replied with a hint of pride as he sat back down. "I spent years perfecting the system that's responsible for the three dimensional characters in all our simulations."

"So Janine is also a computer generated character and not an actress?"

"Janine?" Andrew laughed. "Oh Janine, my favourite 3D, she's a handful isn't she. Yes, totally computer generated. I had a lot of fun designing her."

"She spent the whole morning telling me her life story. It would have taken you years, not weeks to develop such realism. As she was speaking I was searching for any flaws. There were none."

"Thank you. I appreciate the compliment. Well, Janine's memories are totally false. I have developed a system that develops memory from a story. And that's all her memories are, just a story. I coerced the author of 'Trentsworth Terrors' to create Janine's history in story form, which is why Janine refers to the characters of the children's book quite a bit. I then put that story into the memory developer, or as I call it, the MDR, and the result is Janine. Because everyone has pretty much the same learning memories, the MDR inserts all those itself and of course basic instincts. Their social interaction skills are standard, biased slightly by whatever the story denotes about the character. From a recluse that would have very little skills, to a high charismatic 'Mr Popular' who would have all the social skills possible.

"In some respects a person's memory is very complicated. In others it's very simple. The MDR takes a simple memory concept, i.e. A story, and turns it into a more realistic complicated version. Complete with emotional responses to each event. The 3D program then uses those pre-recorded emotional responses to create the response to new events. It then records those responses as more memory and thus compounds the complexity of the original MDR data. The result, as you are fully aware, is very believable. If were possible for them to think, they would probably be fooled themselves."

"They do indeed seem very human. But if Kyndrea is 'on' all the time. When she went to Christchurch, did you..."

"Did we simulate Christchurch for her?" Andrew interrupted. "No, that would really blow the budget on computer hardware. We simply turned her off for the period she was away and then got the MDR to graft a story of her trip into her memory data. Once turned back on, she remembers being to Christchurch.

Simon looked back at Kyndrea. "Is everyone here like Kyndrea and Janine?"

"No, definitely not. The processing power required would be astronomical. No only Kyndrea, Janine and Bob are 3D. The rest of the thousands you see around are various levels of 2D, from the most basic non-interactive to the complex that can have quite an intelligible conversation."

"What's the difference?"

"3D have more data than code and 2Ds are visa versa."

"Just pretend I am not a computer engineer."

"Okay", Andrew slowly replied as he thought of a simpler way to put it. "2Ds have no memory, well not much of one. Their emotions are totally programmatic. I have told them what to do in every situation. Well, the basic ones anyway.

"Let's start with the basic model. They have no memory at all as they are just scene fillers. They were the ones you overheard earlier today. I have to program in their conversations, their movements, etc. They have a basic reactive code that stops them from bumping into moved furniture, other characters, but that is all.

"Then there's the next step up, which has more memory and thus more reactive to situations without needing as much specific code. They react to the basic models' pre-programmed actions in a more random manor, though their conversations are still quite simple.

"Then there is the first grade 2Ds which are a bit more intuitive. They can hold a standard conversation without complex inferences. They are the shop keepers, waiters. Basically any character you or the 3Ds come in contact with."

"How on earth did you managed to create something so complicated in the week or so you had available?"

"A week!" Andrew burst out laughing, then in a more subdued voice. "Beginning to doubt my words now?"

"What do you mean beginning?"

"Well", Andrew continued, ignoring Simon's question, "Through drugs we had you in status for two months. Even that would have been unattainable in the early days. Now I have a complete stock of 2D characters. They're basic enough that they can be transferred from one scenario to another without too much alteration. So I really only needed to set up the 3D characters. Again, now I have developed the MDR to a level where it does most the work, it is much quicker than the earlier scenario set up. I still worked overtime, but as you can see I did manage to complete it. Though, to be honest, some 3Ds were not in place right at the start. After seeing you off that first day, I went straight back to work. Actually," Andrew smirked, "the original Kyndrea and Bob you saw at the plane were 2D versions. Not only weren't the 3Ds ready, but it meant they also behaved exactly how I wanted.

"In fact, to make certain she would be in the main mall for you, we didn't swap Kyndrea programs until you said the first hello. If you were paying attention, you would have noticed how her face became more alive as she continued reading her book. Then it was just down to how well the data was put together, and I think I managed a great job."

"A great job? A fantastic job! Kyndrea, Janine, even Bob are more than just simulations. Have you ever pondered that since you have made them so realistic, that they are no longer simulations?"

Andrew smiled, "An easy trap to get caught in. Many people think they're so human that they are indeed human. But no, take it from me, they are produced by the computer. Just the result of specific lines of code."

"But they respond to the environment. You cannot say to me that you wrote in code 'If Simon confesses, then weep for two hours holding picture, and stare out the window.' You can't have foreseen everything. There must be some outside influence shaping their characters."

"Only your own, Simon. Plus my programming code and MDR data. We had to be certain they would hate your guts when they found out who you were. So there are specific guidelines in the code, but everything else is a reaction to the environment around them."

"Are you saying that they think for themselves?"

"If you call automatic reactions to situations thinking, yes." Andrew paused, looking at Simon. Shaking his head he continued. "If you are thinking along the lines of intelligence, forget it. They're just a computer program, nothing more."

"Some people would consider us as just computer programs."

"People who don't know much about biology. We are much more than lines of code in an array of processors."

"Do you know much psychology?" Simon challenged.

"I have to, to be able to rehabilitate people. I need to know a lot of different subjects. I have doctorates in Computer Science, Psychology, Physics and Physiology."

"You are a smart bastard, aren't you."

Andrew just smiled and let Simon continue.

"So you think you know it all. Well, believe me you don't. You haven't experienced your 'Programs' one on one, have you. I have and I can tell you it is just like talking to you. There is no difference. I know that to you they are just programming code, but Andrew, there is more to them than that. Perhaps you didn't plan it. Perhaps it's some type of miracle. But they are now no longer mere collections of programming code. There is more to them than just a collection of memories. They are intelligent. Just electronic not biological."

"They are only artificial intelligence, not real intelligence."

"No, they are real electronic intelligence. Intelligence is self-awareness isn't it?"

"Self-aware? Who said anything about self-aware? Now you are stretching reality."

"Look at Kyndrea," Simon said, pointing at the screen still showing Kyndrea crying with the picture in her hands. "If that is not a reaction by a self-aware being, I don't know what is."

"Then you don't know what a self-aware being is. You aren't qualified to know. It is an easy trap to fall into, Simon."

"It's easy to fall into, because it's true!" Simon yelled back.

"Believe me. I wrote their programs and I know exactly what they're capable of. Self-awareness is not in the program code."

Simon watched the screen. Kyndrea had got up. Placing the picture back on the side board, she crossed the room to the staircase. The screen followed her movements. Eventually she ended up at her father's bedside. He was asleep, but she held his hand. "Get better dad. I need you now more than ever."

Andrew fumbled mid-air with his fingers as though he was typing on an invisible keyboard. The screen disappeared.

Simon turned and looked at Andrew, "What will happen to them once this simulation is ended?"

'The program data is saved to disks for prosperity and then the computer is erased."

"As I thought." Simon looked slightly worried. "You can restore that data if you require?"

"If I require. I can restore the whole scenario and the 3Ds would continue as though there was no break. Or I can restore just the locality data and use that locality for another scenario. I would think Trentsworth would be restored a few times."

"For your holidays, Andrew?" Simon smiled. For the first time since the plane landed on the lake, he felt a happiness wash over him.

"Now that's a very good idea," Andrew laughed. "At least I can be assured of fine weather."

"But seriously", Simon interrupted Andrew's laughter. "How many three dimensional characters have you created since IVRRAC began?"

"I think Kyndrea and Bob were the twenty fifth and twenty sixth. Janine would be the twenty seventh. She was an afterthought. That's why I got the author to write her story. I didn't have time at that stage, we were already in Trentsworth."

"And I thought I was a cold blooded murderer." Simon looked Andrew in the eye. "You have basically killed 24 people. You are now planning to kill three more and not even blink an eyelid?"

'They are not people." Andrew had become very stony faced as he hissed out his reply one word at a time. "They are merely computer data going through a series of computer codes."

"Are they?" Simon realised his previous statement had hit a raw nerve. There could be a chance he was right. "What if I can prove that they are fully self-aware beings, worthy of life?"

"You prove I am a murderer like you." Andrew looked at the ground, "But, as they are not self-aware beings, they're not worthy of life. It's a mute point."

"But you, Andrew," Simon continued, ignoring the last statement, "have the opportunity to reverse your killings. I want to cut you a deal"

"You make me a deal?"

"If I prove to you, by a bench mark we both agree on, that Kyndrea and Bob are self-aware beings, you promise to keep Trentsworth running and also boot up the other scenarios"

"I don't have enough computer power to run two scenarios simultaneously let alone ten!"

"Well, if you're right, you won't need to worry about that! But if you're wrong, you're going to need enough computer power to run two. Somehow, that is for you to decide. Get the other twenty four 3Ds moved from their scenarios to Trentsworth. Then you only need Trentsworth and the current rehabilitation scenario running."

"And the bench mark is?"

"You decide and tell me. You programmed them, you know what they shouldn't be capable of."

"Interesting proposal." Andrew thought for a while. Simon watched the activities on the water as he waited. He was still not entirely convinced this was all a computer generated reality. If it was he had to take his hat off to Andrew. He did know his stuff.

"Well", Andrew started, "I programmed both of them to hate you. That is once they knew who you really were. If you can get both of them to love you again as Simon Tallsbury, not as Scott Tallburg, that would be definite proof that they have left their programming. And to leave their programming would suggest a self-awareness within the data."

"Sounds too easy." Simon looked at Andrew. "Isn't there something else?"

"May sound easy, but you will find it quite hard in action. If you did succeed, which I very much doubt, Trentsworth will survive and the 24 others will join them."

"Deal!" Simon held out his hand.

"Plus," Andrew added, not taking Simon's hand. "I will also pour more technology into the system, so Trentsworth will survive the massive increase in processing power needed to support these characters with real time speed."

Andrew shook Simon's outstretched hand. Then he looked Simon right in the eye. "But if you fail, and you will, Bob is programmed to hate you so much that he would kill you. And he definitely will without a thought about the consequences. And remember, the way you are linked to the simulation, you will also die in the real world."

"A win, win situation. I was going to kill myself anyway."

"I suppose you have a point there."

"So all I have to do is have Kyndrea love me again as she did before. Then have Bob know who I am and not kill me?"

"Well, both of them to forgive you would be enough." Andrew lent over to get his cup of coffee. "Whether they wish to be with you, that is up to them and you."

"Sounds easy enough," Simon commented.

Andrew looked up to check Simon was not being sarcastic. He wasn't. "You will find out very quickly that their programming is more ingrained than you currently think. It would be easier to float a gold brick in the Lake of Worth."

"You think you know everything about this computer program. But you're wrong, Andrew. It has taken on a life of its own. It has left your minute lines of program code behind and is now running on data, changeable, alterable data. Just like the memories and emotions in our biological heads. Where ever they may be."

"In some ways I hope you're right. I wish I could say I created Electronic Intelligence. But I know you're not, it's impossible. Good luck anyway, I will be watching with great interest."

With that Andrew got up and left through the front door. Simon found himself alone in his lounge watching the tourists walking past on the path outside. Trentsworth had lost its realism now he knew that they were just pixels in a giant computer. It was as though he found the walls were made of painted canvas, but they weren't even that real.

That aside, he had to process what he had just learned. He needed to ignore where he was and get to work. Twenty seven lives hung in the balance. He needed to come up with a plan to win Kyndrea back.

As he thought, out the window it had started to rain. He felt Andrew probably had arranged that for effect. He smiled as he leaned back in his chair. The rain pelting on the windows made him sleepy. It had been a long day and he found himself drifting off to sleep.

Christine's eyes moved from the image of Simon projected on the wall opposite to the door beside the lighted rectangle. "Come in, Andrew." The door opened and Andrew walked in, shielding his eyes from the projector as he made his way to a chair on the far side.

"You want to see me, Christine?" Andrew asked innocently.

"Do I want to see you?" Christine muttered, then louder, "Do I want to see you? No, I don't want to see you. I want to berate you. What right have you to make a deal with Simon? You have no authority to decide on what our equipment will be used for."

"The equipment will be obsolete at the end of this project. You have already signed a budget for all new processors with our earnings." Andrew held up his hand to stop Christine interrupting. "Anyway, he won't win the bet. You said yourself that there is no way these 3Ds are intelligent self-aware entities. I remember our argument last time I brought it up."

"True. I do not think he will win the bet. As for your other excuse, can I play back a bit of your deal?" Christine pressed a button on the desk before he could answer. Andrew's voice filled the room.

"Plus, I will also pour more technology into the system"

"Not all the equipment promised is obsolete."

"I will buy the extra processors and memory. You pay me enough. I had to think of something quick. He would have committed suicide if I hadn't. The psych report must have been wrong. It should never have got to this stage."

"The psych report was right on the button, and you know it, Andrew. You had planned all this. You were up on Peak View before he even got there. All I want is to be kept in the loop. Don't underestimate me Andrew. I know how this system works." Christine relaxed and in a more calm voice asked, "What are you going to do when he fails to turn them?"

"He will see how forgiveness works, or not, as the case may

be," Andrew answered, pleased he had got away with it. "He will forgive himself as they cannot. It's not obvious from the report, but he's capable of that. He will come out of this quite sane and a good member of the public."

"Hmmm", Christine looked at Andrew, directly into his eyes. "You are still up to something, Dr Johnson. Just ask me before you make any more deals."

Freedom

Simon woke up to find himself still in the chair. He smiled as all the past days' events rushed through his mind. It wasn't a dream, it had happened. He told the truth and had lost Kyndrea. He realised he had also lost Trentsworth.

He was amazed; until now this rich man's playground was his prison. Now he had lost it, he realised how much he loved it. He wondered if he could get back the realism. He also wondered if he could win back Kyndrea. He knew it would be hard to win a girl's heart in the normal world when you have killed her mum. Winning back someone who is programmed to hate your guts as well? That was the problem, he knew Kyndrea was self-aware, that was obvious. To prove it, she would need to do something even real people would not do easily. So he thought of the most common start. He rang the florists. Always start an apology with flowers.

Kyndrea awoke to the sound of her alarm, 'Time to get dad his breakfast.' She got up and grabbed her dressing gown. She looked at it and shook her head. 'Not today. Today I live life,' she said to herself. Placing it back on the hook, she walked straight into her ensuite and turned the shower on.

Fifteen minutes later she bounded down the stairs and into the kitchen. The world always seemed better after a shower. Why waste even a day over a creep like Scott?

Bob awoke to the knocking on his door. Kyndrea came in with his breakfast. "You seem chirpy this morning."

"Just pleased to see you getting better, dad."

"I always get better. You know that." He thumped his chest. "Take more than that to get rid of Robert McKenzie."

"If you're so better, will you be coming down for lunch then?"

"I think I could manage a stroll down the stairs. Besides, I'm out of touch with the soccer."

"I could have brought a screen up here dad."

"The bedroom is not the place for television."

"It hasn't been the place for much else either."

"Kyndrea!"

"Well dad, it's been ten years."

"We'll discuss this later. Don't you dare try and win over me while I have the disadvantage."

"Okay dad." Kyndrea smiled as she placed the tray on the bed. "And don't think I'll forget to bring it up later. This is too important."

Kyndrea walked downstairs, looked at the front door and thought, 'Why not.' "I'm off out for a bit!" She yelled up the stairs and then walked out into the street. She needed to do a bit of grocery shopping anyway. She felt the sun shining on her face. A slight breeze flowed over her body. It was good to be alive. She couldn't imagine living anywhere else than Trentsworth. None of the other places she had been ever felt as real as this moment now.

She bought the required groceries and had a look around some of the clothes shops. She decided to stop for a cappuccino. While drinking the warm soothing liquid, she saw Scott ducking into the florists. 'I knew he wouldn't go through with it. The weak never do.' She didn't let it affect her day. He was on parole and the government wouldn't let him stay forever in that mansion. One day he'll be gone, and that would be that. Then she could go and meet a decent man, a man with all the right qualities.

It seemed to get colder so she picked up her bags and took a taxi back home. She made salad for lunch. Bob and her had a conversation basically about nothing as the afternoon wore on.

While making dinner, there was a knock on the door. "I'll get it dad!" She yelled, as she wiped her hands on a kitchen towel and walked to the door. It didn't surprise her to find a courier holding a bunch of flowers in her hand.

She grabbed the flowers, said thank you, and then closed the door.

"Who was it?"

"No one, just a delivery," Kyndrea answered, trying to hide the flowers from Bob's view. He didn't turn around from the screen. The game was obviously at an exciting point.

Once in the kitchen she pulled the note from the flowers. "Please forgive me. Simon/Scott"

"How dare you!" She cursed under her breath, so her dad wouldn't hear. She tore the note up into small pieces, then saw the knife that she had been using for cutting the chicken.

The next day, after having breakfast, Simon heard a sound at his front door. He got up and opened it. On the doorstep there was a pile of shredded petals and leaves. 'What did he think? One bunch of flowers, and "I forgive you for destroying my life"'?

He decided to go to town and look for something. While there he placed another order at the florists, this time a week's worth. It would be a long week. He thought he would be safe hanging around the new town as Kyndrea obviously liked the old town. So there shouldn't be much chance of bumping into her. It was too soon to try and persuade her to forgive with words.

He walked into the book store and looked around. He wondered if Andrew realised what he was looking for. He looked all over the kid's section and then he found it, one copy of a book, proudly proclaiming it was called "Trentsworth Terrors".

On the front cover it had an illustration of Trent's castle with a foreboding storm above it and a lightning bolt hitting the tower. He went to the counter and paid for it. He then went to the café and with a cappuccino he started reading. 'Lightning streaked across the sky. It was quickly followed by a loud clap of thunder. For a split second it lit up the entire scene. A large man running up a shingle road followed, not too far away, by two boys....'

Kyndrea decided the house needed a full clean. It was the

housekeeper's day as well, so together they started from the top and didn't finish until the final ornament was cleaned and dusted. Bob spent the day recuperating in front of the television. Still he felt as though he was in the way. He wished he was strong enough to fly or even walk. He'd rather be out and about while Kyndrea was in one of these moods. It was his first inkling that there was something wrong between his daughter and Scott. He knew it was best to wait until she approached the subject, but it didn't stop him being concerned. It was around five o'clock when the doorbell rang.

Bob let Kyndrea answer it. As the door opened, he heard her sigh. He turned to look, but she had already disappeared into the kitchen. He heard her cutting something up, which puzzled him as she had already ordered pizza over the phone. But then one does strange things when one is in love.

The next day after cleaning the front doorstep from the mess his second bunch of flowers had made, Simon caught the tram to the workers' town. He wanted to see Mark's house, the tunnel system, the Trackers Den and the other sights written about in the children's adventure book he read the previous day.

It wasn't everyday you got a chance to live in a town which was the setting for a fictitious story. Besides, he had to do something to keep his mind off the task at hand. Patience was the key. Whittle down her resistance before striking.

Kyndrea was cursing. She had almost forgotten an appointment with a group of businessmen from Europe. She rushed around the house getting ready for the tour. She would be late if she didn't hurry. Mr Gousing was quite well known for black marking a person's name for being late. He believed absolutely in being punctual.

The tour took all day and Kyndrea arrived home just in time to head off the courier with the flowers.

"You are a popular lady," the courier commented. "You are very lucky to have someone this interested in you."

"You can have him if you want", she grumbled back as she grabbed the flowers. How long before Scott got the message? Flowers would never win her heart. Nothing that bastard was able to do, would.

It's All in the Telling

The next morning, cursing him in full voice, she dumped the shredded remains on his doorstep. This was not really the way to start the day. She decided to continue south and wander into town. Perhaps looking for new fashion arrivals might get rid of this sour taste in her mouth.

She was in the most renowned shop for the latest in fashions when she bumped into Janine. She didn't recognise her at first. It was a shock to the system. "Janine! What have you done? You look fantastic."

"Really?" Janine smiled and looked down her feet. "I still feel half naked, but Richard thinks it makes me look wonderful."

"Richard?" Kyndrea looked at Janine in wonder. "We must discuss this over some coffee."

They walked out of the shop and into the busy main street. They eventually found an empty table and sat down. Janine told Kyndrea all about meeting Richard. "We're just good friends, but I do feel so alive when I'm around him"

"Just good friends?" Kyndrea asked in a sceptical tone.

"Okay," Janine smiled, "Very good friends at night, but we're keeping the rest of the relationship as plain friends."

"That's playing with fire, Janine."

"Since when have you known me to be careful?"

"Good point," Kyndrea laughed then stopped and looked Janine in the eye. "But seriously, if you have crossed that line, you're either lying to yourself about what your true feelings are, or you're using him. Which ever it is, it will cost you the friendship."

"Don't be such a sourpuss," Janine laughed back.

"Think about it. Any relationship built on a lie will fail. If I was you I'd just dump him. It's not worth the angst."

"You are a bit down on it." Janine looked slightly concerned. "Dad said you didn't have the usual zing yesterday. I've seen Scott, I know you're going through a rough patch."

"That's the understatement of the century. It's over, Janine. There is nothing in this world that would make me talk to him again. Let alone get back together!" Kyndrea shivered, "Even the thought makes me queasy."

"What on earth did he do? You and him were inseparable. I hate to think what could be bad enough to split the two of you up."

"You want to know?" Kyndrea stopped. This could be her revenge. If she told Janine, the whole valley would know by nightfall. It would certainly stop the flowers. The florist would refuse to send them for one thing. There would be a lynch mob at his house by midnight.

He would have to leave then. The government would have to pull him out and she would not even have to lift a finger. Janine could be the perfect weapon, one that was so easily wielded. Kyndrea herself could never tell the public about Scott, it would demean her as a gossiper, she would come out looking just as bad. But with Janine doing the dirty work, she would become the innocent victim. Oh, this was good. This was perfect. Scott would curse the day he ever laid a finger on her mum. "Did you know I had met him ten years ago?"

"He did mention that you had met previously in Auckland, but was it that long ago? A lot of water has passed under the bridge since then."

"And blood," Kyndrea completed.

"Blood?" Janine looked at Kyndrea.

"Yes, blood. Simon, I mean Scott, is not a nice man." She started having second thoughts. 'Did Scott really deserve to be an outcast? What was she thinking? Of course he deserved it! He deserved everything that will be visited upon him and more.' "Ten years ago my mum was murdered."

"And Scott was there but didn't help?" Janine finished for Kyndrea. "Kyndrea, it can happen so fast. People freeze. You can't blame Scott for not trying to prevent it."

"Trying to prevent it?" Kyndrea laughed loudly. People turned to look at them and then as quickly turned away again. Kyndrea quietly continued in more of a hiss than a whisper. "Scott didn't try to prevent it, well, because he was doing it. His real name is Simon Tallsbury. He's here as part of his rehabilitation."

"Rehabilitation for what?" Janine's mind was awash with confusion. Was Kyndrea saying what she thought she heard? Surely she was mistaken.

"Rehabilitation for murdering seven", Kyndrea held up

her hands with both thumbs and an index finger curled away. "Count my fingers, Janine. Seven women. My mum apparently was the first. I looked up the Christchurch papers after he told me."

"Scott? Our Scott? A murderer?" Janine laughed. "He hasn't even got enough guts to use a can of insect spray. You must be mistaken. Perhaps he just looks like the photo in the paper."

"You didn't hear me. I said I looked up the papers after he told me. He confessed to me that he had killed my mum. Right to my face, he said it in no uncertain terms. He was Simon Tallsbury and he murdered my mum. He murdered her while I watched. He murdered her with my own knife. He murdered her." Kyndrea paused. Her face had turned red with sadness and anger. "He murdered her."

Janine watched as Kyndrea bounded from the table in tears. The chair fell to the ground as she left, the metal making a loud clang against the crusty black seal of the street, accentuated by the smashing of the china cup that she had also dislodged in her hurry to exit.

'Scott. A murderer?' Janine thought to herself. Perhaps she, too, needed to read that paper. She wanted to make certain of her facts before she did anything more.

Simon, having decided that today would be a day to pretend to be a tourist, was paragliding above the lake. The wind rushed past his ears. He felt like a bird watching everyone below him going on their daily business. The boat slowed down for some unknown reason as he flew past his house, which brought him low enough to recognise Kyndrea running along Springfield Rd. She was in a hurry, but she ran right past her house and kept on going. This interested Simon, and he watched her carefully as she ended up on a bench in the park beside the lake outlet. In fact it was the very bench that he had, on that dreadful morning days ago, spent sleeping before putting his terrible plan into action. The boat suddenly sped up and he climbed higher.

Kyndrea loved this bench. It was her place. The place she went when she needed to avoid people. No one used this park much. She had done it; she had started the chain reaction. Janine would start gossiping and that would be the end for Scott. Why did she now feel guilty?

Scott had brought it upon himself. He's the criminal. He should pay for his actions. Something inside her, though, was saying she had gone too far. She had betrayed his trust, but what is the trust of a murderer worth? Nothing, he was nothing, and deserved everything he got. Her guts were all twisted with confusion. She felt like a child who just accidentally broke a window as the owner came up the path. She had all the justification in the world, and yet she knew she had done wrong.

It was a while later that she got up from the bench. All she had managed to do was tie herself up in even more emotional knots. She felt deathly ill. She had a headache. The last thing she needed was a courier to deliver his flowers as she arrived home, but she knew she had to get there before her dad answered the door.

The courier was at her front door as she arrived out of breath. The courier handed her the flowers, "You're fast becoming one of my regulars," she said as Kyndrea roughly grabbed them from her. The courier continued, "Yet you never seem that pleased. They're obviously guilt flowers. He must have done something really bad."

"You don't know the half of it," Kyndrea grumbled, on the way to her front door. 'But you will by tomorrow,' she continued in her head. 'Then even you'll probably refuse to deliver them.'

Kyndrea didn't get much sleep that night. She had ordered in Thai for dinner; there was no way she felt like cooking and all those spices didn't help her knotted stomach. She kept thinking of scenes from Frankenstein, all the Trentsworth populace outside Scott's house with pitch forks and flaming torches. "Kill the monster, Kill the monster", the chant drumming in her head. 'Well, he is a monster. Only a monster could murder a woman like that, in front of a thirteen year old girl. He deserved what he was going to have to go through the next few weeks.'

Simon woke up the next day and walked down the stairs. He was up late that morning. He had spent the night partying hard, trying to forget things for a moment, but it had failed. The first thing he did was open the front door.

He was surprised to see there were no flowers waiting for him. Surely she could not have succumbed so easily. Perhaps the florist forgot, or she talked the florist into stopping the deliveries. He remained perturbed about it all through his brunch.

Then came the knock on the door. He stood up suddenly, almost knocking his mug onto the floor. He went to the door and opened it. Standing behind it was Kyndrea holding a shoe box.

"Will you stop sending the flowers, you monster!" She opened the box and threw the mess of petals and leaves all over Simon. "Your secret's out. I told Janine. The whole of Trentsworth probably knows by now. I would get your officer friends over here quick smart and make them put you back in jail where you belong." She had to say it. She wanted to see his expression, but he just stood there dumbfounded. A slight look of being betrayed came over his face.

"Whatever happens, Kyndrea", the look dissolved away to a kind, gentle face, "I forgive you. I still love you, and I always will." Simon closed the door.

Kyndrea stood there for a few minutes aghast, 'What right has he to forgive me? He is the monster, not I, whatever happens today he deserves every minute of it.' She stormed through the gate and back home.

Simon had just got comfortable again when there was another knock on the door. "That was quick," he commented aloud as he got up. It was not Kyndrea but Janine on the other side. "Hello Janine."

"Hi Simon", Janine greeted as she came through the doorway, closing it immediately behind her. "I saw Kyndrea leaving as I was walking down from the hotel. Still no luck with the flowers?"

"None, but she is talking now." Simon followed Janine to the chairs by the windows, "Even if it's just to announce that you have told all of Trentsworth about my history."

"She always took me for a gossip", Janine commented as she sat down, "Perhaps I was before I met you. A lot has changed this past week."

"You can say that again!" Simon sat next to her.

"Which is why, I guess, I didn't announce to all and sundry your secret. I know there is a lot more to you than a simple mindless killer."

"You are very trusting Janine, coming here, knowing my past." The phone rang and Simon answered, "Hello?" He handed the phone to Janine, "For you."

"Yes, I'm fine," she paused, listening to the ear piece. "No, I'm not spurting blood all over the place. Yes, my head is still attached to my neck." She laughed. "No, no, half an hour is fine. Okay twenty minutes then. Bye." Janine put the phone down. "I'm not an idiot either. Richard's going to ring me every twenty minutes to make certain I can still speak."

"Okay, maybe not so trusting."

"It was Richard's idea. Yes," she continued, noting Simon's look. "I told him and I swore him to secrecy. He is my best friend so I trust him. You see he looks out for me. Personally I know you wouldn't try anything. One, I realise you've changed and two, all seven were done in public areas even if you hadn't."

"You have been studying."

"I like to know my facts. Knowing you must have a parole officer here, I tracked down Andrew. He's got a wonderful house, difficult to access, but totally worth it. Not only for the view, but the interior was wonderfully designed."

"What did Andrew have to say?"

"Quite a bit." Janine smiled, remembering the previous evening. "He was very talkative, and he knew a lot about who you are. Probably more than you do. He also asked a lot of weird questions about myself. I put it down to his psychology background."

"No," Simon laughed. "He's just weird. Though in a good way; he did help me to get my life back."

"And you've helped me more than you could ever imagine. I know your secret. I know why you killed Kyndrea's mum. Knowing that now, I realise I must have hit every raw nerve in your body when I came here that day, and yet instead of being a revenger, you were a saviour. Instead of spilling my blood you spilt my tears.

"To be honest, I wanted to. In truth, I was under hypnosis so I couldn't"

"It wasn't the hypnosis that stayed your hand Simon", Janine laughed. "Andrew also told me about that. It was mostly hype. You were only hypnotised just enough to make you think about your actions. You were just no longer blinded by the rage that previously led you to kill. You saw behind my rich exterior to the true Janine. You showed me my real self. You gave me the knowledge of what made me tick."

"I wish I knew what made me tick. What made me kill Kyndrea's mum."

"Andrew said you will in time. When you are required to know, but he said I can tell you that it was not for a good reason. It was understandable, but not at all right and you knew it; you wanted to be punished. But they didn't, the law put you in a home for wayward youth. You wanted prison. You probably even wanted death. The unpunished guilt of that murder drove you to do it six more times. Each time you secretly wanted to be caught. You weren't careful. You weren't secretive. It was just plain luck that no one saw you until the last one and each time your guilt doubled, making you angrier and more unsociable. "That was the real reason you did not kill me. You had been caught. You were being punished. You didn't want to be here. This was a prison to you, a punishment of having to live with all us rich folk. And as the cloud of guilt was fading away, you saw my true self.

"What I want to know", Janine queried, "Is why it took a stranger to tell me. Though I have many friends here no one ever told me the truth."

"It is easier for a stranger to be truthful than a friend who has been playing along with the lie for years."

"I suppose that sounds viable. Now to the reason I came." Janine paused as the phone interrupted. Simon just passed the ringing handset to Janine, "Yes, I'm still breathing. You too? Good. Shouldn't be too long now. Lunch at The Boulevard? Sounds great, half an hour? Perfect."

Janine smiled sheepishly as she put the phone down. "At least he cares."

"Which is more than I can say about Kyndrea."

"Don't jump to conclusions, Simon. A wise man once said, "Love and hate are opposite sides of the same coin." You would need to worry if Kyndrea took your flowers, put them on the sideboard and forgot about them until they were withered and dead. That she is taking time to chop them up and hand deliver them to you, means she has a lot of feelings towards you. Albeit the wrong ones at present, but that is why I came. I offer my services to you. Get Kyndrea to flip that coin once again."

"And what can you do?"

"What can I do?" Janine looked affronted with the question. "Why, I'm the greatest organiser in this valley. I know everyone that you need to know, and everyone you don't.

Just tell me what you think Kyndrea will not be able to resist and it's yours."

Simon thought back to his initial conversation with Kyndrea. He was so filled with hate that day; he was amazed he could remember anything she said. She told him what would he need to do to win her heart and he remembered what.

"I know", Simon announced, "This is what you need to do, and the sooner, the better."

Janine listened to Simon as he told her of Kyndrea's comments and what he thought would come close to those ideals. At the end Janine nodded, "You are quite brave. She is either going to despise you forever, or find her love for you once again."

Their half hour was up and Simon saw Janine to the door. She kissed Simon on the cheek as she left. She didn't have much time to organise the event, but he knew she would pull it off.

Kyndrea had spent the day re-cleaning the house and fussing over her dad. She was too scared to go out into the world. Everyone would stare at her. Everyone would pity her. People would ask her how she's coping. She would have to be polite to these well meaning strangers, inwardly wishing they would mind their own bloody business.

'At least I won't have to field off flowers today,' she consoled herself. The doorbell rang, Bob was out on the patio, so she got up and opened the front door.

On the other side was the courier.

"I swear these bunches are getting bigger", she said as she handed Kyndrea the delivery, "It must be like the botanical gardens in there by now. You have really struck it lucky with this guy."

"You haven't heard?" Kyndrea asked in surprise.

"Heard what?"

"The man who sends me these flowers. Who he is? What he did?"

"No", the courier's eyes lit up, "What. What's the goss?"

"He", Kyndrea started. What was she doing? She was more than a town gossip. "He loves me very much." She rushed inside and slammed the door. How dare he make her feel that way? She slammed the flowers onto the kitchen bench and immediately took a knife to them.

As she was furiously cutting away, her eye fell on a bowl she had found in the fridge, some leftover sauce from a past meal. She smiled to herself.

The next day, after meeting Kyndrea at the door, Simon had his second shower that morning. At least she was putting in some effort.

Kyndrea slammed the door behind her. She walked straight into her father. "What was in that bowl?" He pointed at her hand.

"Just some leftovers, I thought Scott would like them."

"Good idea." Bob took the bowl from her hands and walked her into the lounge. Placing it on a coffee table he gently pushed Kyndrea towards a chair, "You do know it's customary to leave the leftovers in the bowl? And not all over the grateful recipient?"

He turned around towards her, leaning right over her. All the humour suddenly went from his face. "I warned him. I threatened him. If he hurt you in any way, he would know nothing but pain. What did he do to you, Kyndrea? Why have you been so miserable this past week?"

"Don't go over there, dad." Kyndrea looked up in horror, watching this face filled with rage. She had never seen him so angry since that dreadful time ten years ago. If he was this angry over her being upset, what would he be like when he heard the truth about Scott?

She had no doubt now that he would kill Scott if he found out. She couldn't let him find out. Not now, not while he was still recovering. The drugs he was taking were not helping his anger. "It's just a silly misunderstanding. I'm waiting for a verbal apology. That is all dad. A lovers' tiff. He loves me, dad."

"He loves you?" Bob sat down in his favourite chair. "He has a funny way of showing it. Just a lovers' tiff?" Bob eyed the bowl, "Well, I'd hate to see what you would call a full blown argument. Perhaps Kyndrea, it might be best for all concerned not to wait for a verbal apology. And get him back over here for tea. I miss his unique way of seeing the world." A smile emerged on his face.

"It'll still take time dad," Kyndrea sighed. She felt like she had just defused a nuclear bomb. A bomb that could still go off. She suddenly remembered Janine. 'Dad would find out anyway from her. Yet if she did everything according to my plan, where are all the phone calls? The well meaning visitors?'

A little bit of hope emerged in Kyndrea's heart. Perhaps there was time to turn back the clock. She rushed up to her bedroom. Picking up the phone, she dialled Janine. She still hated Scott, but she didn't want her father ending up in jail for the killing this snivelling murderer.

Judge Not Others

Simon had just got redressed when the doorbell rang again. He was getting popular. He opened the door. Expecting to see Andrew, he was surprised to find a strange man on the other side.

"Scott Tallburg?" The man asked.

"Yes, how can I help?"

"I've a piece of information you maybe interested in," he answered, a slight English accent showing through. "It maybe worth some money to you."

"Richard, isn't it?" Simon smiled and moved away from the door, "Come in. Any friend of Janine's is a friend of mine."

"How did you know?" The man walked into the lounge and made his way to the seats. He looked slightly worried.

"I recognise your voice from the phone call yesterday", Simon semi-lied. He did recognise the voice, but not until he had figured out that this man was the fourth 3D. Janine wouldn't be able to have decent conversations with a 2D.

"Don't worry, I won't kill you," Simon laughed, misinterpreting the worried look on the Richard's face. "So what is this information you want me to see?"

"Ah, well you see." Richard said composing himself. This was not going according to plan. He cursed himself for not putting on a fake voice yesterday. He decided Simon knowing who he was, would not matter. "Janine has told me everything."

"I'm aware of that, otherwise the phone calls yesterday would be quite weird."

"Of course." Richard paused, and took some folders out of his briefcase. "Janine also gave me the evidence she gathered on you."

"You were slow to believe her?" Simon asked. He was slowly getting a picture in his mind. Where did Richard come from? Andrew didn't have time to create a 3D for Janine.

"No. She wanted to brag about how clever she was. If I hadn't taken them, she'd probably show others to prove her cleverness."

"You think she's that immature?" Simon was starting to dislike this man. He was attempting, very poorly, to turn him against Janine.

"She is, Simon. She is."

"So you have come to give me the papers so Janine won't be able to?"

"Well, since you ask." Richard handed Simon the folders, "You see, these actually are photocopies. The originals are in my hotel room".

"So I guess the answer is no, then." Simon leafed through the papers. Most of them were various newspaper articles printed after his trial. A few of them had poorly reproduced photos of him. Singularly not proving anything, but together it was obvious that Simon and Scott were the same man.

"I will hand them over to you. But first, since these documents have been taking up space in my small room, there should be a discussion about certain storage fees."

"Storage fees?" Simon looked at Richard. He thought so. Did Janine know what sort of person he was. No, of course not. "You can't have had them for more than a day!"

"My hotel room is quite expensive. If you think about it, the space these take up in my drawer is quite valuable."

"How much money?"

"Oh, lets see." Richard paused to feign thoughtfulness. "I'm a firm believer in the supply and demand method of valuing. I guess the government must have set you up with a reasonable amount of money. You having to live on this side of the valley and all. I think a thousand an hour should be sufficient."

"A thousand an hour? That's extortion!"

"Ah, finally we're on the same wavelength." A smile covered his face. "Janine said you were a smart cookie. You give me twenty thousand dollars for the storage, I return the papers to you for you to store where you like."

"And if I don't think your storage is worth this fee?"

"I will have to relocate them to a cheaper storage area. Say, the editor's desk of the Trentsworth Tribune. I'm sure they're hungry for a piece of decent news which doesn't involve entertainment, thrills or dining out."

"And should that worry me?"

"I think we both know what will happen if they get read by the Trentsworth locals. You're already a celebrity by virtue of your so called inheritance."

"I repeat, should that worry me?"

"Oh, you are a cool one. I suppose you have to be, to murder seven people. I'll tell you what. I'll give you another twenty four hours to mill it over. Of course my hourly rate stays at a thousand an hour. The longer you leave it, the more it'll cost."

"What if I tell Janine about this conversation. I'm sure she'll find my account very interesting."

"You have no proof. I'll deny it of course. Don't ever try and blackmail me my dear lad, even if she did believe you, with twenty thousand it won't take me long to find another girlfriend." Richard got up, "Well, I'll be seeing you. I'm at the Trentsworth Plaza, room seventeen oh two. And I don't accept personal cheques." Laughing, he let himself out, closing the door behind him.

Simon just sat there with the documents on his lap. He had never been blackmailed before. He wondered what to do. Should he tell Janine, would she believe him? She probably wouldn't, why should she.

He could go to the police. He didn't really want them

involved. It would be quite well known Janine was associated with him. It would not be good for her business. So Simon was back to the question about telling Janine. He didn't want to see her hurt. He wasn't worried about the documents. He deserved everything he got. He wasn't going to pay money to cover it up. There had been enough deceit already.

The next morning, Kyndrea had decided to prepare a special cocktail for Simon. She got up early to do it, so her dad wouldn't see. With the kitchen extractor fan on full she started boiling the broccoli that she had frozen the night before.

Even with the fan on, the smell was still quite overpowering. She added the remains of the previous night's floral delivery. Stirring, she put in some old sago pellets she had found at the back of the pantry. She couldn't ever remember buying them, but they made the stew extra slimy.

Finally she poured it into a bucket that already contained some foul smelling items from the garden. Stirring vigorously she mixed it all together. 'If this doesn't stop him, nothing will,' she thought to herself.

She placed the bucket outside and went upstairs to shower. After breakfast, she waited until she was certain her father was engrossed in the sports before she snuck out and walked over to Simon's. He had obviously been watching out for her as he opened the door before she had a chance to knock.

"I'm well aware you want me dead." Simon announced before Kyndrea had a chance to say anything.

"Well die then and save yourself the money for flowers." Kyndrea positioned the bucket ready for tossing.

"I did almost jump off Peak View."

"I know, it was a nasty surprise seeing you still alive. That would have done us all a favour." She looked at Simon, into his eyes. Curiosity got the better of her, "Why didn't you jump?"

"Knowing that by doing so, I would be killing another love of yours, I couldn't do that to you." Then Simon closed the door.

Kyndrea stood there dumfounded. Those words struck her like a slap in the face. She threw the bucket contents away. She marched up the path, but less decidedly than before. The words played over and over in her mind, 'I couldn't kill another love of yours.'

Simon was glad of two things that afternoon. Firstly, that Kyndrea had taken to heart what he had just said and secondly, he closed his door when he did. That slop could only be described as liquid fertiliser; it stunk, even through the closed door. Time was right for Janine's little job. He hoped she could organise such an event over only a couple of days.

When the flowers arrived that evening, Kyndrea accepted them and placed them in a vase. They were very beautiful, and not their fault they were sent by a jerk. 'I couldn't kill another love of yours' repeated in her head again as she rearranged them.

She was haunted by them all day. No matter how busy she was those words kept repeating themselves. She knew the reason they irked her was that they spoke the truth. She hated him, but she hated herself even more for also loving him.

The next morning Richard woke up. He was surprised that Simon hadn't rung yet. The time was getting close. One thing about the blackmailing game, you had to go through with your threats. He got up and had a shower.

There the thought came to him. He could give the information about his conviction to the newspaper, but withhold the part about Kyndrea. The useless local reporters wouldn't connect her with the daughter in the first murder. Then after showing Simon he means business, renegotiate the deal about leaking Kyndrea's history to the press.

Simon may not care about himself but he definitely cares

about Kyndrea. Janine's frantic ringing around the valley for Simon's great performance was enough proof of that. After two nights of missing Janine's company, he was quite happy to make Simon's life a misery.

He dried himself off and walked out of the bathroom. He looked at the clock. It was time. Still wrapped in a towel he opened his suitcase and released the false bottom. Reaching in he went to grab the papers. His fingers felt nothing.

He frantically pulled all his clothes out of the case and ripped the false bottom away. It was completely empty. "Where the Fuck!" he cursed, as he rummaged through the clothing. Then he went to the hotel drawers and started tossing all the contents out.

As he was doing this, he slowly became aware of a quite chuckle behind him. He looked around. There was a man there dressed in jeans and a T-shirt. In his hand were two folders.

"Looking for these, Richard?"

"Give them here, you bastard!" Then a look of recognition came over Richard's face. "'Ere, ain't you David's parole officer?"

"You remember me then?" Andrew asked.

"How could I forget. You seemed to know everything David and I cooked up. You were always one step ahead of us." The anger showed in Richard's face. "It was because of you David went straight. He was going to be the finest extortionist ever, until you came along."

Richard slowly felt around the drawer he was last searching and pulled out a gun. "Well, Mr Andrew, I think you had better return those papers to their rightful owner."

"I am planning to do so, Richard. Simon will be quite relieved to get them." Andrew didn't move an inch. He was showing no fear, only a mild amusement.

"I meant me." Richard was getting even angrier. This Andrew fellow was always a thorn in his side. He should have guessed he was the same Andrew Janine spoke of. Only David's Andrew could pull off a scam this big. He pointed the gun right at his opponent's head. "You may be smug because of a bullet proof vest, but what about your face?"

"Oh it's bullet proof as well!" Andrew chuckled. "You have no idea what you are dealing with here. How far do you think you could get after shooting me? Do you think I would enter a known blackmailer's room without backup?"

"I've escaped your crones before. I can do it again. Now hand over the papers."

"My crones weren't guarding every exit before, Mr Coster. Now put down the gun and promise me you will not bother Mr Tallburg again."

"Why should I?" Richard immediately said, but he knew why. Andrew was right, he was very careful with his extortions, they couldn't pin one on him. But murder, that was completely different. Besides, he may threaten, but he wasn't a murderer.

"Because if you do, I will leave with these papers. Then you can get on with your life, and I with mine."

"Aren't you going to arrest me?"

"Arresting you would just mean putting Simon and Kyndrea through the hell I'm trying to avoid. I'm sure after today, knowing I'm about, will cease any more of these fiscal arrangements."

"Oh definitely," Richard replied. He realised he was sweating, yet he was the one holding the gun. A quiet chuckle left his mouth as he put the gun on the sideboard.

"Besides," Andrew continued. "Janine would be devastated

to learn of your past vocation. It would be best for both of you if you retired. You have enough money to live modestly here. Why not enjoy the valley. The lifestyle."

Before Richard could answer, Andrew strolled past him and let himself out. Richard looked at the mess behind him and the gun on the desk. 'One day Andrew, one day. I will retire, but not before I dig up all your dirt. I won't even bother asking for remuneration.'

The knock on Simon's door came at noon. 'Quite late,' he thought, 'for the flower delivery.' He was quite surprised to see Andrew standing there. In his hand were two folders.

"I thought you might be interested in seeing these, extracted from a certain hotel room."

"Richard?"

"Richard won't be bothering you anymore." Andrew shook the folders and they exploded into dust. "I love that trick. Do you feel like lunch?"

"Why not," Simon agreed and walked out his door, closing it behind him. "So, Richard isn't here anymore?"

"Oh he's still here. He's too involved with the scenario now to be deleted, but he knows, well some of, what I am capable of. He won't bother you ever again and hopefully he will leave others alone as well."

Simon followed Andrew up Springfield Road towards the station. "He's from another scenario, Isn't he?"

"You catch on fast." Andrew paused, after he almost tripped over. "I'm on a treadmill to simulate walking," he explained, "Can we discuss this once we're seated? As you see I find it hard to walk at this speed on a treadmill I can't see, and talk at the same time."

There was a table vacant with a view over the lake. The table belonged to a more upmarket style of café, bordering on an actual restaurant. A waiter quickly came over to hand out the menus and take any drink orders.

They both ordered the house dark beer. Once the waiter left, Simon asked again, "What scenario did Richard come from?"

"I thought it would be obvious. A couple of rehabilitations ago we were rescuing an extortionist from his dark future. I set it up in an Oliver Twist style story line."

"Richard was Fagan?"

"Correct. Though he only had two other apprentices. But

he sent them out to spy on the wealthy vacationing in the island paradise that they were set up in."

"Island paradise?"

"I have a fantastic job, don't I?" Andrew laughed. "You can imagine what people could get up to on business trips away from their wives. I think it was the first scenario we had to put an R rating on."

"So he fell in love with one of the victims."

"Oh no, we don't ever try to deal the love card, too difficult to untangle at the end. I mean, how do you tell a person their love is just a program in a computer? We would have to kill the 3D off during the scenario and of course the psychological damage could be immense for our subject."

"So you've never played out the love option?" Simon's stomach started feeling heavy and knotted. The waiter came over and placed the drinks on the table and left.

"Never", Andrew drank a sip from his glass and then continued. "You are actually the first to even be told about the actual set up. All the others still believe they were actually at the location we put them. Of course all those locations actually existed in real life, unlike here, so there was no real reason to inform them of what actually happened.

"Just like you towards Kyndrea, he cared for a victim's wife. He realised that there were other parties involved, not only the victim. He came to realise the hurt extortion can wield on the innocent and therefore he was cured. We stopped the scenario and I stored Richard and his two other trainees onto disk.

"Then Janine needed a lover. I went through all the past 3Ds to get a match, and unfortunately the only one that came close to what Janine would be after was Richard. As you obviously guessed, I didn't have time to create a new one for Janine's morning meeting, nor, unfortunately, have time to check whether the system could handle a fourth 3D."

"So I was meant to only care for Kyndrea?"

"What do you mean, meant to?" A worried look came over Andrew's face. "Tell me you haven't actually fallen in love with her."

"She's so wonderful. Just knowing that there is a chance she could forgive me. Just knowing she loves me enough to hate me."

"That sounds like one of Janine's philosophies. Snap out of it Simon! She's only a computer program. It's like falling in love with a character in a movie. She's not real."

"She is real, Andrew." The anger started showing on Simon's face, "That is what I will prove to you tomorrow night. She will forgive me Andrew. She will show you she is not just mere programming. Her forgiveness will save her kind."

"The deal was Bob as well, Simon. His programming is more ingrained."

"I will see you after tomorrow night. You will know then that Bob is just a matter of time." Simon got up, "Thank you for the lunch."

"We haven't ordered anything yet."

"Thank you anyway. I need to go home now, save up my energy for tomorrow."

Simon walked away and Andrew sat there smiling to himself. "This is so easy."

A Flareful Night

The next day Simon walked back home from Janine's office smiling. They had discussed the final details for their plan. That she had managed to arrange so many people in such a short time amazed him. He was certain it would work. After tonight it would only be Bob he need worry about.

It was a usual calm warm summer's evening and Bob was busying himself getting the gas barbecue lit. "Are you sure the flint doesn't need changing or something?"

"Here dad", Kyndrea said, as she placed a salad on the patio table. She went over to her father and ignited the gas with one single turn of the knob.

"Obviously heated it up for you," Bob muttered as he sat down on a chair.

Kyndrea laughed, "I'll get the meat dad and then you can play chef."

"Sit down for a bit, Kyndrea," Bob commanded. "The grill needs time to heat up. You've been fussing around this house for the past couple of days. You need to rest."

"But dad the house was..."

"The house was perfect", Bob interrupted, "And now it's even more so. I'm not saying it's unwelcome. I enjoy a spotless house. Even one to this extreme, but you can't work yourself into a frenzy like this. You must face your concerns head on."

"He has to apologise first."

"I've seen the flowers, two lovely arrangements, in the lounge. Isn't that enough?"

"Nowhere near, dad, sure he's spent money at a florist, but nowhere on the note is there an 'I'm Sorry' or 'I apologise'. Spending money is easy. I should know." Kyndrea forced a weak smile, "Saying those two words. That's the hard part."

"I see your point, but it doesn't mean you have to spend the rest of your life fussing over me and the house, not that it isn't appreciated."

"I'll get the meat!" Kyndrea got up and walked into the house.

The subject was not brought up again over the meal. Kyndrea and Bob just sat on the patio drinking coffee, watching nature's own special lightshow fading behind the mountains. Kyndrea was just about to get up when suddenly a couple of red flares erupted on the opposite shore.

Then several fireworks reached up into the sky and lit up the valley. More and more fireworks were launched, exploding high above the valley. The echoes could have woken the dead. "This is unexpected," Bob muttered, "but fantastic."

"As though it was created just for you and me, dad," Kyndrea laughed, and sat back to watch the show.

After about ten minutes everything became dark once more as single vertical line of flares lit up. Then four more flares lit up on either side to form a capital "I". The letter moved to Kyndrea's left and as it moved, more flares lit up where the "I" originally was. Slowly, a scrolling word began to take shape.

There seemed to be around fifteen to twenty letters lit up before the "I" disappeared. The lighted message began, "I am lost without you."

Kyndrea suddenly felt very nervous. 'He couldn't. He wouldn't,' she thought as the rest of the message started taking shape.

"I am lost without you. Please forgive me. I know what I did was unforgivable. Believe in yourself. You have the power to forgive even this. The whole world should know how much I love you, Kyndrea." The last four words stayed in place until the flares died away naturally. Then the valley was dark.

She stood there, silent. She was furious. How dare he embarrass her in this way. Well, she could do the same. She could tell the valley what she was supposed to forgive. Then see what happens. She thought back to how relieved she was when Janine had kept it to herself. She didn't want to go through that again.

'Janine!' Her mind took a sharp turn. 'You had to be the one organising this. Yet you knew what Simon had done. How could you Janine? How can I Janine?'

"Well, if that's not an apology", Bob broke into her thoughts; "I don't know what is. I think it's time for you to have a word with Scott."

"You don't know what he did, Dad!" Kyndrea shouted back. Bob saw the anger in her eyes.

"Well, tell me then!"

"He's the one who," Kyndrea paused, looking at her dad. He was angry at her for not patching it up. She imagined his heart racing ten to the dozen. It would not be good for him to know, not now. Not so soon after the last attack. "Who invited Janine out to tea last week. Without telling me."

"Is that it?" Bob looked at her confounded. "Women!" He cursed. "You go over there right now young lady and accept his apology. He doesn't love Janine. He loves you."

"I'll go then!" Kyndrea walked through the house to the front door and exited. Bob smiled, he liked seeing Kyndrea with Scott. There was an obvious connection, like it was meant to be. She had spent the last ten years moping around the house. He didn't want to let this chance go by, Scott held a special place in his heart. There was something about him.

After closing the front door, Kyndrea looked to her right. No way would she talk to him tonight. Let him suffer. Let him wonder what was going on. She walked to her left, towards the outlet park. Sitting on the bench, she could hear the crashing of the water as it hurried to leave the valley and make its long journey east to the ocean.

Scott was right, she still loved him. That made her even angrier, how could she love her mother's killer? What would her mum be thinking if she knew? It would be the greatest betrayal of all time. She could never love Simon. What would everyone think? 'Hi, this is my husband Simon. You may know him. He killed my mother.'

It seemed like some warped relationship out of a badly written black comedy. It would never work. She could never explain it to her mum's memory. She could never explain it to her dad. He would have never sent her out of the house, if he really knew the truth. He would have gone himself with knife in hand. Bob would disown her. Was Scott's love worth losing her dad over? That scenario was not possible. Her dad would win every time. No, she could not go back to Simon. She just had to close this part of her life forever. Lock it and place it in the deepest dungeon of her mind. She could live without Simon, she had done so before. She could do so again. Forget he ever existed, forget the love she held for Scott. "Live life!" She told herself out loud, "Run free, enjoy the moment. Put the past behind you."

"Unfortunately, the past has a way of biting you in the backside."

Kyndrea turned and saw Scott standing behind her, "How long have you been there?"

"Not long", Simon smiled and sat down beside her, not waiting for her invitation. "I saw you leave the house. I guessed you would come here."

"How did you guess that?" Kyndrea asked, suddenly remembering why she was here in the first place. Her face screwed up in anger as she turned to face him full on. "What the hell gives you the right to plaster my name in flares so the whole valley can see?

"What on earth is got into you? You know I cannot go out in public now? You have made me a prisoner in my own home. You never think of others, do you? You never consider the consequences. Now I have my father on my case. He wants me to make it up with you."

"You haven't told him?"

"Of course I haven't told him, he's just had an attack. Do you think I want to kill him? I will tell him when he is strong enough to take it and then you're dead. Why can't you just go and leave us alone?"

"I am a prisoner of this valley and for me it is real, not because of imagined social pressure, but because if I step one foot outside, I break parole. I will be placed in prison."

"Well that's where you belong."

"It was where I belonged." Simon looked into Kyndrea's eyes. "I have changed now. If I hadn't, you and your father would be dead and I'd be hot tailing it back to Auckland."

"Pardon?"

"I had it all planned out, my escape. I got to know you, Kyndrea, because your father had a plane. It wasn't because I was attracted to you." Simon, noting the look of horror on Kyndrea's face, quickly continued. "That came later. As though it was an avalanche, I fell deeply and rapidly in love with you."

"You used me?" Kyndrea looked at Simon in disgust. "You used us?" He was worse than she thought.

"In the beginning, yes I did." Simon smiled quietly at Kyndrea, she didn't return it. She stayed sitting there beside him, as still as a statue, her arms crossed, staring him down. "Then I got to know you, and then I got to know your dad. Even though I felt trapped here with your people it was my personal hell. I decided not to escape, but stay here with you. My love for you was so great, Kyndrea, I would spend a lifetime in hell, if I could spend it with you."

"Well, you'll have to go there without me."

"And once I found out who you were, I mean, who your mum was, so um, I had to leave. I had to go away, so you would never know, but then it was either my escape or your father's life. Well, you know the rest."

"Okay, so you didn't kill us, so what? Simon, you killed seven people! Seven people's lives are ended because of you.

How can I love a person who maliciously destroyed seven families? How can I love a man who killed my mother? What does that make me?"

"Human," Simon answered.

Then there was silence. She looked at him, he looked at her. She broke into tears, "Scott I love you, I always loved you. But..."

"But, I know your but. I had to deal with that 'but' for ten years and didn't even realise it, until you came along. You loving me hasn't condoned those seven deaths. It has saved other lives. If you weren't here, if you didn't love me, I would have been lost in my erroneous thinking.

"I would have escaped prison, and then kept on murdering. Thinking, knowing, I was in the right. I have to live with those seven deaths on my hands. This is for me and me alone to bear. Not you. Even if you go away and never see me again, you can know you have saved lives by showing me your love. Don't forgive me for what I have done. Forgive me because of your love. The love that rescued me from disaster; the love that saved my life; the love that saved countless lives from my insanity, the insanity that you alone were able to stop."

"But what if people find out?"

"That is your vanity. They should congratulate you for being able to forgive in the face of absurdity. I know deep down they will think you are a great woman, which you already are Kyndrea, the greatest woman I know."

Tears flowed down Kyndrea's face as she unfolded her hands and wrapped them around Simon, "Thank you Scott," and hugged as though she needed to squeeze the life out of him.

It was early in the morning that Kyndrea and Simon walked together up Springfield Road. Kyndrea kissed Simon as they parted at her gate. She walked dreamlike through the front door and into bed.

The next morning she got up early and fixed breakfast for her father and herself. Humming as she did so. Bob awoke to the sound. He smiled to himself, 'Finally, we can get back to normality.'

When Kyndrea knocked on Simon's door he was still asleep. He walked down and opened the door and smiled when he saw her face. She watched his eyes. It seemed as though they were new lovers again.

Simon smiled. He wasn't sure if she had actually forgiven him or just chose to forget. He felt he hadn't done enough to have her love him like this. Sure it took a lot of guts to do what he did, but it took even more for her to forgive him. Now it was done, his part in it seemed too simple.

They spent the day together in Simon's house. They talked about what was going on around Trentsworth, what things had happened over the past week. Simon didn't mention Richard's extra enumeration schemes. Within a couple of hours of conversation it seemed that they were never parted.

What is Reality

The next day Kyndrea, much to her annoyance, had an appointment with a tourist party. Simon went to Peak View, hoping that he might bump into Andrew up there. Sure enough, standing on the deck admiring the view was Andrew.

"I still amaze myself, how realistic this view is," Andrew commented as Simon came closer. "It's a bit of a cheat though, the mountains about five back are just a backdrop."

"So, are you going to close down Trentsworth?"

"You haven't finished yet." Andrew turned and looked at Simon. "Or is Bob too difficult for you to even try?"

"I just thought Kyndrea would be enough." Simon looked at Andrew, "Surely if Kyndrea can go against her programming, so can the others. I know Janine has already, you're not admitting it, but I know she has. She must have, she's changed so much."

"You're just scared. Terrified you won't turn Bob." Andrew challenged back. "I don't blame you. I did say you may not survive the shock when he kills you in this world."

"Yes, you did, I remember that vividly. No, I'll try." Simon looked out at the view. "But Kyndrea won't let me approach the subject until he is fit to fly again."

'That is fine, that won't be long. IVRRAC is prepared to put the game on hold."

"It isn't a game, Andrew!"

"It is if you lose, and you will. You have until the next day after his first flight."

"For me to talk to him, or for me to turn him?"

"Both. I would talk to him immediately afterwards. If he doesn't kill you, which he will, he definitely won't forgive you."

"Twenty four hours is not long enough!"

"It has to be, do you realise the amount of computer power

necessary to generate all this?" Andrew waved his hand over the valley. "Look down; you can see the cars and buses. Even the people, moving, doing what the computer says they should do, reacting to the environment and to the 3D characters. To think, ten years ago one movie frame, with nowhere near half as much detail, could take 9 hours to create. And now you are in a real time simulation that is way over a thousand times more complex than a picture in a movie."

"It is pretty unbelievable," Simon agreed. "I still feel somewhat that you are fooling me. I can't even see a pixel; surely it would be obvious if I looked."

"You are thinking of the arcade versions of Virtual Reality. Remember, here you aren't seeing through your eyes, your senses are being fed straight from the system. That is why it is so risky for you to die in this world."

"I could die because you have made it so real?"

"Basically, yes. We needed to, else you wouldn't be fooled, the rehabilitation would fail. I have a program set up that calculates the data from a model or detailed plan. For this I was fortunate to have access to a scale model of Trentsworth, the same one that the author of the adventure series uses for his inspirations. But even with the immense computer power we have on hand, we are still restricted to what gets simulated. Our white van was a very useful tool while simulating your trip to Trentsworth. We only had to design the interior and a small section of exterior for both airports, and the inside of a plane and van. The train trip was done with the NBS system that we also used for your flight over the Alps."

"NBS?"

"'Nothing But Scenery,' Kevin thought that one up. He's my assistant. He also designed most of the code. We used a special camera on a tour flight of the Alps for in Bob's plane and the Transalpine Express for the train trip here. Though we couldn't use it for the commercial flight, we ran out of time to get that recorded and with all the security now, it would be a nightmare getting the okay to do it. Besides, it would be even more data for the computers to handle and they're groaning now."

"You make it sound so limited, and yet it doesn't seem to be."

"That is because, for you it is unlimited. We designed the barriers to be invisible to you. In the case of this scenario, the barriers are basically the surrounding mountains. For Richard's first scenario, it was the ocean."

"I suppose that was obvious. So large in scale that even you have lost control. Look at Kyndrea for instance; I have proved that she is now more than you originally programmed her to be."

"Well, semi-proved. The data does allow for forgiveness. She hasn't called you Simon since the night before last. I think that is because she can love Scott, and hate Simon. If you get her to call you Simon and still have her loving you, then I will be equally impressed in your social skills."

Tour of the Soul

That night Simon invited Kyndrea out. He got the name of one of the best Trentsworth Restaurants from Janine and through her connections managed to obtain a table.

The restaurant was quite busy. It was located above the ticket office for the Yohanne. It was primarily a fish restaurant, though Simon had a steak. Kyndrea ordered half a crayfish. They passed a tank of live ones as they got to their table, so she was assured it would be fresh.

Their conversation was just a general mix of what each of them had done that day. "I should see next time if you can take part in the tour. I would like you to see how my actual professional spiel goes. Would you be interested, Scott?"

"I would love to," Simon replied, then added, "You know, you can call me Simon if you wish. No one's called me Simon in ages now."

"I", Kyndrea started.

"A rock lobster for the lady and a steak, medium-rare, for the gentleman," the waiter interrupted, placing the meals in front of them.

'Thank you," they both replied and they started eating. The subject of the name was not approached again that evening. Simon felt he may have been a bit quick to mention it. He realised he was still treading on egg shells with Kyndrea as he hadn't earned her full trust yet.

After a pleasant walk back down Springfield road, they got back to Simon's gate. "Well," Simon said, not knowing what to do next.

"Well", Kyndrea noted as well. They looked into each others eyes and their lips touched. Suddenly the warmth flowed through both of them as the kiss became more passionate. After a while Kyndrea gently pulled away.

"Do you want to come inside?" Simon asked gingerly.

"I would love to, but." Kyndrea answered. "It's still too soon. I have loads to do tomorrow morning anyway. Have to report to Janine's dad on the past tours and get new appointments. I can arrange to get you on one at the same time, though."

"Sounds good", Simon commented, the disappointment showing through slightly. "See you tomorrow afternoon?"

"Meet you in the mall, at the wharf. Twelve thirty?"

"Great! Twelve thirty then." They kissed again, slightly less passionately and parted.

The morning seemed to drag on forever as Simon played himself in a couple of snooker games. He even decided to go for a couple of laps in the pool. He might as well use the facilities while he had them. Once Bob had been turned, he would probably have to leave the valley.

Simon wondered what would become of Kyndrea and Bob. He couldn't stay here, could he? Was it right to lead Kyndrea into loving him again when he couldn't continue loving her? Perhaps Andrew could create another 3D to emulate him. That would be the best solution. Then it would only be his own heart that breaks at the end. He deserved it anyway. He would survive, he was a survivor after all. He was a loner, an outcast, what could he bring to a relationship anyway? Kyndrea was better off without him. His 3D replacement could be improved to be what he could never be.

Back to Auckland he would go; back to reality. As Scott he had no history, no past to stop him getting a job. He would live as a normal, dutiful citizen until he had done his full quota. But there would be no Kyndrea, no one to welcome him home each evening. No one to kiss passionately after a wonderful evening's meal out, no one to tell all his deepest secrets to. But then he did take these special people away from seven others. He didn't deserve to have one himself, did he?

Well, he had Kyndrea now. Why worry about the future? Let Andrew worry about that, he needed to live for today, not just for his sake, but also for Kyndrea's. She needed someone there for her. She needed that love he stole from her ten years ago. He was the only one to give it back to her, through himself.

It was twelve thirty when Kyndrea came bounding up towards him on the wharf. "I just got us tickets on the wildest jet boat ride ever. We have just enough time for a quick lunch."

They returned to Simon's front door both wet and exhausted. "I've never been on such an intense thrill ride." Simon commented as he opened the door.

"Great wasn't it," Kyndrea agreed. She followed Simon into the house. "Do you know what I feel like now? A nice hot soak in a bath."

"How about my spa pool?" Simon suggested. Kyndrea's

face lit up.

"Perfect." She smiled, gazing at him lovingly.

He looked into her eyes, he couldn't take his eyes off her face. Her smile was so full of wonderment and love. It was as though he had just given her the world. It was a smile that could only be shared between two lovers. A smile reserved just for him.

He didn't want to disturb that look, the gleam in her eyes. But he was drawn closer and he placed his lips on hers.

"I checked with Mr Gousing", she commented as their lips parted, "you can join the tour tomorrow."

"Huh?" Simon was still in the moment that he wasn't quite ready for a change of topic.

"You okay?" Kyndrea asked. She felt a twinge of pride that he was so taken with her. "I said you can join my tour tomorrow, is that okay?"

"Yes, definitely."

Simon led Kyndrea through to the pool room. He found the controls for the tub and got the system working. He looked up from the control panel to see Kyndrea stripping off her wet clothes. He decided to follow suit.

Simon was right, she did have a beautiful body and he couldn't help but watch her as she slipped into the bubbling froth. She, too, seemed to watch his every move as he carefully stepped into the pool. She smiled innocently at him.

Moving over to her side, he lent forward and kissed her mouth. She moved her hand over his hair and pressed him closer. The kiss instantly became more passionate and he felt her wrap her body around his. He let his own passion overtake the moment and moved his arms lower, feeling the smooth skin of her back.

Kyndrea woke up early the next morning and saw Simon lying there in his bed. She smiled as she remembered the previous night. He started stirring and looked across at her. She looked at the clock on the bedside table beside him. "I have to fix dad some breakfast. I want to make sure he's okay, I've got time for a quick shower first."

"I'll stay here then," Simon smiled, as he cuddled back into his pillow.

"Tour starts in two hours; you might as well get up and have breakfast ready for me on my return."

"If you say so." Simon sat up and stretched out his arms.

Kyndrea watched the skin tighten over his chest. He wasn't well endowed with muscle, but he didn't have any fat either, so the muscles he did have were very obvious. She suddenly wished she didn't have the tour that day.

Simon had made it to the lounge when she emerged from the bathroom fully dressed. "Shouldn't be longer than quarter of an hour," she said as she headed for the front door.

"See you in fifteen minutes then, miss you already."

"Now you're being ridiculous." Kyndrea laughed as she closed the door behind her.

Simon joined the group of tourists. They seemed fascinated with Kyndrea's vast knowledge. Simon was fascinated just with Kyndrea. Their relationship had moved to a higher level. Her eyes sparkled each time she started a new piece of local knowledge.

Kyndrea found it hard that day to keep her mind on the tour. She was basically running on automatic, her mouth playing the same old recording she used every tour, while her mind was on the night before. Suddenly all doubt that Simon and her should be together had gone as easily as a wisp of smoke.

They had connected on a new level last night. She looked at Simon's eyes following her every move. If she died today, she would die happy. Her life was suddenly complete with Simon, she knew he would be the one she would marry and spend the rest of her life with.

The day passed quickly for both of them as the tour wore on. Finally, it was getting to four o'clock and Kyndrea was winding things up at the wharf by the mall. Simon was looking forward to another evening with Kyndrea. He felt like another hot tub when a sight made his stomach suddenly feel very heavy.

Behind Kyndrea, as she spoke about what other things the tourists might wish to spend their money on, was something he had hoped he would not see for quite a while. Landing on the Lake of Worth was the amphibian plane. It was time for the next phase.

He had just got to know Kyndrea, regain his love for her and now it was time to throw it all away. He felt anger at the world. He could have been given a few more days, but then would that be enough? Would even an eternity be sufficient to say he had spent enough time with Kyndrea?

After the tourists parted and went their separate ways, Simon asked Kyndrea, "Your dad back on his feet?"

"As though nothing happened," Kyndrea laughed. "He was already up getting my breakfast when I got in this morning. He didn't realise I wasn't even in the house so he was fixing me the full hot breakfast. He was feeling extremely hungry. He does that, one minute dying, the next bright as a button. He had made an appointment with the local doctor this morning. He obviously got the okay to fly. I'm so happy for him. He's a lot less grumpy after he's been around the mountains a few times." Kyndrea noticed the look on Simon's face. "What's the matter, you don't seem so pleased?"

"Well, I promised myself I would break the news when he made his first flight. If I don't I might never tell him and unfortunately I have to or we will all be living a lie. I cannot live another lie, ever."

"Why now? Give us another week at least!" Kyndrea stormed off the wharf into the mall. Simon chased after her.

"In another week someone else may discover my secret, Kyndrea. Bob himself may find that paper. What does he do when he's not restricted to the house?"

"He goes and catches up with everyone he knows. I suppose he goes to the library as well, looks at the papers there."

"Then I had better get it over and done with." Simon grabbed Kyndrea by her shoulders and looked deeply into her eyes. "I know. I, too, wanted this to last for an eternity. Even another week isn't enough to spend with you, Kyndrea. Even just one lifetime seems to be a mere slice of what I really want."

Simon released her shoulders and started walking back to Springfield Road. Kyndrea followed and wrapped her arm around his waist as they walked side by side. "Okay", she said, "I understand. There is no real reason for me to say no."

"Ask him to come around tonight. Tell him I need to ask him something."

"You are playing with fire." Kyndrea smiled, "He will be hoping you're asking for my hand in marriage. After one night of me being at your house, he'll be expecting that. You know how he jumps to conclusions."

"You never know, he might say yes."

"Before or after he kills you?" Kyndrea released her hand from Simon's waist. This would be the end of their relationship. Her dad would never forgive him, and she would be forbidden to see him. She remembered her other relationship. That ended when she had to choose between her dad and her boyfriend. "Are you sure you shouldn't leave it for a month or so, let him get used to you being a part of his life?"

"Sorry, Kyndrea, it has to be tonight," Simon stated, cursing to himself, 'Damn Andrew and his deadlines I wanted longer with Kyndrea.'

They parted at Simon's gate with a couple of perfunctory goodbyes. Neither of them wanted to start something they could never finish. This seemed to be the end, the end of something that could have been so wonderful.

The valley was getting dark as the sun sank beneath the western mountains. Simon had sat placidly watching the activity on the lake die down, until there were only the lights from the cruise boat gliding along it.

Lying in front of him on the coffee table was a kitchen knife, a bottle of liquid, a wad of tissues and a folded note. The wait was becoming unbearable. He had thought he had bad moments in his life, but this was the worst. So much hinged on him being able to pull this off.

Twenty seven lives hung in the balance. He knew they were lives as there was no other explanation. Andrew was wrong. Somehow life had been created here. Simon had to make certain he would preserve it, but really it was all up to Bob, not himself. All Simon could do was to state his case. Bob chose whether they lived or died.

There was a knock at the door. Simon got up and let Bob in.

"Kyndrea said you had something to ask me?" Bob smiled.

"Unfortunately my question is not what you may be thinking. I need to tell you something before I can get anywhere near what you're thinking of. We need to sit down first. My request requires your full attention."

The lights of the computers flashed all around Andrew as he watched the screen on his desk. The image of Bob smiled as he took as seat by Simon. "And so it starts," Andrew said to no one in particular. "You may not think it but I am for you winning this bet. But sadly I still reckon you are too hung up in VR to know what is actually happening."

Kevin, wearing a white smock, entered the room, "Resuscitation equipment is ready, Andrew. I hope we can bring him back. He wasn't such a bad guy after all."

"Most people aren't, Kevin," Andrew smiled. "That's how our system works. The secret is to forget the prejudices and look for the human being that is in all of us."

"Pity we can't say that about the 3Ds, we wouldn't need all that equipment I just set up."

"He will stick to the program, Kevin."

"Kyndrea didn't."

"Her program wasn't that exact. It couldn't have been or she wouldn't have fallen in love with Simon in the first place. No, Bob is black and white." Andrew replied, but Kevin noted a slight doubt in Andrew's voice.

Simon rejoined Bob with two cups. "There you are, white one sugar, right?"

"Good memory, Scott. Thank you."

"You're welcome, Bob. Now, before I ask the question. I wish you to indulge me in listening to a story of my past. It will make asking my question easier."

"You make it sound so serious. I have all night. To be honest, Scott, you are a mystery to me. I would like to hear about you before Trentsworth. The papers were quite vague on it when you arrived."

"Well", Simon paused, using all his strength to keep going. "I grew up in a rich neighbourhood. My dad was the CEO of a very large company and through my first ten years I wanted for nothing. Actually, to be honest, I was a spoilt brat and somewhat a mother's boy.

"I didn't fully realise it, but I did sense there was something of a gap between my mother and father. The occasional yelling match when I was in another room. They were very careful not to argue in front of me. I continually had the feeling that something was not right.

"Then, when I just turned twelve, my dad left mum for another woman. This home-breaker had recently become widowed and had piles of money. So practically out of the blue my father left us."

"You must have been devastated."

"Not as much as mum. She just stayed in bed all day and I had to do all the work around the place. Mum was not inherently rich. To be honest, she was a bit of a disgrace to my father's parents. Dad tried to turn me against mum as well. He invited me over to meet his new wife and step daughter. But I knew mum would die without my help. She could not take another betrayal. Once he realised how I felt, he severed all ties with both mum and me."

"You must have so much hatred for your dad. I couldn't ever imagine severing ties with Kyndrea."

Simon paused and looked at Bob. He really saw the injustice in his life. He realised by talking to Bob, finally being able to tell someone the full truth, the memories started becoming clearer. What had previously laid hidden to him was slowly coming to light. He didn't care if Bob was listening now or not. He had to keep going. He had to see this through. He knew the answer, what Janine had referred to, was finally in his grasp.

"Yes", Simon continued. "I hated him for what he had done to mum. With the grief he had caused, mum was starving to death. I could do nothing to save her. I tried to feed her, she refused to eat. Then we started falling behind on the mortgage with her not working. I couldn't afford to buy food. I was only twelve, for Christ's sake. How could a twelve year old be expected to talk to bank managers, get a six hundred dollar a week pay cheque?

"My dad knew people high up. The rich protect each other. He didn't have to pay child support, he didn't have alimony payments. His rich lawyers made sure of that. He made sure my mum suffered. She suffered all right, straight into a hospital bed.

"Dad refused to take me in. I refused to go. I was put in a welfare home. A dirty, underpaid, rat infested welfare home. The owners tried their best, but the money was never enough for the number of children they had. Then finally they took me to the hospital, to see my mother for the last time.

"She laid there. A shadow of who she really was. It wasn't my mum, it was a skeleton. She had no muscle, no fat, just skin and bones. The only thing I recognised was in her eyes, the love she held for me in those blue eyes.

"Then the blue faded and the nurses took me away from her as others moved the sheet over her head. I screamed, I didn't know what to do. I ran as I released myself from the nurse's hands. I ran and ran. I didn't know where to. I had no destination. I only knew I had to get out of there. There was no one left in my life who loved me. Do you know how that feels? No one. My father had been stolen from me by a rich bitch. My mother now dead. All I could do was run and I did, as fast as my legs could take me. I ran from the hospital towards my old house. It was all I could think of. I ran past a collection of shops pushing my way through the multitudes of rich shoppers, not caring if they fell into the gutters or onto parked cars. I had to get away from those people. I was the only one that mattered now. Just me. Then, as the shops disappeared into the distance, I saw her." Simon paused as the realisation overtook him. A look of horror flashed over his face. Bob sat there transfixed to what he was saying.

He had to continue now. "I saw her and his step daughter," he paused for a moment in thought, "well, I thought I did. I saw a rich mother and a daughter, but my mind said it was them. All that anger, the anger for my dad, the anger against her for stealing him away over took me.

"I became a different person, gone was the mothers boy, the spoilt brat. The anger made me into a monster; a terrible revenge-filled monster. I ran over to this lady and her daughter. I grabbed a knife out of the girl's science project.

I stabbed her mother. Once for every month my mum laid ill in bed."

Simon paused and looked away from Bob's horror filled face. Then Bob stood up suddenly and moved away from Simon, grabbing the knife on the coffee table.

Simon continued, seemingly oblivious to what Bob was doing "I then looked at her. Who I thought was my father's step daughter. I then saw she wasn't. I realised I had made a mistake. I heard the teachers coming for me so I dropped the knife then ran and hid under a hedge. I didn't know what to do. I'd murdered an innocent lady. I'd revenged the wrong person."

"Maybe", Bob hissed, "But I know I have the right person in my sights, Simon, Harold, Tallsbury!"

"Yes, you do, Bob. I won't blame you if you kill me. I was so filled with hate all my life. Hate for the rich. Hate for what I did. Then I met your daughter. Do you know how clearer your mind becomes when you are in love?"

"I used to. Then you came along," Bob softly stated, the knife in his hand shaking with pent up anger. He studied Simon's face, thinking, 'I should have recognised him immediately. Those eyes. I need to go now. If I stay he will be dead, but is that a bad thing? Yes, Kyndrea would be left alone with me in jail. Can I stop myself? Haven't I been waiting for this all my life. Finally I have Margaret's murderer to myself.'

"I wrecked your life, and I want to pay for it, so I have written a suicide note. See that solution?" Simon pointed to the brown bottle on the table. "It will wipe away your prints and you can place the knife in my hand. You can dispose of the remaining solution easily in your toilet. No one will know the truth. Kyndrea won't tell, she can't live without you.

"You can have your wish and I won't stop you. I deserve to die and you won't go to jail. I've already attempted suicide, so the police won't argue. It will be just a failure at rehabilitation. Which is ironic in a way, as strange as the technique seems, it worked.

"I can never bring back those seven people. Now, since something changed in me after meeting Kyndrea, I can't live with myself knowing I wrecked seven families. You killing me will be a godsend. If I can't forgive myself for what I have done, why should you?"

"Damn right! How can I forgive you for killing Margaret? How can I let you, her killer, take my daughter away from me?" Bob approached Simon. "I have been waiting for this for ten years. Do you know how angry I was when you got off by being a juvenile? I reckon that was the day my heart condition started, weakened by the immense emotion that flowed through me."

Bob took the knife and moved over to Simon. "Finally, I get to do what the law should have done years ago. You ask me to forgive you? You ask me to forget those ten years of anguish? How could you even conceive the idea that I would even consider it?"

"Kill me, then. I promised I wouldn't stop you. I deserve to die."

Andrew looked at the monitor, "Quick! Kevin, man the machines, he's going to do it, lets see if we can save Simon."

"Doubt it. His heart is already racing ten to the dozen." Kevin cursed as he ran into the adjoining room.

"Pity, there was a point there I thought Simon may have actually pulled it off," Andrew said. To himself, "There was almost a glimmer of hope."

Bob pressed the knife into Simon's chest, "Simon Harold Tallsbury, I sentence you. I sentence you to," his voice quivered, the knife shaking as Bob pressed harder.

Simon felt the blade pierce his skin. 'Now I know how they felt,' he thought and closed his eyes, just waiting for the darkness to engulf him. 'May Jesus forgive Bob and myself for what we have done.' Then he heard a sound of metal hitting the window glass.

He opened his eyes. Bob was kneeling on the floor. Bob was definitely a person you wouldn't expect to see crying, but he was. "I have wanted to do that for ten years. Every night I dreamt of pulling a trigger, stabbing or even drowning you. Now I have the chance, I fail. I have failed Kyndrea. I have failed Margaret.

"I am not a murderer. Unlike you, I cannot condone what you have done, no matter what the reason. No matter how reasonable, there is no excuse for murder. I cannot live with this hatred that has built up within me any longer. For myself, I need to forgive you and get on with my life."

Andrew called in Kevin, "Break open the Champagne! Order a couple more super computers, we are going to be world famous, Kevin, world famous."

"You forgive me?" Simon asked, to be certain what he heard.

"I do. At least now I can understand what madness overtook you when you killed Margaret. I forgive you your actions, but there is a condition." Bob stood up and looked sternly down at Simon, "You must never see Kyndrea again. When you can, you must leave Trentsworth and never come back. You are not a man I would want to see ever again."

"I will be required to leave anyway, once my parole is finished," Simon confirmed as Bob walked towards the front door.

"Remember", Bob said as he reached for the door handle, "Don't place a foot anywhere near our house, or my daughter. Good Bye!" And with that Bob left, closing the door behind him.

"I would hold fire on the drinking, gentlemen," Christine announced as she walked into Andrew's office. "The deal was that Kyndrea and Bob forgive Simon totally for what he has done."

"Yes, and Bob said", Andrew started.

"He also said the word 'condition'." Christine sat down on Andrew's messy desk, shifting aside a few electronic boards and papers. "Where were you in Sunday School? True forgiveness is unconditional."

"The forgiveness is not conditional, he just doesn't want to see Simon again, is that so bad? Christine, you're splitting hairs."

"No, Andrew, I'm not. Any scientific analysis needs to be exact. If you're going to write your papers on electronic intelligence, you need to have definite proof. Proof is not a mere three words. Proof is actions continuously going against the programming."

"Kyndrea Margaret McKenzie!" Bob yelled at the top of his voice. "You come down here at once!"

"I won't stop seeing him!"

"Right, my dear." Bob walked purposely up the stairs. "While you're in this house, you obey my rules. And not seeing your mother's murderer is one of them. What are you doing?" Bob questioned as soon as he walked into Kyndrea's bedroom.

Kyndrea was placing dress after dress into one of two suitcases lying open on her bed. "I knew you would lay down the law, so I'm moving out."

"You couldn't leave here for old what's his name, why should I believe you can do it for Simon Tallsbury?"

"Because I love him, dad!"

"You loved the other guy as well and he didn't kill your mother."

"Not like this. I realise now I didn't really love Martin, now I've experienced what I have with Simon. I've forgiven Simon dad, I had to, besides he's a different person now."

"Forgiven? How can you forgive such a person?"

"You asked me to, for one." She angrily shoved more clothes tightly into the suitcase.

"I didn't know who he was then. Don't try and put it back on me. You could've told me at the start when you found out."

"You would've had another attack. Two attacks within a day, you'd never regain your pilots licence even with the most advanced autopilot."

"You knew who Scott was the day I had the attack?" Bob's asked in a more calm voice.

"Simon told me just after the ambulance left."

"Oh Kyndrea, You must have had a terrible time."

"Worst day of my life since coming here, dad."

"And I actually told him I forgave him, the bastard!"

"It wasn't Simon's fault!" Kyndrea stopped packing for a second and looked at her father. "You said you forgave him?"

"On condition he never sees you again."

"Oh, how magnanimous of you!" Kyndrea opened up her top drawer and started filling up the second suitcase. "You didn't forgive him. You just said that to get rid of him."

"Yes, I forgave him."

"Oh sure." Kyndrea stopped again to look her dad straight in the eye, "If you did, why are you here forbidding me to see him again? Think about it carefully while I'm away."

"You won't go."

"Just watch me." Kyndrea started on the second drawer down, throwing the clothes in from where she stood.

"I will, I'll watch you right to the front door." Bob tried to smile. "Kyndrea I know you better than you do. How many people leave their lover's bed to get their father breakfast? You have spent the last ten years with me. You cannot live any other way. Once you get to the threshold you will see you can't live without me."

"Dad, you don't understand. I still love you." Kyndrea closed the two suitcases. "I still want to be with you. I'm not leaving you, I'm just going to stay with Simon. It's up to you whether I can see you again or not."

"My door's always open." Bob held out his arms and Kyndrea moved towards and embraced him. "Once you leave Simon, you can come back anytime."

Kyndrea pulled away. "You don't get it, do you dad?" She grabbed the cases and walked as quickly as she could down the stairs, the suitcases bumping on the occasional wooden stair from their weight.

Bob caught up with her at the doorway. She had opened it but could not go any further. Crossing the threshold would sever ties with her father for what, at the moment, seemed forever. Bob was pig-headed; he would not give in on his stance.

"Come back inside, Kyndrea. Let's both have a good night's sleep and talk about it in the morning. You don't want to leave me, do you?"

"No dad, I don't want to leave you." Kyndrea forced a smile through the tears welling in her eyes. She hugged her dad. "I love you, dad. I will always love you."

Still Work to Do

Simon was relieved and upset. He had saved their lives, but it didn't do him any good. But then did he really deserve happiness. He had been sitting there for the past ten minutes just pondering on what he finally realised, if Bob was based on the real father of Kyndrea, would he want to ever see him again?

Yes, he would. Bob had changed as well, changed completely. No wonder the real Bob had felt so guilty. For some strange reason Simon couldn't feel any joy in knowing how his father had died. Perhaps it was time for him to forgive, also.

He got up and put the knife away and tipped the bottle of water down the sink. It was then he noticed the red stain seeping through his shirt. He immediately went upstairs to his on-suite and fished a sticking plaster from the medicine cupboard. The cut was not large but bled furiously. He cleaned himself up and was walking down the stairs when there came a knock on the door. Simon paused.

Then he rushed down, and opened it, hoping. "Oh, its you," he said, not hiding his disappointment as Andrew walked in.

"You were expecting Kyndrea? She would never choose you over her dad, you know that. She loves him too much to hurt him that way."

"I do, but hope is not logical."

"Very true." Andrew looked at Simon gravely, "Unfortunately science is."

"What do you mean by that?"

"My boss, Christine, you remember her?" Simon nodded. "Well, she's a sucker for being exact and apparently the deal was full forgiveness. Bob is required to rescind the conditions before IVRRAC can accept their self-awareness."

"What!" Simon yelled, "He forgave me. Isn't that enough?"

"Apparently not. I can't do anything about it, Simon. My hands are tied."

"He has to accept me as Kyndrea's boyfriend before

tomorrow afternoon?"

"The deal was twenty four hours after the first flight," Andrew smiled, placing an envelope in Simon's hands. "This is an official document stating you're required to depart from Trentsworth in four weeks. Since you have made such headway in the past two weeks, we have extended the timeframe. You are required to spend at least a week here with Kyndrea loving you as she did early today and Bob loving you as if you were his own son."

"Three weeks to turn Bob around?" Simon asked, taking the envelope.

"Correct, you have until fifteen hundred hours, Friday the ninth of April."

Simon pulled the papers from the envelope; the top page was a calendar print out, "Good Friday? Shouldn't you be home on holiday?"

"Just the way the dates fall, Simon and I never have a holiday during rehabilitation, no matter what holidays there are. The time is due to Christine wanting to get away early. Even if you fail Simon, after those four weeks, I have a job for you in the real world. You would fit in well with our small team here. You are extremely intelligent, and I should know, I have had your brain in my computer for the last several months. We could use your unique insight."

"I would be too tempted to watch Kyndrea's progress if I succeed or too devastated if Bob didn't turn. I don't know if I could handle being around this process either way."

"Very true, said you were intelligent. I would have been surprised if you had said yes. I can, though, get you a university degree in whatever you want to get you on track for another job. And a glowing reference. You'll need to keep being Scott. Simon still died in the van explosion. You have a clean slate; the world's your oyster."

"Thank you, Andrew. Thank you for saving my life. Now the question is can I save Bob's?"

"Remember Scott, anything's possible." Andrew opened the front door. On the other side was Kyndrea. She was placing the right suitcase on the ground. Andrew turned to look at Simon, a slight surprised look on his face. "Anything, Simon. Follow your heart, not your logic. Must go, nice seeing you again Kyndrea."

"Come in", Simon welcomed, kissing her on the lips. She gently returned the gesture, but Simon could tell her heart wasn't in it. She was upset over something.

"I can't live without you, Simon", she stated, as she gave the suitcases to Simon and walked towards the easy chairs. "No matter what dad wants."

"You don't know how happy it makes me to hear you say that." Simon just left the suitcases and followed Kyndrea. "But I am not worth losing your father over. I have to leave Trentsworth in a month. Andrew just delivered the bad news in that envelope."

"I will go with you, Simon." Kyndrea wiped her eyes with the back of her hand. Simon pulled a few tissues out of a box to her left and handed them to her. She gratefully accepted them. "I must admit I did falter at the doorstep, but now I have said my farewells to dad and told him how much I love him, I could follow you to the end of the world and further."

"If only you could." Simon looked at Kyndrea. She stared back. Their lips touched and they kissed, it was the most loving, the most sensuous kiss he had ever had, it seemed to last for days. If only she could go past the ends of this world and into reality.

The next morning Kyndrea woke up beside Simon. She looked at the clock and immediately thought she had to get back to make her dad's breakfast. She felt awful as she realised the nightmare of the previous night was no mere dream but reality. She had left Bob for Simon so there was no going back. Kyndrea decided to make Simon and herself breakfast instead. She got up and walked down the stairs. Bringing the breakfast, she woke up Simon; once he had sat up she placed the bed trays over him. She then got into bed and grabbed her tray off Simon.

That day Kyndrea busied herself unpacking her bags and tidying up Simon's wardrobe. "Leave a man here for a couple of months and the place becomes a pigsty," she muttered, smiling though as she did.

By the end of the week Kyndrea had made herself at home, and Simon had learned what it was like to have a female touch around the place. They had fast become an inseparable couple, but Simon knew that the clock was ticking. In three weeks he would be required to leave. Andrew's last comments, though, stayed in his mind playing with his hope. What did he mean, anything's possible.

Simon thought of Bob. He would need to approach the subject at some stage, but he felt he needed to let things settle for a bit. Show him how happy Kyndrea was in her new life.

The next week they spent as much time as possible together, a month was not a long time so he had vowed to make the most of being with Kyndrea. This week would be solely focused on her. Next week he would worry about Bob.

Kyndrea, too, was trying to forget what it was like living with her dad. She kept him out of her mind, busying herself reorganising the house. She knew, though, that living with Simon was the best decision she had ever made, although she knew it could be better, he was holding back for some reason. It was as though he didn't think she would leave the valley with him.

She had tried time and time again to convince him she could leave, but he still resisted giving in to her. She knew eventually he would and if it was this much joy living with him like this, what amazing feeling it would be when he did relent and throw all caution to the wind, allowing himself to be taken by her.

The week ended with Kyndrea and Simon even closer. On Friday Kyndrea had a phone call from Mr Gousing. "Simon, he's got a job for me tomorrow. Is that okay?"

"It's Good Friday, Kyndrea, doesn't he know that?", then to himself, "It's Good Friday, oh my, and I haven't done anything at all, it came so fast."

"This is Trentsworth, Simon", Kyndrea laughed. "There is no such thing as holidays here. The tourists still come no matter what day it is. Besides, the council make the most of any holiday. This helps pull the people out of Christchurch and into the valley for a few precious and expensive days."

"That's fine, Kyndrea, it's not as though I have to go to work on Tuesday. You get out there," Simon yelled softly finishing with "At least it'll keep your mind on other things."

The next morning the alarm woke up both of them. Kyndrea got up and went off to the shower. Simon lay there thinking. With her away that day, it'll give him a chance to see Bob, he had been thinking of what he could do all night and hadn't had a good sleep.

Kyndrea came out of the ensuite drying herself. Simon stopped thinking, seeing Kyndrea seemed to put his mind a rest. He watched this wonderful angel slowly cover her beautiful body with garments seemingly designed to accentuate the beauty no longer seen. She knew how to look fantastic, but that morning it made him feel sad. Sad, that this angel was being torn away from her happiness by one selfish man, he felt a lump in his stomach.

It wasn't long before she left the house. Simon got out of bed and had a shower. The lump in his stomach was growing. He knew Bob would not be pleased to see him, but this nonsense had to stop. Kyndrea would miss this part of her life and it would eventually tear her apart.

He walked out the lakeside door of his house and walked over to the patio doors of Bob's. He was in the lounge sitting in his chair reading a book. Simon knocked on the glass.

Bob looked up and then continued reading. Simon knocked again; this time there was no response from Bob. Simon tried the door handle, it moved and opened. He walked in, to Bob's obvious shock and horror.

"What part of, never talk to me again, don't you understand?" Bob yelled, standing up. At his full height he was slightly taller than Simon, and far more menacing.

"The first word," Simon replied, "If it was just me, I wouldn't bother, but Kyndrea is miserable without you."

"She can come back to me anytime she wants to."

"She doesn't think that." Simon stared straight at Bob's eyes, "She reckons you will have nothing more to do with her."

"She knows I love her." Bob was slowly making his way towards Simon.

"You think?" Simon firmly replied. "If that was so, she would be here instead of me. She thinks you hate her because she chose me over you."

"You're going to throw that in my face are you. How you managed to steal her away from me?"

"I didn't steal; she came of her own free will."

"You still stole her, you," Bob paused, he was lost for descriptive words.

"I did not take, you pushed her at me. Anyway, I have to leave in a week's time. The rehabilitation people want me to leave, so they can start recuperating their funds tied up with the house. Now I have officially been rehabilitated."

"She's leaving the valley with you?"

"Yes, well she wants to. But there is something she doesn't know, something that will stop her leaving."

"What? You have a family? You do not love her?"

"I love her, and I wish to marry her, but it is impossible for her to follow me out of the valley. Let's just say it is very much to do with the rehabilitation technique."

"Oh," Bob looked perplexed for a second, then his resolve came back. "Well, tell her that she is free to return here at any time. Once you go away."

"I won't, you can if you want." Simon turned to leave. "I will tell you, though, you have an endless invitation to come over and see us. Once you've grown up and can see both of us can share Kyndrea's love." With that Simon left and walked back home.

Bob stood there, his mind racing. 'How dare he come into my house and accuse me. He has no right, he lost that right ten years ago when he killed my Margaret. This has gone far enough, I can't even wait a week longer for Kyndrea to come back, if ever. 'She's pigheaded just like me. She will find a way around this rehabilitation limit. She will leave the valley for good. I need to talk to someone. Someone who could make the problem go away. Someone who is an expert at stealing boyfriends.'

It was mid afternoon and Bob waited patiently at the café's table. He had a pint of beer half drunk in front of him. Janine came through the crowds and sat opposite. "Hi. You needed to see me?"

"You want anything to drink?" Bob asked out of politeness only.

"Wheat beer."

"Waiter!" Bob waited until a harassed looking man came to their table. "A pint of wheat beer, whatever fancy name you call it, and another one of these."

"Certainly, sir." The waiter disappeared back into the crowds.

"Now Janine, I hear you fancy Scott."

"Sorry?" That question came totally unexpected. She was not sure where this conversation was going. Bob had never spoken to her again since the Martin episode. "Yes, I tried, but I failed, okay? Scott is madly in love with Kyndrea. You have nothing to fear."

"On the contrary, Janine. I have everything to fear. Simon, I mean Scott has already taken Kyndrea away from me, and there is a good chance she will leave this valley with him."

"Simon's leaving?" Janine's face fell.

"Yes, he is and you are the only one who can stop him." Bob paused and then his mind clicked over what actually was said. "You know who Simon is?"

"Yes. Obviously Kyndrea's told you as well."

"No", Bob took another drink from the glass, "Simon did the decent thing and told me himself. Was I the only one here not to know?"

"No. Only Kyndrea, Simon, Richard, Andrew, you and me."

"Andrew? Richard?"

"Richard's my very close friend and Andrew's Simon's parole officer."

"Andrew? I might need to have a word with him. He could stop this nonsense."

"What nonsense?" Janine asked as the waiter brought over the two drinks.

"Kyndrea has gone to live with Simon."

"Good on her."

"No it's not, she won't speak to me. Simon's turned her against me."

"I can't believe that." Janine took a drink from the glass. "Simon would want you to be included in anything they did."

"Well, I don't want Simon included. How can I spend time with my wife's killer? What monster would that make me?"

"Do you think Kyndrea's a monster then?"

"She's just a bit confused at the moment."

"Confused?" Janine laughed, "Someone here's confused, but it isn't Kyndrea. Tell me, what would your wife want in all the world?"

"To be alive again. Not to have been stabbed to death by some insane teenager."

"That happened, you cannot change the past. I don't think that would be what she wants. I doubt whether there is any regrets after death. She would want something else, and you know what I'm talking about."

"Of course she would want Kyndrea and me to be happy, but not at the expense of her memory."

"What are you actually afraid of, Mr McKenzie?"

"What do you mean, afraid?" Bob yelled back. The talking stopped around them as Bob calmed down. They waited until the babble of voices surrounded them once again.

"You see Kyndrea happy. You see she has finally met her true love. And yet you want to wreck her happiness? I know why you wanted to see me. You wanted me to steal Simon away from your daughter. I should be insulted and offended that this is what you think of me. And I am in a way, but I have already forgiven you, Bob. Primarily because you were correct, a few months ago I was a slut who would pinch a boyfriend out of Kyndrea's grasp. Yes, I even tried it. Do you know why? Because, ever since high school my so-called friends have treated me as though I was a slut.

"Each time I enticed a boy over to my place, they applauded me. I gained popularity by sleeping with any willing partner, within reason of course. To my father I am a very successful businesswoman, which is what he wants me to be, but to everyone else I was a joke. To them my business success was proportionately related to my nocturnal success.

"Totally untrue, I never mixed business with pleasure. If you call selling yourself for attention, pleasure. I was so scared of being alone, I distanced myself from any true friend, thus I was alone anyway. Do you know who allowed me to see the dark spiralling downward tunnel I was in? Simon. He listened to me. I pushed every wrong button possible and he still saved me from myself.

"I won't help you tear those two apart, Mr McKenzie, but I will help you to see that they should be together. Even you can't be blind to the happiness they share, how Kyndrea is now so alive. The only thing stopping you sharing this happiness is your fear. What is your fear? What are you afraid of?"

Janine stood up, leaving her half full glass on the table and walked away. Bob was left there staring into the crowd. 'Me afraid, how ridiculous.' He sat there for a while longer finishing off his glass. 'Robert McKenzie is never afraid.'

Simon looked at the clock, one thirty. Kyndrea came in and saw him looking apprehensive. "What's up?"

"Do you think you should go over to your dad's and see if he's changed his mind?"

"If he has, he can come over here. Now stop thinking about him and think of something to do tomorrow. It's a holiday weekend, we should be enjoying ourselves. Besides, we only have another week and a half here in the valley."

"True." Simon looked at the clock again, four forty. "I don't want to leave without you and your dad reconciled."

"He'll see sense before we leave. You told him the date we're leaving when you snuck off behind my back. Didn't you?"

"Yes I did. How did you know?"

"The tour started on the lake. I could see our patio doors quite easily. You should know, you cannot hide anything from me."

"Very true", Simon smiled. Inside he knew the truth. Kyndrea could not leave with him, and if Bob did not call around in the next fifteen minutes she wouldn't stay in Trentsworth either.

"Must defrost the chicken," Kyndrea excused herself. Simon was not in a good mood, and he didn't seem to want to tell her what the real reason was. He would open up in time. She decided it would be best to let him sulk for a while.

Simon looked at the lake as a clock on one of the sideboards chimed three times. He looked up at the sky expecting the sun to turn red, the mountains disappear or something. Bob had not apologised so he had failed Kyndrea. He had failed all of them.

There was something else he could have done. There must have been. Bob and Kyndrea were self-aware. Should they be punished for their own pigheadedness? Should they be punished because Simon had failed to bring their human side out to the open?

Simon marched into the pool room away from the kitchen and started yelling at the top of his voice, "Why bother keeping it going, Andrew? It's over. It's all over, IVRRAC wins! They get all their stupid computers back. I failed, I failed all of them. Get me out of here!"

His life was full of failure. He failed as a son to his dad. He failed as a man for his mum. He failed as a decent human being for those seven innocents. Not once in his life was there a time he could be proud of. He failed at being human and because of that more lives would perish. "Where are you, Andrew? Get me out of here now!"

There was a knock at the door. Simon wondered why Andrew even bothered to keep up the pretence now. Trentsworth was ended. He walked back towards the door to the lounge and as he opened it, he saw Kyndrea at the front door.

"Dad!" Kyndrea yelled in happiness as she slammed the door wide open.

"I have come to apologise, Kyndrea", Bob said. "I have been acting the fool."

"Come in, come in." Kyndrea smiled as she closed the door behind Bob.

"I was so scared of losing you I forced you away. Ironic isn't it."

"Do you want a drink?"

Simon closed the door and walked down to the snooker table, "Too little, too late, Bob." He grumbled throwing a couple of the red balls into the cushions opposite.

Bob looked at Kyndrea, his eyes welling up, "No, just sit with me Kyndrea." They sat on a couple of the easy chairs. Bob looked out onto the lake as Kyndrea looked into his eyes. "I had a very interesting talk with Janine yesterday afternoon."

"Oh?"

"She's quite the intelligent one, isn't she."

"She's been surprising many people these past few months."

"She asked me what I was afraid of. Can you believe that? Me afraid?"

"Never", Kyndrea smiled. She felt glad to see her father again, but he was slightly different. Something had changed in him.

"Yet she was right. There were a few things I was afraid of. Losing you as I have already said, but upon discovering that, I realised there was something else was holding me back. I've been wracking my brains over it since this morning. You know me, once I get a sniff of something I can't let go. Then it came to me, and it was so clear. I was scared of losing Margaret a second time. I felt if I let Simon into my life I was destroying Margaret's memory. Margaret was meant to be at a meeting that afternoon. It was a meeting about getting more volunteers for prisoner pen-pals. You know, people who befriend prisoners to help them rehabilitate?"

"I know dad, I wasn't that young and naive."

"Well, I thought, if that was Margaret, how could forgiving

her murderer be tainting her memory? By my actions over the past few weeks I was forgetting whom Margaret was anyway so why be scared of it. I then remembered the look on your face the day after the firework's display. The joy in your soul the day you first met Scott.

"If a man can make you feel so happy within yourself then why come between you? I said to Simon 'No matter how reasonable the action, there is still no excuse for murder.' And I now realise that includes the murder of true love.

"I wish, oh how I wish Simon didn't mistake Margaret for his father's girlfriend. I wish Simon didn't have to experience his mum dying in that way, but you cannot change the past. In the same way the past shouldn't dictate your future.

"Vengeance is no reason to make my future a living hell. By not really forgiving Simon with all my heart, the only person I was punishing was myself. I realise that now. I hope you can forgive a stupid old man, Kyndrea."

"No, I can't", Kyndrea replied, "But I can always forgive an intelligent, wise and the bestest father in the entire world. Come here dad!" Kyndrea gave Bob a big hug. Bob smiled, a small tear running down his cheek.

Simon threw more balls across the table. Ten minutes too late, just ten minutes earlier and the world would have been saved. "Ten Minutes!" He yelled. "In the movies it's always the second before, but no, in my life it's ten minutes late!"

"Do you really think we're that strict?"

"Sorry?" Simon looked around. An image of Andrew seemed to be projected on the snooker table's green felt.

"We are not idiots, Simon. Bob forgiving you ten minutes late does not remove the fact he did forgive you. We'll just delay your departure so you can still spend the required full week with Bob, Kyndrea and yourself."

"He did it? I did it? We did it!"

"Still a week's trial to go. You need to put your mind to the best option for ending your rehabilitation. You need to get yourself sorted. Work out your priorities. Get it so Kyndrea and Bob will be the least affected, but don't lie to yourself Simon. That's the worst thing you could do. Be true to yourself and the rest will follow."

The image faded and Simon was left there holding a red ball in his hands. He placed it gently onto the table and sat on one of the wooden seats against the wall. 'Anything's possible. Be true to yourself. What was Andrew trying to tell him?' he pondered

One Blissful Week

Over the weekend the three of them joined in the festivities around Trentsworth. As Kyndrea had said, the Trentsworth District Council did make a big thing of Easter as with any national holiday and they found a small carnival set up on the lake shore near the mall.

Simon had never been in a family environment for over a decade and he forgot how wonderful it could be. With those secrets no longer between them, the three bonded even closer. Simon still had one secret, one he could never let Bob or Kyndrea know. He rationalised, though, that it was not so much a secret, but an extra piece of knowledge that no one in Trentsworth needed to know. After all he never needed to know he was just a pile of chemicals reacting to one another to know how to live. It wasn't the chemicals that made him Simon; it was his experiences and miracle of self-awareness and freewill.

In that respect Kyndrea and Bob were exactly the same as himself. He proved it, even to the sceptical IVRRAC team and now for a week they could just live life as it came, appreciating every moment they had together.

"Dr Johnson, please report to the CEO. Dr Johnson, please report to the CEO," Christine's voice rang through the IVRRAC's PA system.

"Why doesn't she use the telephone like everyone else?" Andrew cursed, as he left his chair and walked towards the door. He took a quick glance through the window on his right. The other side was set up similar to an operating theatre.

On a peculiar looking table was Simon's body covered with a sheet. Disappearing under the blankets was a multitude of tubes and wires. His body moved slightly in reaction to the alternating air pressure mattress.

Andrew continued out into the corridor, turning left. At the end was a door marked "CEO" and Andrew knocked.

"Come in Andrew"

He opened the door and walked in. Again he was blinded by the projector. "You wished to see me Christine?"

"What are you up to Andrew?"

"Just tying up the loose ends, Christine."

"Yes, but using what knot? I noted your last two conversations with Simon. Both times you alluded to something. What is the next deal you're thinking of? You have already cost us a whole new array of processors and even more memory."

"Yes, but the publicity is worth more than the mere cost of electronics."

"We may not want publicity Andrew. The whole basis of our technique is that the subjects do not know what it is they are in. You of all people should know that."

"Do we want to continue rehabilitating then? We could branch out into VR rental."

"I knew it. Oh I knew that was the deal you're thinking of. No Andrew! N. O. The precedent could destroy society as we know it. We set up as a rehabilitation institute for a reason, Andrew. Think of what Simon's life would have been like without our help.

"Think of the others we have helped to realise what life is all about. We have used false reality to show these unfortunates the real reality. We are not in it for the fame or the money. Your skills have made our system the most advanced virtual reality in the world.

"We could have gone public years ago and made immense amounts of money on royalties. We didn't because of two reasons. One, we would have to stop the rehabilitations. Two, your worlds would be worse than drugs. At least drugs lose their potency after a while.

Imagine being in a world where you have no problems. Where you could be king. Where you could be a god. Why would you ever return to the real world?"

"They said the same about television. It did not destroy society."

"Some would disagree with that statement; however it definitely made a huge dent. A virtual reality is a hundred times more addictive and the program never ends. No, Andrew I will not be responsible for releasing this onto society. While it is kept here it's a blessing. Once released into the world it'll be a curse."

"Okay I promise not to push for publishing my findings. But you must agree to one thing, precedent or no precedent."

Even though Bob, Simon and Kyndrea were enjoying their new found relationship, Kyndrea could not help but notice that Simon was being slightly distant. There was still something bothering him.

She decided to approach the subject over dinner one evening. They had gone out to the Peak View restaurant. Bob had decided three would be a crowd and refused to join them. Kyndrea felt it was a great opportunity to talk seriously. "Simon, what's the matter?"

"What do you mean?" Simon asked. He knew what she meant. Should he tell her? What would she think? He had to come up with some explanation.

"Don't get me wrong, this last week has been wonderful, but I know something has been bothering you."

"It's Andrew." Simon decided to be as honest as he could without wrecking Kyndrea's universe.

"What about Andrew?"

"You know I have to leave Trentsworth? Well, I have to leave by myself. No companions. No one from my rehabilitation can leave or visit me ever again." Simon looked straight into Kyndrea's eyes, "And that includes you."

"Can he do that?"

"I am going on actual parole soon, and one of the conditions is to leave Trentsworth and all relationships." Simon amazed himself at how quickly he came up with that story.

Kyndrea stared out the window. The mountain peaks were bathed in orange as the sun set. "You know I will miss this place. But even that can't stop me from leaving, why do you think they can?"

"They are the government; the law. Do you want me to be put back in prison? That's what happens when a person breaks parole rules."

"Even stupid rules?" Kyndrea argued, she was getting very upset.

"I know you love me, but you can't leave Trentsworth with me. They will not allow it."

"I do not give in that easily Simon."

"I know you don't. But IVRRAC has more power than you could ever imagine." Simon thought over in his head, 'What would Andrew do to stop her leaving? He can't control her mind, he admitted to that. Perhaps he would kill Bob? No, not after what I showed him, surely. Maybe there's a 2D character that will keep her here.

Making up that there were parole rules wouldn't last for long; she would find a way around that. Simon reached out and held her hands. "I know when I leave here, you will lose me. I'm going to leave, there is no other choice. But before then

I want to spend the next few days spending one hundred percent of my time loving you. Not fighting Andrew. Not fighting IVRRAC. Just being with you."

"You want to leave me?"

"Definitely not! But the world is against us, believe me. Let us just have the best days of our life."

"I'm going to speak to Andrew!" Kyndrea announced, "He can't have that much control over your life. He has to give you some slack. You're rehabilitated, for Pete's sake."

"You don't know how his hands are tied, Kyndrea. He admitted to me that he would love us to stay together, if it were up to him, but it isn't, Kyndrea. Andrew isn't the boss. He has to obey the rules as much as we do."

"What's his phone number," Kyndrea asked getting out her cell phone. She sat there poised to take action. Simon just looked at her. She started getting even angrier, "Well?"

"Um," Simon paused, he didn't know Andrew's number. He had only used speed dial on the home phone. It would look strange if he didn't know it, "03 184 4152," he blurted out. It was a possible Trentsworth number and hoped Andrew was paying attention.

"Hi Andrew," Kyndrea started, "Look! You, Simon and I need to talk. Your regulations are getting ridiculous. Surely Simon and I can stay together. What? It's possible? You will see us tomorrow at our house? Two PM? Fine, it's a date." She put the phone down and looked at Simon. "Andrew is coming around at two. Remind me to get some cakes before lunch will you?"

"I don't believe you, Kyndrea," Simon smiled.

"What?"

"You are angry at him, yet you can't help playing hostess."

"No need to be impolite." Kyndrea smiled. "I'm sure Andrew is trying to do all he can. Besides, he reckons he can fix it for me and you to be together. But he said you would need to make a sacrifice."

"What?" Simon yelled. He looked around the restaurant in slight embarrassment. He continued, quietly. "That means? No, it can't be that. Could it be? Wow!"

"What does it mean, Simon?"

"No, that wouldn't be possible, the government wouldn't allow it. We wait for Andrew and hear what he has to say."

They continued the evening talking about their dreams for the future. He wondered what sacrifice Andrew was talking about. He hoped it was the one he was thinking of, for that was not really a sacrifice, not for him anyway.

The next morning Simon woke up next to Kyndrea. He looked over at her, wanting to kiss her, but not wanting to wake her from her slumber. She was so peaceful in her sleep, like an angel sent from heaven. He lay back down on his pillow and tried to go back to sleep.

He felt her arm move around him and a voice spoke quietly in his ear, "What time is it?"

"Only seven o'clock", he whispered back as her arm pulled him towards her. He felt the warmth of her body. Her arm started exploring his own, running down his side to his hip. He turned around so he was facing her and their mouths touched.

The downstairs clock struck ten as Simon made his way to the kitchen. He knew he would miss the love between him and Kyndrea. He would definitely miss the physical relationship. He realised, though she was not actually human, she was more human to him than any other lady in his life.

He would sacrifice anything to be with her. That was what love was all about, knowing that you would put your life on the line for the life of the other.

After breakfast, Kyndrea decided to clean up the house for Andrew that afternoon. She asked Simon to go to the bakery. He left the house and headed for the mall. Once he got there he observed Andrew sitting at a café table. In fact it was the one where he first met Kyndrea.

"I noticed you managed to select my favourite table," Simon commented, sitting down.

"Being in charge of the whole place has its advantages, Simon," Andrew replied.

"I suppose so. What are you doing here?"

"I need you to answer me a few questions."

"What questions?"

"I have been talking over the last few days with my boss about this possibility, quite heatedly at times. Our lawyers have gone over the contracts involved with a fine tooth comb. This could be a very bad precedent if the public found out, so we cannot afford to have any legal battles.

"It seemed like my hands were tied. Christine was firmly against the idea, but the lawyers managed to perform a miracle and now I can offer this choice. You need to decide before the meeting this afternoon. I need to organise a few things if you agree to the terms."

"What choice? What terms?"

"You stated before that a real person doesn't belong here, but that aside, do you wish to stay in Trentsworth?"

"Of course I do!" Simon yelled. He must have misheard. Why would they want him to stay here? "Really! You're being serious?"

"You will need to start working for us in an office I will set up. You are required to pay for the physical upkeep of your real body."

"Sure," Simon could not believe what he was hearing, it was better than winning Lotto.

"Doesn't knowing that the world you are living in is fake, faze you at all?" Andrew queried, his face taking on a warning tone. "Are you sure a real person can spend the rest of their life in a computer generated world?"

"Kyndrea is not fake, and she loves me and that is all that matters. So what if a grocer wont remember me from one visit to the next. True, I know the truth, I know there is more out there. All I want is in here. I love Kyndrea, I want to spend the rest of my life with her."

"Good, I thought that would be your answer." Andrew grinned.

"Will she grow old?" Simon suddenly asked. He had never thought of that before. There was no need for her to do so.

"Yes she will. She needs to, she knows people age, so if she doesn't she will start doubting the world. Besides I said before, this world follows physical properties, and ageing is a physical thing."

"Do I need to sign anything?" Simon asked.

"No, your verbal agreement is all we need. This conversation will be kept for future reference. Now I need to go off and finalise the last few things before seeing you this afternoon." Andrew grabbed the folder in front of him and walked off towards the train station.

Simon continued on toward the bakery and purchased a selection of cakes. When he got back, he wasn't surprised to see Bob and Kyndrea laughing away at some private joke.

"You're staying for lunch Bob?" Simon asked as he went to

put the cakes in the kitchen.

"If it's okay with you Scott."

"It is definitely okay with me. Kyndrea tell you my parole officer is seeing us this afternoon?"

"She mentioned it. I will be gone before then, don't worry."

"Oh, I don't think Andrew would mind if you were here, but it's up to you."

"He wants to get an afternoon flight in, Simon", Kyndrea interrupted, "So he's leaving straight after lunch anyway."

Simon played Bob at a few games of snooker while they waited for lunchtime to come around. Bob was very good and Simon lost each time, but each time they laughed and joked about something. Simon was sure he had made the right decision. There was nowhere else he could enjoy life this much.

After lunch Bob left and Kyndrea started cleaning up the house. Simon sat in front of the window watching the lake. Eventually there was the knock at the door and Simon let Andrew in.

Kyndrea came out with a tray of coffee and cakes as they

sat on the chairs overlooking the lake. "What is this solution of yours?" she asked, offering a cup and cake to Andrew.

"I have discussed things with the parole board. If Simon can secure a job in Trentsworth he may stay, and I have organised an interview already with a firm in town. Their offices are in a prime position in the station, overlooking the mall and wharf. The job is well within Simon's capabilities." Andrew looked at Simon. "You don't mind working in an office, Simon?"

"Not if it means I can be with Kyndrea", Simon immediately replied.

Kyndrea smiled. She could see the love Simon had for her. She loved him then even more for that. Her business brain suddenly kicked in. "What about this house?"

Simon will have to either move from or buy it. The government needs to reclaim the money."

"How much do they want for it?" Kyndrea asked.

"What they bought it for plus 10 percent, house values have gone up again."

"I haven't even got enough for a deposit on that," Kyndrea replied sadly.

"But we're staying!" Simon yelled. "Kyndrea! We are staying together in Trentsworth."

"Yes, we are", Kyndrea smiled.

"Cheer up," Andrew remarked, "Perhaps Simon will win the Lotto this weekend. It's a big draw this time, just happens to be large enough to buy the house freehold."

"Yeah right!" Kyndrea sarcastically replied.

"You never know." Andrew winked at Simon. "Thanks for the coffee and cake, I must be going. I will ring you with the exact time and location of the interview Simon."

"Okay. And thanks Andrew." Simon got up and let Andrew out the front door.

"Well!" Kyndrea breathed out. "You can stay! And I suppose we can move in with dad until we can arrange another house."

"If Bob doesn't mind, neither do I." Simon answered. "Though I think I will enter the lotto draw, just for fun."

"You won't win, no way. It's a fool's game Simon."

"You're probably right," Simon smiled. There were definite advantages knowing the guy in control. "But I will anyway."

"Only a cheap one then, you only need one line to win."

"This is true." Simon smiled to himself. "Well, I'll choose my own numbers then. They will include eight, eleven, thirty six and thirty eight."

"Why?"

"I met you at the café at number eight the mall, at eleven o'clock. You lived at thirty eight Springfield Rd and now live at thirty six."

"Oh, how sweet." Kyndrea wrapped her arms around Simon, "You'll definitely win with those numbers." She kissed him and they held each other in a long, romantic embrace.

"I shall go and purchase a ticket then," Simon confirmed as their mouths parted. "Today will go down as the third best day of my life."

"Only third best?" Kyndrea took a step back, a playful frown on her face.

"Well, the day I first met you was the second best."

"And the best day of your life?"

"The day you become my wife, if such a day will exist." Simon grabbed Kyndrea and held her tight. He looked closely into her eyes. She looked at him in wonder.

"Is that a proposal?" Kyndrea knew eventually the question would be asked. She couldn't believe he asked so soon though. She kissed him again.

"Yes", Simon answered, once their lips parted. He got down on one knee and looked up at her. "Kyndrea, will you marry me?"

"Of course I will!" she smiled and laughed. "Now get up, you look silly." She looked at her left hand, "Haven't you forgotten something?"

Simon looked perplexed then smiled, "I need to ask Bob's permission first, then I'll do it properly. Besides, buying jewellery is definitely something I am not acquainted with."

"Perhaps I can help, give a few suggestions?" She pulled Simon up and embraced him once more. She pulled him tight, resting her head on his shoulder. "I love you Simon."

"I love you too. Thanks Kyndrea for making my life complete." Simon gently lifted up her head and looked into her eyes.

They just stared at each other in silence. He ran his hands through her hair. She was worth staying for.

Kyndrea soaked in the love that poured from Simon's eyes. She wanted this moment to last forever. Their lips got closer together and slowly met. The passion exploded as they hugged each other tightly. Kyndrea felt Simon hard against her as his hands moved gently over her back.

She pulled him even closer to him as though they could become one body. The embrace seemed to last for hours, neither of them wanting to let go. Eventually Simon relaxed a bit. Kyndrea felt the cool air on her perspiration.

They smiled at each other and after a few small farewell kisses Simon exited the house. He was so filled with joy. He hadn't ever felt this way before. He knew he would win the Lotto, he knew he would get the job. He was almost certain Bob would agree to the marriage.

He purchased the ticket at the mall mini-market. The owner was serving him, "What ticket would you like sir?"

"The smallest one", Simon answered.

"Sorry?" The owner looked puzzled. "They're all the same size."

"Huh?" Simon looked perplexed, then he laughed. "The cheapest then."

"Very good sir. Good luck tomorrow."

Simon took the ticket. "Luck has suddenly become my best friend. I think you'll be seeing me on Sunday with the winning ticket," Simon laughed with the owner, as he paid.

He walked out and looked for a good wine shop. Suddenly the reality of his decision came to him. He was in a fake world and every so often he would be reminded by the non-sensible answer of a 2D. True, more 3Ds would be introduced but he also realised that he never asked Andrew if all the 3Ds were law abiding.

How many were there like Richard, but what right had he or Andrew to decide what 3Ds lived and what 3Ds stayed in perpetual sleep. The valley would change as more people had freewill, for better or even for worse, but then it would also be less fake.

He was an experiment, would a real person survive in a computer generated world. He was going to prove one could. 'What was that quote?' he thought to himself. 'I am real and everything else is a figment of my imagination.' Who was to say the real world was the real world anyway.

At least Simon knew where he was and what purpose he was fulfilling. No matter what experiences were in store for him in the future. He knew he was there to be a husband to Kyndrea, and a father to their future children. He was also the one who had saved twenty seven lives.

The End